THE LAND BEYOND THE MAP

Miles to the west we could see the canyon widen to a spreading valley; the granite uplifts on which we stood sloped away to hilly rolling country. Behind us the snow ranges reared, a piled and awesome jumble. Still, it didn't seem right. I should have recognized peaks, but they were strange.

There were patches of timber below us, some spruce, but broadleafs too, in variety. They shouldn't have been there. A small band of elk drifted across an open space. They were familiar enough, but out of place.

"Denny," I said, "You've flown across to Yakutat. Where are we?"

"Vin," he said, "I never saw those peaks. There's no country like this west of the St. Elias." He rubbed his nose and stared into the distance, into the west. "This is funny business."

STEPHEN TALL is the *nom-de-plume* used for his science fiction novels (of which this is his third) and for his short stories (of which there are about thirty-five) by Compton N. Crook, Ph.D., biologist and ecologist, professor emeritus of Towson State University of Maryland. Obviously his writing tends to reflect his personal involvement with the natural wonders of the world, an involvement which has resulted in travel and research in many of the remote corners of the Earth, including the Andes, Antarctica, and the Yukon (the region that is the launching point for this book). When asked to characterize himself as either a writer or a scientist, he commented: "Why don't we just say that I'm a field ecologist who happens to write science fiction. That's about right, isn't it?"

THE PEOPLE BEYOND THE WALL

Stephen Tall

DAW BOOKS, INC.
DONALD A. WOLLHEIM, PUBLISHER
1633 Broadway, New York, N.Y. 10019

Cover art by Gino D'Achille

DEDICATION

To the memory of

My Mother

Who would have liked it, I think

FIRST PRINTING, MAY 1980

1 2 3 4 5 6 7 8 9

Chapter 1

We had looked forward to it for weeks. And finally, it was now. We were in the air, high above the fantastic twisting ice stream of the Kaskawulsh Glacier. Our tiny plane was a speck, a mote among the vast rock masses that bordered the great canyon. On into the St. Elias we droned like a lost bumblebee, out onto the awesome plains of snow and ice that are the Icefield Ranges.

I sat in front with Phil. Denny lay back on the duffle behind us, pretending to enjoy the ride and the view, but gripping his shoulder straps so hard his big knuckles were white. Denny, who would climb anywhere, was deathly afraid of small planes.

I wasn't too happy myself. I watched Phil, lounging at ease in his harness, one hand on the wheel. Continually he made small adjustments of the gadgets in front of him. Every ten minutes he pulled forward his microphone, reported position to the operator at Kluane. Phil was the only one having fun. He was lean and dark and weatherbeaten—and nuts. All bush pilots are nuts.

But he did what he said he would do. He took us on over the Divide, past the incredible snow-and-ice-sheathed massif of Mount Logan, down onto the white stretches of Seward Glacier.

"There," Phil said.

It was easy to see. It looked about as wide as two fingers, a dark, jagged, irregular crack in the endless snow sheet. We knew it for what it was, though. Phil and Jack Wilson and Pete Swan had watched it for a month. It was new, and it was already famous; the great-grandfather of crevasses.

Phil brought us down. He swung into the wind, dropped his flaps, and set the little plane on her skis as neatly as a duck settling on a pond. We glided bumpily, then the snow stopped slipping past. The black edge of the crevasse showed off our left wing.

"I said to within fifty feet," Phil said. "But I doubt if it's more than forty. Want to pace it?"

"I want out!" Denny said. "Just lemme out! Then you can play games with this kite!"

Phil looked amused, but he helped us unload. The tent, the extra food, the little primus stove; these we covered with a canvas, piled snow around the edges. We figured to use them, tomorrow perhaps. We set up a marker, for there's plenty of snowfall here in late May; plenty any time, for that matter. By the time we got back the whole cache might be drifted deep.

We checked our pack frames, our thin, strong nylon ropes, ice axes, pitons, karabiners, and a couple of slender steel stakes, more than two feet long, that were our special devices for climbing ice walls. With the contents of the packs we could survive for weeks if we had to.

Phil walked the few paces to the lip of the crevasse. It wasn't a crack, but a great gaping rent in the ice, twenty-five or thirty yards wide, a good mile long. Phil peered over the edge and shuddered.

"Nobody in his right mind would go down in there! You guys are nuts!"

"Exactly what I was thinking about you," Denny said. He stamped his booted feet, onto which he had just clamped and buckled crampons. "At least this is solid. That thing," he jerked his head toward the plane, "just ain't safe."

The pilot grinned.

"It got you here," he said. "If you are out by day after tomorrow, it'll get you back. If the weather gets rough, hole up. I'll find you."

We watched him taxi the little plane about, figure his run, then take off like the ski jumper he was in effect. In a few minutes he was a soaring, faintly purring speck in the sky, and we were alone in a land the Abominable Snowman would have loved.

I won't belabor our descent into the crevasse. We had done it before. Never anything this big, but we knew how. Fortunately, the break wasn't sheer. There were ledges and splintered outcrops and plenty of spots where crampons could cling. We made it to the bottom with everything in good condition, but when I looked up from the floor of the crevasse I wondered how. It was a rugged sight. According to Denny's altimeter we had come down a four-hundred-foot ice wall. Looking up, I believed every foot of it.

There was plenty of room at the bottom. It was rough and broken, but walking was possible. We had taken ice samples as we came down the wall. Now we took time to label the bottles and cache them. Then we coiled ropes, packed up in trail order, and set out to explore the crevasse. As we worked our way along we took more samples, leaving each bottle at the sample location to be picked up on the way back.

It soon was pretty evident that the crevasse was more extensive than it showed from the air. Before long we had hiked a mile. The opening narrowed above us, then closed over entirely, bridged by snow, and from a craggy and glistening ice canyon we walked in an apparently endless, vaulted ice hall, bathed in delicate blue and pink light as the ice filtered and broke up the sun's rays.

Then the crevasse divided. There had been no hint at all of this from above. But now there were two ice corridors to choose from, both definitely sloping downward, burrowing westward into the glacier.

Denny was leading. He paused at the fork and looked back and down on me. His pack frame reached high above his heavy shoulders, but he stood at ease. He said nothing, just looked at me. I gestured with my free hand.

"The wide one," I decided.

Denny led on.

I guess we both knew we had come far enough. But we were young, and this was different. We were properly and warmly clothed. We had emergency rations. We went on.

We could see that we were far deeper than when we began our hike. We had walked for miles now, sloping steadily downward. I regretted that we had used up our sample bottles. The composition of ice at this depth probably had never been studied from undisturbed sources.

The open end of the crevasse had been new, but this glistening ice corridor had a feel of permanence. The walls were no longer splintered, but were smooth as glass, as beautifully molded and curved and rippled as transparent marble. The ice showed more and more undisturbed clearness, and we could look deep into the sides of our frigid covered canyon, literally peering into the heart of the great glacier.

It wasn't cold. When we touched bottom at the end of our

climb into the crevasse, Denny's thermometer registered 21° F. An hour and maybe a couple of miles later it showed 18°. When the crevasse had roofed over and the altimeter showed us 300 feet deeper, it was up to 20° again. No air movement, but the air was fresh. It was good to breathe. I never felt better, more energetic, more rested.

It didn't seem like it, but four hours went by. We had covered maybe ten miles. We thought we were having a rare bit of luck. We never had heard of anyone hiking *into* a glacier, on down into the belly and bones of it. We couldn't bring ourselves to turn back yet. Our incredible corridor looked old as time, old as the vast ice mass itself. And still it sloped down.

We knew that on the Kaskawulsh-Hubbard Divide the ice sheet had been determined to be at least 3000 feet thick. We were down to 2000. There was more to see. More to know. This would be a trip to remember.

That ice had been accumulating since the dawn of man's history. What a place to make a study of glacier ice unprecedented in glaciology! We weren't glaciologists, but we were assistants to a good one, and at our respective graduate schools they thought we had promise. Actually, I suppose we were just brash young snow prowlers who were really here for the opportunity to explore and climb in the snow ranges.

We still had light. We might have expected it to dim, to grow shadowy, but it continued to glow with a soft, steady radiance. By now our ice walls were clear as mirrors. And the corridor, while it had no tracks or other evidence of use, was smooth and worn, as a trail over rock is worn.

"Vin," Denny said, "we've come far enough. This is getting a little hard to understand." He placed his hand against the transparent wall and leaned. "What say?"

I grinned at him. I knew he was right. I knew, too, that he was just making sense. He wasn't afraid. Yellow-haired Denny, with his chubby, little-boy face, his clear blue eyes as innocent as a six-weeks pup, and his great tapered body with its lean flanks and wrestler's shoulders—no, Denny wasn't afraid. Once I had watched him wade cheerfully into a raucous mob with no weapons but his big clenched fists, and I had seen the demonstrators fall away before even one got the slug. Denny looked like a cherub, but nobody got the idea he was one.

I knew he was right, now, but it came hard. I tried to spin it out. Somehow, this ice world drew me.

"Fifteen minutes more," I proposed. "Fifteen minutes, then back we go."

Denny glanced at his wristwatch, looked quizzically at me, then stepped off without a word. I shrugged into my pack and followed.

It didn't take fifteen minutes. Five hadn't gone by. We rounded a turn in the corridor and could see it looming darkly ahead. It didn't move, and it took us a minute to realize that it wasn't in the corridor at all. It was deep in the ice wall, frozen most naturally, and it had been there for many centuries.

We walked slowly forward until we were opposite it. We dropped our packs and stood looking up. It was a sight no modern man had ever seen. Our Pleistocene ancestors, though, must have skulked after it often, with baffled, eager, hungry eyes and slavering jaws.

It had to be a woolly mammoth. The vast body, covered with long, coarse, reddish-brown hair, the long curling tusks on either side of the thick, muscular trunk, the great, high, almost naked forehead, the small, dull, piggy eyes staring at nothing—it was a mammoth all right. The pictures in the books are pretty good.

We looked, but didn't comment.

"Denny," I said finally, "I want a fifteen-minute extension on my fifteen minutes. There's still stuff along this trail we ought to see."

Denny looked at the awesome bulk of the specimen in the ice wall, down at the smooth trail under our feet, then back at me. His clear, little-boy eyes lighted happily, recklessly, as he made up his mind.

"Feel free," he said. "Take an hour. Take all the time you want."

We understood each other, Denny and I. We knew then that we weren't going back to where the crevasse was new, not until we knew the story of the corridor into Seward Glacier. We had chocolate and iron rations. We wouldn't freeze. We were going on.

The next half hour was like the rest had been. Then there was a change. The trail, which had been smooth under our feet, became choppy and broken. Chunks and splintered pieces of ice lay on it, and the canyon-like walls were seamed and translucent again. Then, ahead, a jumbled ice jam seemed to block the corridor. Great shattered chunks lay on each other in haphazard confusion. A first impression was that this was newly done, but when we looked closer, we knew it couldn't be.

That jam choking the corridor may have been there as long as the mammoth had been. It was an old, old jam. A fossil jam.

The trail over it, though, was newer. We could see where it led, smooth spots here and there, worn where something had pulled itself up over block after block. The jam, after all, wasn't more than fifty feet high, and the corridor vaulted above it for hundreds of feet more. We put on our crampons and gloves. Then clambering over was a cinch.

After the blockade, evidence of trail use increased. Still no tracks, but we didn't need any. Feet had polished the floor of that corridor. Not recently, that we knew, but sometime, something had used it.

It felt chillier. When Denny looked at his thermometer again it was down to 5° F. The ice of the walls was clear again, and deep in the distance, like peering through water, we could dimly discern dark shapes, some erect, some sprawled, some strangely distorted. There were none near the corridor, though, and we never got another good look.

Then the corridor began to taper. The vaulted roof sloped swiftly down, the walls drew together. Within ten minutes we barely had head room. The corridor was a tunnel, maybe seven feet high, three or four wide. But the floor under our feet was polished again, and we could still go forward at a rapid walk. And the light glowed with a soft radiance, pinkish and bluish tones giving life to the clear, fluorescent-like white.

Denny strode along ahead of me. No hesitation here. He almost acted as if he knew where he was going, the thrusting self-confidence with which he did everything never more in evidence. I followed, because it was my turn to follow. But on the trail, over the ice fields, up the cliffs, I always led my share.

The light began to fail. It was scarcely noticeable at first, but the gloom intensified rapidly. Denny led on. The smooth ice under our feet became broken, then almost mushy. The air, crisp and exhilarating for so long, grew wet, dank, musty.

There were dark discolorations in the corridor walls, which soon became mud, stones, unidentifiable rubbish.

"Moraine, I think," Denny offered over his shoulder. "We've walked right out from under Seward, Vin."

It was a good guess, but somehow it didn't sound quite right. Seward was bigger than that. The light was so faint now we were practically groping our way. Denny fished his flashlight from his pack. It was a little hand-squeeze generator, flaring when the grip was pressed, dying on the spring return. The gloomy, dripping, muddy walls, the sloppy mess under foot, appeared and vanished as he worked the grip. And the smell was like a charnel house. Not putrefying, not rotten. No, it was too old for that. But now the rubble was mixed with bones, some of them of unbelievable size. At one spot a rack of ribs thrust out into the tunnel so far that we had to squeeze around it. And each rib was the size of my upper arm.

The slush under our feet became running water. Soon we were wading ankle deep. It was icy, but our boots were waterproof. The tunnel widened. On one side the wall was now solid rock, a fine-textured granite that sparkled in the flashlight's beam. The tunnel was skirting a cliff. It vaulted high, spread wide. Around a curve, far ahead, we could see light. Daylight.

Quite suddenly the spreading tunnel became a canyon. On both sides cliffs loomed high, but there was blue sky above them, and across the narrow ribbon of it I saw an eagle wheel in a slow, soaring circle. Behind us a great ice wall reared, but it was the canyon and the stream that claimed our attention.

The stream was ten, fifteen, twenty yards wide, the cold milky water rippling over slime-covered, smooth-worn stones. Here and there big boulders obstructed, and behind them little sandbars stretched downstream. But the incredible thing was the bones.

Piled in water-jumbled rows along each cliff side, jack-strawed across the stream among the stones, there were bones, huge bones, by the many thousands. A paleontologist would want three lives just to sort them all. There were more bones here than in all the museums of the world. And, I don't doubt, of creatures not known by even a single specimen.

We were pretty well speechless—and it takes a lot to stop

us from talking. We splashed through the freezing water to a big flat rock that was touched by a spot of sun. Gratefully we climbed up, shed our packs, and stretched out. We'd been hiking almost without a break for ten hours.

The sun was high. The short Arctic night had passed. In spite of the skeletons our surroundings looked normal. At least it was a situation we could relate to. We'd been in a lot of canyons, climbed many rock walls. For a minute a mountain goat showed, threading its way across a ledge high on the sun-splashed cliff.

We ate a few raisins and a bit of chocolate. We were dry inside, but we figured we'd wait for water. The stream water probably wouldn't have harmed us, but it looked too much like Monday soup. And uncooked, at that.

Chapter 2

We slept. Lying there on that hard rock, pack-sacks for pillows, we slept like babies. When I opened my eyes again moonlight had replaced sunlight in the slit above, and the river had a chilling, spectral feel, especially when the light glinted on the vast skulls that sometimes dwarfed the boulders. In a few minutes Denny stretched, yawned, and sat up. He grinned at me.

"Your fifteen minutes are up," he said. "What do we do now?"

"Change socks," I said. "We should have done it yesterday. My feet are getting sore."

The boots hadn't leaked, but feet do sweat, and even good wool can take just so much. Dry socks made us feel better, and a few mouthfuls of iron rations made us fit to go. We still didn't care to drink the stream water. We knew we'd find a seep from the cliffs farther down. And we knew we intended going on downstream. We didn't even discuss it. When we were ready I splashed back into the stream and took the lead. It was my turn. We didn't discuss that either.

The stream bed widened, the cliff walls lowered. The Arctic dawn was showing again. The air was crisp, but it had lost the ice chill. The bones in the stream were fewer and smaller. There was spruce and juniper in the rock crevices above, and several times I heard bird song. Then the stream had a trail over the rocks along one bank, a game trail. We followed it gratefully. It was rough, but at least it was out of the water. And we knew that sooner or later it would probably lead us out of the canyon.

This it did within a mile. A fissure knifed sharply back into the cliff to our right. The trail turned into it. We climbed steeply, wound around jutting cliff walls, and wondered what we would do if we met a grizzly coming down. It was strictly a one-way trail.

We had to stop often to catch our breath. It was at one of these stops I found it—or maybe them would be better. We were long past the last of the giant skeletons. The rock around us was clean and sharply fractured; igneous rock. It would hold no life remains. It amused me, then, to see the half-handful of tiny bones, bleached and weathered, spread across the shelf-like ledge against which I leaned to rest. A chipmunk's bones, I thought idly, or a rock squirrel's.

Then I saw the skull. Little bigger than a Ping-Pong ball, there still wasn't any doubt as to what it was. It was perfect, a nicely shaped skull with fine high frontal plates, the lower jaw still attached, all the teeth in place. And the rest of the skeleton fitted. There were graceful leg bones three inches long, a well-sprung rib cage still partly assembled, wee vertebrae like bleached, carved beads.

Silently I tapped Denny on the shoulder. Still silently we both bent over the tiny remnants. They were mature bones. Most of them were still there. And they weren't synthetic. Nobody was playing a trick. They were real.

"Human!" Denny breathed. "A little man!"

"Or worse," I said. "Maybe a little lady!"

I could see that Denny didn't appreciate me.

"Vin," he said slowly, and his small-boy face wrinkled comically as he thought, "Gulliver was the last man to see people this small. We know they don't exist. But I don't for a minute doubt these bones."

"Nor I," I said. "But," I added, "I don't think I'd believe a live one. This one has to have come from the ice, like the big things down below there. Something brought it up here while it was still whole."

Denny reached past me and lifted an object from a crevice in the rock wall. It was wedged in, on end, and his big fingers probed carefully before he could free it. He set it on the ledge and delicately raised the lid, which turned on ornate hinges infinitely small. It was a box, maybe ten or fifteen inches long. It was of some pungent, aromatic wood, probably cedar. It sat on four carved wooden feet, and every outside surface was etched with a dainty tracery of stylized carving, still perfect after who knows how many years. Inside, it was lined with an iridescent cloth, soft and delicate, but sturdy and strong. In one end there was a pillow the size of my thumb, tied or sewed into place.

"From the ice too, no doubt," Denny said.

I said nothing. I lifted the tiny skull and placed it gently on the pillow. Bone by bone I returned the little skeleton to its coffin. The vertebrae were too small to pick up so I scraped them onto a slip of paper from my pocket notebook and gingerly poured them in.

"We can't take a megatherium or a mammoth on the plane," I said, "but this goes back!"

"Don't you feel like a ghoul?" Denny asked. "Up there there might be a whole cemetery of them. This was certainly carried away by something."

I filled the little coffin with crumpled tissue. It had had a catch. I could see where it was broken. But I fastened the lid down firmly with heavy rubber bands and stowed it in my pack.

"If anyone owns it," I said, "he has only to ask. Let's go up."

It was still a long pull, and another hour before we made the top. But it was worth it.

What a view! Miles to the west we could see the canyon widen to a spreading valley; the granite uplifts on which we stood sloped away to hilly rolling country. Behind us the snow range reared, a piled and awesome jumble. Still, it didn't seem right. I should have recognized peaks, but they were strange.

There were patches of timber below us, some spruce, but broadleafs too, in variety. They shouldn't have been there. A small band of elk drifted across an open space. They were regular elk, not caribou; familiar enough, but out of place.

"Denny," I said, "you've flown across to Yakutat. Where are we?"

The big fellow pushed back his cap, and his curly yellow hair poked out over his forehead. With his china-blue eyes he reminded me of an enormous baby. It was a serious baby, though.

"Vin," he said, "I never saw those peaks. There's no country like this west of the St. Elias." He rubbed his nose and stared into the distance; into the west. "This is funny business, boy."

"Plane'll be back tomorrow," I reminded him. "When we don't show at the crevasse, they'll circle for us. After all, we're only a day's hike away. They can cover that in minutes."

"Maybe," Denny said dubiously, "maybe. But I got a feeling. And it don't include a plane pickup."

"You think Phil can't set down in that elk pasture? He'll be sad. He's a bush pilot. He can land where it's really rough."

"*If* he finds it. Which, somehow, I doubt. That's oak down there. It don't grow in the Yukon. Not forty feet tall, it don't."

"Doesn't," I said absently.

"Thank you, professor," the big fellow said. "The trail leads down. Shall we follow it? We can always come back."

We had had a good drink from a seep halfway up the fissure, and we had each eaten a survival ration we were testing. Still, I could have used a chicken leg or a small steak. I loosened the .357 magnum in its holster.

"If we can get close to one of those elk," I said, "what say we have breakfast?"

"I'll join you," Denny said. "Just watch out for the game warden."

By now the sun was high and warm. It was beautiful country. And every stride we took, every turn of the trail into the lowlands, emphasized the fact that this wasn't Arctic. High latitude, sure, but temperate.

From back of me Denny's big hand clamped onto my shoulder and I was yanked down behind a convenient boulder. I didn't make a sound; didn't even move to rub my bruised knee and backside. I knew emergency. I waited for Denny.

"Stay low," he said softly. "Sneak a look around the rock. Coming across that meadow to the left."

I looked, and caught my breath.

"The game warden!" I said.

Denny snorted like he does when he's amused.

"Yeah," he said, "and in one way he sets my mind easy. He couldn't fit in your coffin. Look at that guy! He could play linebacker for the Colts."

There was nothing to compare him with, but we could tell he was big. And I've never seen a man move so easily, so much like a cat. He poured himself across the meadow, hardly rippling the grass. It wasn't long before we realized that he knew we were there; had probably known long before we saw him.

Denny admitted it by standing erect and leaning against the boulder. I rubbed my knee for a minute before I got up.

"You crippled me for nothing," I growled. I shook the .357 in its holster, making sure it was free.

"Apologies," Denny said. "When we finish dickering with our friend here you're entitled to one free kick. Barefoot, of course."

If we had been stupid, we might have thought this fellow a savage. There wasn't much to his outfit. He wore brief breeches of a neutral brown, a sleeveless, vest-like top garment the same color, and high, soft moccasins, probably of elkhide leather. His clothes were cloth, though. They had been woven. His only weapon was a four-foot oak club, maybe as thick as my wrist, neatly trimmed, and worn from much handling. Only that, excepting a small, thin knife in a sheath against his thigh.

He stopped ten feet from us and simply stood, looking us over with complete composure. He was a lot of man. About Denny's height, which would put him five inches over six feet, he was less thick, his belly was board-flat, and every muscle showed quality. His black hair was cut square at the shoulders, banged across his high forehead above interested blue eyes. He had no beard, which meant he shaved. His skin was whiter than ours.

He spoke a few syllables in a deep, smooth voice.

"Sorry, old buddy, no savvy," I said.

"Sorry, old buddy, no savvy.' He played it back instantly, even imitating my tone. He grinned, and it was impossible not to grin back.

He motioned, then started off across the field.

I looked at Denny. He shrugged his shoulders.

"What have we got to lose?"

The man led with his gliding stride and we followed, first me, and then Denny. And I distinctly heard the fellow say, experimentally, under his breath, "What have we got to lose?"

What, indeed? Offhand, I could think of several things, like maybe my chances of becoming an old man. I didn't look forward to that, but I wanted it to happen, in time. And while this fellow seemed intelligent and friendly, there was no way of knowing. Like the oaks and the elk, he was out of place. He was neither Indian nor Eskimo, but in spite of his white skin he wasn't Caucasian, either.

I matched his smooth, gliding stride. He must have been going about six miles an hour. I stay in good shape, but there wasn't any doubt that if we had far to go he was going to walk the ears off us. After a half hour I was beginning to drag.

He seemed to sense this. We had been going across country, but now we cut into a well-traveled trail. The terrain still sloped downward, with patches of timber and grassland in between. Sugar maple was common, and elm, and poplar in variety. Small birds were plentiful, and looked familiar. The rabbits that popped up and bounded away were cottontails, not snowshoes.

Our guide came to a halt on a knoll. We could see the trail winding down through the broken country. We dropped our packs and stood panting. The man eyed us with open amusement. His big sleek body showed no stress whatever. We could hardly see him breathe.

He let us rest for a few minutes, then led off again. But he cut his pace. At four miles an hour we could go all day, and I thought for a while we were going to. Quite suddenly we were skirting a tilled field—full of cabbages, no less. But no fences and no road. Just the trail leading on.

Then there were other fields, with squash, beans, and green stretches of what must have been some kind of grain. It was young and grass-like, but I'm no expert on crops. There weren't any people or work stock, and no sign of farm tools. But the plants were in rows and in good shape.

The man had not spoken since our first exchange a couple

of hours back. But by a bean field he stopped and addressed us with confidence.

"Your speech is called English," he asserted. His accent was good, with maybe a little Britisher in it.

"You know it!" I said fervently. "Boy, you had me worried! I thought we were going to have to make do with sign language, and that's overrated, in spite of what you read."

"Yes, I do know it," the fellow said. "You speak it differently, however. I suspect sayings outside my experience."

"He means," Denny said, "that you talk like a bum. Show him your college side."

I grinned, and our guide smiled politely. I don't think the words meant much to him.

"We've been following you," I told him, "because we didn't think you could understand us. But now maybe you can tell us where we are."

The man looked back toward the towering snow ranges, then speculatively at us.

"You will tell me, I think, that you came from there."

"Right," I said. "We came across to Seward from Kluane by aircraft. We were dropped off to explore a new crevasse on Seward and, by golly, we walked right out from under the blasted glacier. Came out in the river down in the gorge back there, the one with all the outsized bones."

The big fellow didn't look frightened, but his face was very serious.

"You came from the River of Bones?" You could hear the capitals in the title as he gave it.

"Is that bad?" Denny inquired. "There're relics down there I wouldn't want to meet alive, but what're left now aren't problems."

"It is a place where men do not go," our guide said simply.

"We didn't pick it," I said. "It's where we came out. I thought it was pretty interesting, though. Never saw a melt-out like it."

The man eyed us with a respectful intentness he hadn't shown before. Evidently we had changed status. Before, we had been a couple of guys in funny clothes who couldn't travel very fast. Now we were men who had been unharmed while violating a taboo. Perhaps we were somehow related to the taboo. We could see that he was dubious.

"You will be guests," he said quietly. "When you have been made welcome, have eaten and slept, then you must tell your story to the Primate. He will dispose." He hesitated, seemed to glance toward the ranges. "It will be my honor to be with you. I am called Elg. I do many things, but my greatest pleasure is to make plants grow."

"This is Denny," I said. "I am Vin."

Elg gravely grasped his left hand with his right, barely inclined his head toward each of us in turn. I looked at Denny, then we each did the same thing toward him. I felt like a fool, but "When in Rome. . . ."

Anyhow, it seemed to satisfy him.

He swung back into the trail, and our curiosity had to wait. We followed him, this man who looked like a savage and at the same time had a poise and grace most of our friends couldn't match; this man who spoke easy English with a British accent, and whose formal greeting ritual was closest to what you might see in a prize-fight ring; this man with a body like a decathlon champ who identified himself as a farmer.

He didn't look back, but the trail wasn't to be much longer. We could see it in the distance on a small plain below us, laid out with a perfection I had never seen in a town. Elg paused at an overlook and waved a hand.

"Chan-Cho-Pan. My garn. My society," he said.

"Society?" Denny said it, just ahead of me. "Looks like a town. A town with no suburbs. No urban sprawl. Why society?"

"We shall learn from you," Elg said. "Thus he translated our term garn. He said it was most like."

"I'm lost," I said. "Who's he?"

"Before my years. The one who came from the snow ranges as you have come, but not from the River of Bones. The man called Smith. He gave us English, and paper, and a music called jazz. Those of few years like it, the elders find it trivial."

"Sounds right," I said. "Grandpa loved jazz, but not after he was Grandpa."

"You know of jazz?" Elg was eager. "Perhaps you know also of the man Smith?"

"Where we came from," Denny broke in, "there are plenty of Smiths. The world is full of 'em."

"Many? Many men with the same name? Does this not make difficulties?"

"I'll say this for Smith," I said, "he taught you a lot of English. You talk like a book."

"Books," Elg mused. "Yes, he spoke of books. There were many sheets of paper with symbols on them, all held together by an edge. He had some such. I have not seen them. They are in the Primate's keeping."

I looked from Elg's noble figure and clear, interested eyes to the distant town. Town it had to be, but I would have bet that there wasn't another like it on the planet. It looked like a sand-table model; as if somebody had drawn it onto the plain with a straightedge. It was a rectangle, almost if not square, and it didn't straggle. Beyond its edges the open country stretched away, unblemished by field or building. Within the boundaries it was divided into squares, row after row, with a building in the center of each. The middle of the town was a large open square, obviously a multiple of the smaller ones. Trees dotted it, and indeed the whole town seemed extensively wooded. It needed a closer look before we could see why this was so.

"Garn. Smith. Primate." I brought my eyes back from the town to Elg. "You're giving it to us too fast, friend. Everything you say has to be explained. We never heard of this country. We never saw a town like that. Our people fly across the St. Elias regularly, and nobody ever reported you."

Elg nodded. He didn't seem surprised.

"So said the man Smith. Except he did not speak of flying. He spoke of many people, many more than all the ten garns, and of a thousand things which we never imagined. Some were wonders, some unbelievable, some appallingly silly."

He smiled suddenly, and turned to the trail.

"The sun is low, and you are weary. Later we will talk slowly. Each thing that is strange can be explained. You have time."

We fell in behind him. Soon the town grew bigger ahead. We looked with interest, but that last little remark of Elg's nagged me. He sounded so darned sure.

Chapter 3

You would have thought, even around a town of only four or five thousand people or so, that there would be traffic, noise, bustle. But we were close before we heard any sounds worth mentioning. Our trail dropped into a wagon track. The wheel marks were plain. It was plain, too, that the beasts pulling the vehicles were split-hooved, too small for oxen, with slender, graceful tracks.

The road wound around a little hill, then the city limit was just ahead. It was a clean gravel road, neat as a pin. We were approaching a corner of the rectangular town, and the corner was a sharp, true right angle. Evidently the road bounded the town on all sides, and at it the town stopped.

There was no bustle, but we could hear people. Just murmurs though, no shouts. Conversation level, no more. In the distance I could hear a mellow pounding, as if someone were using a hammer in a perfectly normal way. But it was a quiet town. Its peace seemed to reach out and gather us in.

From afar we had noted the checkerboard design of the town. At hand, we could see how it was done. Each home plot was maybe a quarter of an acre. It was square, and had a gravel road on every side of it. No sidewalks. No footpaths. The building or buildings were near the center of the plot. A single tree occupied each corner. Each was carefully pruned and shaped. In fact, neatness was the keynote of this small city, the garn Chan-Cho-Pan.

We were watched now, as our guide strode easily along the gravel street and we followed, gawking.

A young man ran from one of the home plots into the street ahead of us. He was big, as Elg was big, flat-bellied, and muscular, and he moved with the same gliding grace. There was frank curiosity on his open face as he came toward us. But he waited until he reached us before he spoke—unrecognizable syllables in a deep, smooth voice. These people almost never shout.

Elg replied in kind. The young man looked us over as though we were new, strange animals—which I guess we were. Elg turned to us.

"This is Orb," he said. "This ten-sun he greets guests." And to Orb he said, "Vin. Denny. They speak only English, as did the man Smith."

Orb clasped his big left hand with his mighty right and gravely bowed his black head.

"You are guests," he pronounced. "I welcome you."

We went through the ritual and I said, "Thanks. You are kind to take us in."

That seemed to go over. Orb smiled, and Hollywood, look out! In repose you'd have had to call his face strikingly handsome, but that open grin was a sunburst. No doubt about what the girls would, and undoubtedly did, think about him. He was about the most man I'd ever seen.

"The guest house of the White Pines," Orb said to Elg. "The couches are freshly renewed. The house of Garn the Artisan can provide food. They roast an elk haunch, and there are new potatoes. I smelled them as I came by not long since."

I suppose he spoke English for our benefit. His British accent was pretty much like Elg's, and the stilted phrasing made me wonder. Had there really been a man here who had taught a people to speak graceful English, or were we being given the business? There wasn't time to give it thought. Orb said "Follow!" and he and Elg set off again, striding as only they could.

There were people in the crisscross of streets, but just singles, all men, all dressed pretty much like Elg and Orb, all striding along like big cats. No women, no children. Later we found out that this was just happen-so. It was the time of the evening meal, and families were in their homes.

Our walk took only a few minutes. After all, the town wasn't that big. Orb led us into a sturdy L-shaped house of fieldstone, with shutters swung back from wide windows and a big front door half open. Nobody seemed to be home. This wasn't surprising, as we soon discovered. Nobody lived there. It was a guest house. The community maintained several of them. The current greeter of guests, a post that apparently rotated, saw to it that they were maintained, and assigned guests to them as he saw fit.

Orb was brief but cordial. Seemingly he hadn't yet grasped the fact that we had no knowledge of guest houses.

"Choose a couch," he said. "There are coverings in plenty. Water for bathing in the large vat; for drinking in the small. Food will be brought in a short time. Have comfort!"

And before we knew it the two big men were gone, and we stood in the middle of the sleeping room looking at each other.

"I've had my fortune told a dozen times," Denny said reflectively, "and none of them mentioned this." He tested the bounce of the nearest couch with his knuckles. "Nice."

"Wouldn't have to be much to beat that rock in the river we slumbered on last night," I said.

There were four couches in the room, wide and low, each covered with a soft, woven, blanket-like coverlid and what looked like a folded skin at the foot. Pegs studded the wall by each bed, and at waist level a wide shelf with legs under it, a sort of attached bench. A number of big four-legged stools were scattered about. Not one had a back. No easy chairs for guests, apparently.

I smelled the food before I saw it and drooled in a way that would have made our hosts happy. But when it came into view I forgot about it. I've told you about the men. Then you know what the women almost had to be like.

I could describe her, this slender lithe girl who came through the half-open door without knocking, carrying a big tray expertly in one hand. I could, but it wouldn't mean much. The whole was considerably more than the sum of its parts. You wouldn't get the impact. She smiled slightly, her amazing, long, almost slanted eyes glowed, but she said no word as she glided across the room and set the tray on a big table by the double windows. Then she turned, grasped left hand with perfectly shaped right, bowed a beautiful head crowned with a jet-black coil of hair.

"Be refreshed," she said. The words were a formula, but the low voice matched the rest of her. "The food is good. I prepared it. I am the daughter of Arn the Artisan. I am called Oo-ah."

"I can see why," Denny blurted.

I punched him, and he remembered his manners. We both grasped hands and bowed heads.

"You are kind to strangers," I said.

"There are no strangers," the girl pronounced. "My father says that they are only people we have not yet learned to know."

"Your father is a wise man." I was still pompous.

"I know." Oo-ah brushed it aside. "Come eat. The meat is best hot."

We sat at the table and she served us. Smoking slices of roast meat on worn wooden trenchers which she took from a cupboard on the wall. Hot boiled potatoes, skinned, and covered with a cheese sauce. Good cheese, too, but fresh tasting, without tang. Flat round cakes that smelled like, and were, cornmeal. Milk in wooden goblets that had been turned on a lathe. And to eat it all with, two knives, one wide and flat like a spatula, one slender and curved with a keen edge. With them was a sharp oak skewer, whittled to a point, the other end like a handle.

I guessed that the stick was to hold the food to be cut. I used it so, cut off a bite of meat, scooped it into my mouth with the spatula. It was easier than chopsticks. I could have used a fork, though.

The girl watched us gravely for a few moments. There was, perhaps, a twinkle deep in those long, almost golden eyes.

"From Orb I learn that you know nothing of us, that you came from beyond the ice, like the man Smith. My need to know hurts me, but one does not inquire of a guest."

Denny couldn't take his eyes off her to eat.

"You sit there and be beautiful," he directed, "and we'll tell you all about Whitehorse and New York and the Bicentennial. You won't be asking. We'll be volunteering everything."

She smiled, but shook her head.

"It is not custom. You need food and are weary. When you have slept I may listen." She tapped the tray. "Place everything there. Orb will remove it, quietly, so you will not wake."

She glided out, a graceful sturdy beauty in bright blouse and miniskirt. Even her moccasins wouldn't have been out of place in some gatherings I've seen.

When she was gone the food suddenly gained flavor, and we knew how hungry we really were. She had brought plenty, but there wasn't much left but utensils when we stacked the tray.

She was right about the sleep, too. We were ready for it. If we had been worrying types, maybe we might have had trouble dropping off. But we knew darn well that thirty-six hours before we had been at Kluane, and I suppose we figured that anything done could be undone. Anyhow, I hardly remember peeling out of boots and breeches and tumbling onto the nearest bunk before I was out like a light.

Chapter 4

The sun was high again when I awoke. That didn't mean much, because at that latitude in June we only have about four hours of darkness. But I was sharp again, so I knew I had put in enough time.

Denny was gasping and blowing in the room beyond the sleeping area. I went to the door to look. Denny was having a bath. We had seen the water vats when we came in, but there hadn't been time to be briefed on custom.

The larger vat was nothing but a hollowed-out log half, a wooden trough set waist high on a foundation of rough stone. Denny stood in a depression in the floor lined with loose gravel, his big naked body glowing and shrinking as he dipped and poured water over himself with a long-handled wooden dipper.

He saw me, set down the dipper, and shook like a wet dog.

"Towels are unheard of," he said. "You're supposed to rub dry with your palms."

"Who told you?" I asked. "Oo-ah?"

He grinned. "Orb was here. We thought you were dead, so he's probably gone to make funeral arrangements."

He stepped out of the gravel and waved an arm. "Want to try our Stone Age shower? Water just four degrees above freezing. Exhilarating. Circulation stopping."

"Anything you can do, I can do," I said, and peeled off the little I had slept in.

I did it, too, and lived through it, but just barely. No wonder these people are mighty. The puny young die early just taking a bath.

My teeth weren't through chattering when Orb returned. He had an armful of fresh clothing which he tossed on the nearest couch.

"Be refreshed," he said. "Clean garments are pleasant. These should be suitable in size."

He had a good eye, for everything fit. We didn't even ask where he got them. In a couple of minutes we looked like natives, except for my relatively short six feet and Denny's yellow hair.

That day we saw Chan-Cho-Pan. And, naturally, it saw us. We grasped our hands and bowed our heads a hundred times as Orb or Elg spoke names. There were faces at every window as we kept pace with our striding guides along the gravel roads. Children, suntanned and supple and usually clad only in shorts or briefs, grinned at us from home plots, but the grins vanished when we looked their way, and they clasped hands and bowed as politely as any elder.

Occasionally I remembered, and looked up and listened. This was the day Phil was to pick us up on Seward. But the only things in the sky were eagles, and an occasional gull that must have come from the marsh country that we had seen from the heights coming in. As for sounds, I could well believe that there wasn't a motor in the world. I heard only people, and even they didn't call or shout. Pet dogs barked, birds sang, and now and then a two-wheeled cart came crunching along in the gravel. The secret of the split-hooved draft animals was dispelled with the first one. They were elk, just plain elk, unaltered bulls stepping proudly, but evidently well trained and controlled.

"There are other towns like this?" I spoke to Elg, as we stood at the corner of what I'd call the town square, or perhaps the town park. It was ten home plots on a side, lightly shaded with scattered trees, and with paths twisting through it.

"In the world, ten societies, ten garns," Elg said. He glanced at me, as though the wonder of me struck him again. "Perhaps I should say our world. Since the coming of the man Smith many years ago, and now you, it is evident that there is more than we know. Things are different somewhere. But between the ice ranges and the sea, where the ice also comes in great masses in season, there have been ten garns since time began."

I watched a gaggle of little boys and three big romping dogs darting and chasing among the trees. It could have been any small hometown park, in the somewhere that Elg could not envision.

"Are they near?" I asked. "Could we visit?"

"The nearest, two sun-spans. You will doubtless be free to go where you will, after the Primate has listened and disposed."

Denny and Orb had detoured by the open pool, a bright clean pond of perhaps half an acre, into which water poured steadily from an uncovered wooden flume. They strode up as Elg spoke of the Primate.

"And who," Denny asked, "who or what is the Primate? You've said the word before. Remember, we know nothing."

"That is true," Elg said. He raised an eyebrow, and I could see that he was amused by his own bland statement. Then his fine face grew grave and respectful.

"The Primate," he said, "speaks wisdom for the ten garns. He is only a man, the most honest, the most learned, the most intelligent of us all. He speaks for the world, by agreement, and his word is the last word. Someone must dispose, or men would fight like the beasts."

I felt myself nodding in agreement.

"In our world," I said, "men fight to be that man. And when one wins the place, almost never by wisdom, others plot to pull him down."

Elg shook his head.

"It is strange," he said. "So spoke the man Smith, it is said. There was a man called a Kaiser who was to be removed. Smith often wondered if it ever had got done."

"It was done," I said. "But, as you say, it was no remedy. Later came a man named Hitler, who did worse things. Millions died before he was destroyed."

The two Elkans—men of the elk, as we now knew them to be—stared at us gravely. It was evident that they knew the meaning of the word millions. It was equally evident that they didn't believe, couldn't believe my statement. There were not millions of people. In the ten garns there were scarcely more than forty thousand.

Yet Orb said graciously, "Yours is a strange story, difficult to believe, yet no one doubts the spoken word of a guest. So, you must speak with the Primate."

Denny shrugged it off. "Why not? I'm no snob. I'll talk to anybody."

Elg missed it. You could see him munch on the unfamiliar term.

" 'I'm no snob.' This has meaning we have not learned. Would you clarify?"

It was a chore, especially since I saw the devil in Denny's blue eyes, but I kept my face grave.

"It has no specific meaning," I said hastily. "Just a saying we have to denote willingness. Denny just means we'll be delighted to speak with the Primate, whoever he may be."

"This was never in doubt," Orb said drily. "You have no choice."

For a moment my resentment flared, but I kept it inside. Who were these, these primitives, to tell us what we could and could not do? Then I glanced at the honest, open-faced giants, and answered my own question. They were the owners of this land, and we were interlopers. No matter how we got there, we still were foreign. I could call the land Yukon, call it Alaska, but from that moment I knew it was neither. I didn't understand. I still don't. But I knew.

"We look forward to speech with your ruler," I said. "He sounds more worthy than most such we have known. We'll be grateful for any advice from him, because I have a feeling that our aircraft will not fly over, nor do I think we can go back up the River of Bones. I think we are here, like the man Smith was. A miracle brought us here. Only a miracle can allow us to go home."

Elg's fine face expressed satisfaction.

"The Primate will not teach you much," he said. "You are wise in your own right. But," he added, "you misuse a term. The Primate is no ruler. He listens and disposes, because of all men he does it best. But he was chosen by the people of all the garns. And when he goes to the White Cliffs, not too far in the future now, another will be chosen. So it has been, and so it will be, as long as the sun is in the sky."

The White Cliffs loomed in the far northwest, a white escarpment very different from the snowy ranges to the east. I had put the binoculars on them. Even a cub geologist would have asked questions, and I considered myself pretty good, as far as I'd gone. Like so many things in the last two days, the White Cliffs shouldn't have been there. From first glance, that was evident. They lifted almost at right angles to the continental ranges, to what I still thought of as the St. Elias. Their white was not the white of snow, for the escarpment rose vertical and stark. And it was more than white that the sun high-lighted on those massive walls. Bands of rose, bands of purple, bands of gray and brown and shadowy orange cut through the gleaming white. Horizontal bands, sedimentary bands, extending on westward until the cliffs were lost in misty distance. A sedimentary barrier in a volcanic land.

I turned back to Elg. For a moment the talk had stopped as we all looked northward.

"They don't seem so far away," I said. "The White Cliffs, I mean. Since I'm here, I'd like to take a closer look. They can't be over a day or so distant. Rocks are sort of my hobby, you might say," I added in explanation.

By the way the Elkans were looking at me, I realized I'd stubbed my toe again. Astonishment mingled with anger on both faces.

Then Elg's stern look softened and he shook his head.

"Truly, you know nothing," he said. "None go to the White Cliffs until it is time. It is forbidden."

Promptly the gleaming sunlit walls became twice as attractive. I was ignorant, so I took advantage of it. I blundered deeper.

"What dangers," I asked with some scorn, "are supposed to be associated with a geologic oddity? To me they look beautiful and completely harmless."

"No danger," Elg said quietly. "But as all know, it would not be considerate to go there without cause. None have ever done this. If we did, we would *be* danger."

"Have you not White Cliffs in your own land?" Orb looked completely puzzled.

"We have them," I said. "From the Badlands of Dakota to the White Cliffs of Dover. But there's nothing taboo about them. We study and climb on them as we do any other. But then," I added, "very few things are taboo in our world."

"Our thoughts are not meeting," Elg said. "There are answers to all puzzles. When you have spoken with the Primate we can have long talks, and each will learn from the other. For now, we but confuse each other."

It was true. We all knew it. And apparently audience with

the Primate came before any disposal of our problems, or, for that matter, of us. So we went back to our sight-seeing tour. Our guides or hosts or jailers, we still weren't sure which, led us along more streets, finally finishing with a complete circle of the town along the outside road. Or perhaps square would be better, as I've said. I never saw such an arrangement.

The way those boys walked made us ready to eat, and when we got back to the guest house Oo-ah was waiting.

Orb had brought breakfast, small corn cakes, syrup, and milk. Lunch had been taken in hand, yellow apples from trees across the garn boundary road and a handful of pungent, fleshy leaves that Orb had ranged into the fields to gather for us. Both he and Elg seemed to consider them delicacies, and ate them with relish. They weren't bad, but I could take them or leave them. They didn't exactly seem to take the place of food.

For dinner Oo-ah had small roast fowls, about the size of ptarmigan. She had a kind of parsnip, also roasted, and white fat joints of some kind of grass, served raw on a trencher, that made an amazingly refreshing salad. We each had three birds, well packed in with parsnips and garnished with the grass. We drank goblets of the rich wild milk, which now we suspected that the elk provided. Oo-ah watched, her long golden eyes gradually growing round.

"In your land, do all eat as you do?" she inquired bluntly.

I smiled at her as I licked my greasy fingers. The fowl were fat.

"All don't have the opportunity," I assured her. "No one can prepare food as you do. In all the lands I have traveled I have yet to see your equal as a cook."

"From Pasadena to Hoboken," Denny muttered. "Oh great traveler!"

But as I felt sure she would, she soaked the flattery up. And it wasn't all flattery at that. She really knew how.

"It is not difficult to prepare good food," she smiled. "It is pleasant to see it enjoyed. You may have more if you choose. Though how you could, I cannot see," she added candidly.

But we'd had enough. We helped her pile the remnants on her tray and she went, slender and graceful and beautiful.

With her going the mood changed. We were alone, not dead tired as last night, and finally our predicament hit us with impact. Where were we? What was the explanation for this whole ball of wax? It made no sense, but for the first time we knew it was real. It wasn't a dream. It wasn't television. We were west of the St. Elias, and everything was different.

"Vin," Denny said quietly, "we've had it. Somehow, we've changed worlds." He sat on one of the bunks, ran his fingers through his yellow hair, then finally lay back and stretched out.

"I know." I didn't, of course, but I had to say something.

"Still," Denny rose on an elbow, "I don't buy the idea that we traveled a one-way road. We can go back the way we came."

I had sprawled back on my own bunk. Oo-ah was right; we had put away an impolite amount of food. That, at least, felt real enough. So did the bunk.

"I doubt if it's that simple," I said. "In the first place, we'd have to get back down to the River of Bones, and something tells me they won't stamp our visas for that. And the mountains are different. Who's to say the tunnel wouldn't be?"

"We can look." I recognized the stubborn tone Denny uses when he really thinks he's being herded. He can be as blockheaded and singleminded as a bull behind a gate.

"Don't get muscular," I advised. "They're as big as you are, and there are a good many more of them. I'll bet you can't even lay Orb on his back. If they say no go, we no go. Face that."

Denny was silent. I guess he was facing it.

"Okay," he said at last, "let's go see the man who decides things here. We'll tell 'em in the morning that we want our session with the Primate. Now! No nonsense! Vite!"

I yawned. Our situation was clear, but I was getting drowsy just the same. All that food!

"That's sense," I approved. "They can't deny us that."

The door swung, and Elg came in like a shadow. He looked down at us with a grin.

"I am told that you have eaten well," he said. "Sleep deep, for with the sun we go to the Primate. It is two sun-spans of good travel. I will be your guide. Have comfort!"

He glided out before either of us could speak.

I smothered a laugh. Denny looked grim, but his sense of humor came to the top in a minute or two.

"So they make the decisions," he admitted. "It's what we wanted, isn't it? Have comfort!"

Chapter 5

The morning came, and with it Elg, Orb, and Oo-ah with more little cakes, syrup, milk, and grapes. There were two trays. Elg and Orb breakfasted with us, and the girl watched, as she seemed to like to do. Not only was she naïve and beautiful, but there was a freshness, an honesty about her which, it seemed to me, I'd never experienced before. Denny always looked at her with completely open admiration. She knew it and smiled back at him with composure. It was right and proper and no more than her due that a vivid young woman should attract the attention of every male within eye range. We knew by now that Elg had a wife, but Orb was all charm and muscles when Oo-ah looked his way.

Elg had said that we would have two days of travel. When once again we were on the trail we soon saw what we were in for. These people were as nearly tireless as people ever get. Elg glided ahead of us like a blown leaf. In an hour Chan-Cho-Pan was far behind us. Elg left the trail and struck out across country, traveling in a straight line that paid no attention to footing. He changed from wolf to stag to mountain sheep as the terrain shifted. Nothing seemed to disturb his gliding stride or to cut his superb wind. What a man!

We floundered, but we stayed with him. After all, we're mountain men, and have covered some country in our times. But even the light single blanket roll on our backs was a burden before noon.

We saw little sign of men. Partly, I suppose, it was the route Elg took, for we cut trails and once a road, but never traveled them. Now and then we saw cultivated fields. One high meadow had new hayricks. No people, though. The land was almost as though men never had touched it. Yet we knew it was claimed, was used. The use was simple, fundamental, and did not distort or change the landscape.

"A jeep, now, or a small helicopter, would improve the

travel situation around here no end," Denny panted, as we slogged up a particularly steep slope. "I suppose these people never ride."

"No superhighways," I pointed out. "And even a saddle elk, if they have such a thing, couldn't stick with our boy up front there. No, I imagine there's only one way to go—and we're using it."

Elg was five yards ahead of us. His ears were as good as his legs, though, and he came to a stop when he topped the rise. He became a tour lecturer while we re-oxygenated.

"We have passed the fields of Chan-Cho-Pan," he said. He pointed southwest. "There lies the society of Char-Che-Po. Its garn is a sun-span from this ridge."

He faced back northwest. In the distance, and clearer, was the remarkable sun-bright barrier of the White Cliffs.

"The society of Che-Chan-Da. With them now reposes the token for best wrestler of all societies. We hope to remove it from them in the Games."

"You use the English word 'society,' " I said. "Why?"

"It seems that thus the man Smith called our word 'garn.' As you now know, there are ten garns, ten societies, ten groups of people whose lives are interwoven for the good of all. One has pride in one's society."

"We used to have one of them," Denny said. "We called it the Great Society. Some were proud of it, but some sure weren't."

"Dissension is not good," Elg said gravely. "When such arises, the Primate quickly disposes."

"Which society does he live in?"

Elg smiled.

"The Primate is not of a society. He places his origin out of his memory, and disposes alike for all men. His home site lies alone, and men come to him when they need. You will see."

See we did, but not before we'd put a lot of country behind us and had spent a not restful night in a chilly camp rolled up in our one thin blanket. A good down sleeping bag can make all the difference between Arctic and arthritis, believe me.

But the lack didn't bother Elg. He was up before the sun, searing little cubes of half-dried meat from his belt pouch over the newly fed fire. They tasted good. The fire unstiffened us, and before long we knew we would live. Then back to the trail—or, more often, the lack of one.

It was gaudy country. Deer in the valleys, marmots among the rocks, a coyote skulking at the edge of a brushy field, big hawks sweeping in circles overhead. I especially liked the little streams, clear as glass, cold and tasty. No sludge, no detergents. At pools big trout occasionally boiled the water. I saw brookies so bright they looked painted, and the tall dorsal fin and gunmetal flash of grayling. I knew they didn't belong together. We didn't belong there either. But there we all were.

The sun tilted steeply to the west before we came to the first of the Primate's fields. They were in a wide valley, pleasant and level, and out in the center, on a knoll of considerable height, we could see the Primate's home. The river responsible for the valley curved beneath and half encircled the island of high ground. Small trees in variety held the slopes and terraces, and as we drew nearer we could see that they were mostly fruit trees, a few already with heavy ripening loads. And this, too, was puzzling, for June was barely beginning. The fields were well cared for, the terraces neat, every tree pruned. The stone walls of the house that crowned the knoll, a pretty extensive house, too, were vine-covered, softened with green. There were wide casements, balconies, and what seemed to be a stone railing or broken wall encircled the entire flat top of the building.

It occurred to me that the Primate did himself rather well.

Elg seemed to pick up my thought, for he said, "Many bring problems for the Primate's wisdom. All must eat, and none must depart until they have rested on the Primate's couches. Food is required, and space. But the Primate is a simple man. His needs are few. The garns send workers for his fields, and when duty allows, he also works there."

I had a mental picture of an ancient patriarch, probably with a long white beard, puttering around and delivering opinions with the arbitrariness of age. Admitted, we hadn't seen such an old-timer since we had come from under the glacier. In all Chan-Cho-Pan we hadn't seen a beard. But impressions fixed during a lifetime don't die in a few days.

The Primate, though, did his best to kill that one. When we stood before the main entrance to his home—great double doors of joined, heavy wood slabs ornamented with bands and scrolls of rough, dark metal—we at least expected a couple of guards to step out. But nothing happened. We just stood there. Denny fidgeted, and I finally turned to Elg.

"Patience," he said. "We were observed."

A few more minutes proved that we were. The big doors swung wide. A man advanced across the stone slab, a big man, and even his slow pace had Elkan grace. He might have been forty. No more, certainly. He was dressed pretty much as we were. Sandals, I remember noticing. Not moccasins. He was thinner, maybe, than Elg or Orb, but his hair was black, his muscles the muscles of an athlete. His face had craggy dignity; his long eyes reminded me a little of the golden ones of Oo-ah.

He grasped powerful hands, bowed his head.

"Denny. Vin. Elg. You are guests." A smooth, deep voice, and English like everybody else, with the same British twist.

We went through the ritual. I admit to a little chill when he called my name.

Elg said, "We are grateful." Then he relaxed and grinned, as though the Primate were his neighbor. He looked around with a farmer's eye. "All seems well. The peaches are finer than for years. I smelled them from far."

"There will be some," the Primate promised. "Enter and be refreshed. You were always a good man before food, Elg, but rumor has it that in these you've met your match."

There you have it. We looked for age and ponderous dignity in the fabulous Primate, and we got a big farmer with a twinkle in deep, knowing eyes, whose first expressed wisdom was to twit us on our appetites!

Still, I picked up the ball.

"We will confine ourselves to one peach," I said. "Elg doubtless is hungrier than we."

The Primate's chuckle rumbled, and he led the way.

It would be hard to say whether we were impressed or disappointed by the inside appointments of the big stone house. We, or at least I, still had that lingering feeling that there ought to be richness, ornateness, luxury. Instead, we saw nothing that couldn't have been in our guest house of the White Pines. Rough tables. Wall pegs. Four-legged stools.

But size, now, that was another thing. Space there was. We followed the Primate down a wide corridor and into a vast room, with great naked beams above our heads three times the height of a man. Along one whole side high casements were flung open. Beyond them balconies jutted out. The valley, the fields and orchards, the twisting river stretched beyond the windows, a grand view. It was the sun side, and the long yellow rays of the setting sun reached to the back walls of the great room.

Couches were scattered almost at random over half the space, all neatly spread. And on the other side of the room was a real wonder, the glint and sparkle of open water. It was a pool, maybe eight feet wide, easily twice that in length. The floor was of wide stone slabs, neatly grouted, and into this the pool was set. Water-worn river stones, from the size of a baseball to that of a man's head, had been cemented to form the colorful sides and bottom. Water ran into it from a masonry pipe. It was within six inches of full, and my practical soul was hoping that there was a drain and that it was working.

The Primate gave us a minute to look. Then he waved a hand.

"Have comfort." The formula didn't change, apparently. "The couch that pleases you is yours. If you would bathe, the water is newly drawn, and changes itself with frequency. Elg knows."

He strode to the farthest of the several doors.

"When the sun is gone, there will be food. —More than one peach," he added gravely, and the door closed behind him.

There are times when you don't know what to do next. This was one. Elg was watching us both, and his fine face had the same amused look I remembered when we first had met, many days before. Or was it only five? Ridiculous! I felt as though it had been months since we had climbed out of the canyon of the River of Bones.

"The Primate finds you of great interest," Elg observed. "He knows you bring wisdom unknown to us. He will expect much talk."

"He knew our names," Denny said. "Didn't seem surprised at anything. Did he pick our brains? Is he a telepath or something like that?"

Elg considered, but we soon realized what intrigued him.

"This is a new word," he said. "I can suspect its meaning, but he does not know what you think. His knowledge comes from runners, who have come to him each day from Chan-Cho-Pan. The Primate must know all that happens, so men come each sun-span from all the ten garns. Now do you marvel that his fields and orchards must be large?"

We both nodded.

"He runs a hotel," I agreed. "Guest house," I amended, as Elg's eyes brightened at another new word.

We were more than a little grimy from the trail. The water in the pool glistened invitingly. But I remembered the ordeal of the guest-house shower, so I guess I hung back a little. Denny, too, didn't make any move in that direction. He wandered about, testing the springiness of the couches. Elg finally broke the ice, and I hoped he wasn't doing it literally.

"This bath is doubtless not familiar to you," he said. "Only the house of the Primate could have one of such size."

He tossed aside his few clothes, slid into the pool and went under. Twice he glided from end to end like some great sleek seal, then finally popped his head up and lay puffing quietly and grinning. He knew what ailed us.

"The water lies long in a shallow warming vat in the sun," he explained. "When it arrives here it is no longer cold."

He sank slowly to the pool bottom, then shot out of the water like a torpedo, landing lightly on the neatly guttered edge. With his hands he stripped the water from his smooth tanned hide.

Denny shed his clothes and imitated him. Then I followed. The water was perfect.

White, roughly woven robes hung from wall pegs. We each took one. Lightly belted in place, it made a comfortable garment. But I had trouble finding one that didn't sweep the stone floor.

Have you ever had trout from cold water, on the table before you within an hour of the time they stopped swimming? Our trenchers each held a whole grayling, pretty close to two pounds of luscious, pink-white eating, partly grilled and partly baked in a way I could only guess at. Small green fruits, tart and full of juice, garnished each trencher. They weren't citrus, but, as we found later, their juice gave point to the mouth-watering flavor of the fish. There was a round platter of baked yellow squashes, another of steamed white corn on the ear, and a mound of the promised peaches, pink and fragrant. The drink, as usual, rich elk milk in wooden goblets.

The man who brought this, little more than a boy but a smooth-muscled giant just the same, swiftly arranged a table near a casement. He placed the food, then clasped hands and bowed his head as Elg spoke names: "Don. Vin. Denny."

Don looked us over with the same open interest everyone showed.

"Be refreshed," he said. "The Primate will speak with you when the sun comes. His duties are many, as Elg will say."

He strode out. We sat and ate, and it was, if possible, better than anything Oo-ah had prepared. We tried to justify the reputation the Primate had given us, and Don took away little but bones and hulls and cobs and peelings.

There was no TV to postpone our rest, no world news to worry about, no jets overhead to break into dreams. We each picked a couch, closed our eyes, and it was morning, the sun streaming through the wide casements.

Chapter 6

The Primate came, but not until after Don had brought our small corn cakes and honey and grapes and milk. When I thought of our world, the one we had left so recently and which seemed so far away, one of the things I didn't regret was breakfast. Here you didn't *need* coffee. Shredded wheat, dry toast—ugh! You slept with few dreams, wakened hungry and alert. You didn't need stimulants or filler. You needed food.

So we ate, and bathed again, and Don brought us fresh clean clothes. They were our own. They had been laundered while we slept. We went out on a balcony and looked far over the fields and orchards. We could see how the river came twisting down from the rolling country to the south and east, and beyond that how the hills rose, dark with timber.

"It is a good land."

The Primate's deep voice sounded beside us. We had not seen him come. I suppose his remark would have been small talk, a pleasantry, if it hadn't been exactly what I was thinking. Not in those words, maybe. But that's what it added up to. It *was* a good land.

"We will speak," the Primate said. "Yours will be a story unlike any I have known, so I will greet no other guests this sun. I must learn all you can tell me."

He had put aside the day. We used it, too. As best we could, we told him about the crevasse in Seward, a fine deep gash that opened up almost overnight. He was interested in our interest in cold wild country. His deep eyes glowed with approval when we described the climb down the ice wall. We were men as he understood men.

But his strong face grew grave, then stony, as we told of the hike into the glacier. Denny and I talked in turn, never interrupting each other, each picking up when the other paused. We work together like that.

"That mammoth," Denny said. "We've had nothing like it in our world for thousands of years. But there it stood, just as it had been frozen into the ice mass, twice as big as animals we call elephants. Does that sound like anything you have here, Sir?" He capitalized that Sir, and it seemed the natural and the only thing to do. There was no form for addressing the Primate. He was just another man. But almost from his first word you knew he was more than that. He was an exceptional man. He was the most exceptional man in this land. He was the Primate.

At Denny's question he leaned back on the rough stool and slowly shook his head.

"We know nothing like it," he said. "One does not doubt the spoken word of a guest, else I should say that it exists only in your mind. Even the man Smith did not speak of things of this kind."

"From all I hear, he came across the range. *We* came *under* it."

"It is a wonder," the Primate admitted. "Yet, you speak as you could not speak if you had not seen. It must be thought about."

I had an idea.

"You can see this for yourself, or at least a part. There are mammoth skulls in the River of Bones, complete with tusks. We can show you."

The Primate did not show fear or anger. His color did not change. Only his eyes, those deep long eyes, betrayed how shaken he was inside. His deep voice resonated.

"It is forbidden, it has always been forbidden, to go up the River of the Bones. It is known that nothing good comes from it. And not even in legend has man ever done so."

"Then how, Sir," Denny again, "is it known to cause harm, when no one has ever done it?"

It was a poser. The Primate would not have been the man he was if he hadn't recognized it. His face grew almost quizzical as he reached across the table, plucked a grape from the bunches piled there, popped it into his mouth.

"It is a belief," he conceded. "A belief that has been with us always. Somewhere, sometime, there was a reason for it. But nothing in our stories of what has gone before tells what the reason may be. I have thought of this. Still, I believe."

"Suppose," I said, "that in a time so far gone that no one remembers some of the great creatures in the River of Bones were alive. Suppose the last ones lived there. Suppose some were killers. Suppose that they even ate man. That would be a reason, wouldn't it? The fear could have outlived the memory."

The Primate looked from me to Denny and back again. I think there was respect in that look.

"You have few years," the Primate said gravely. "Yet you require reasons for what you believe. When a man has lived long, this is called wisdom. In the two of you, what should it be called?"

I grinned. Denny chuckled aloud as he got the drift. Even the watchful Elg, impressed by his opportunity to sit in on this day's talk, relaxed and smiled.

"Stubborn? Pig-headed? We have a saying, 'Fools rush in where angels fear to tread.' Do you think that fits us, Sir?"

"Some of your words are strange, but meaning comes through. All of our English came from the man Smith, as you must know. He never spoke of angels, but we know well the meaning of fool. There is another word: courage. Do you think we might use it here?"

It was a graceful compliment. If we had any lingering fears of Elkan savagery, that dispelled it. The Primate was a genuinely wise man.

Denny stood up and stretched his big body. Those stools weren't easy chairs. He loomed for a moment over the Primate, who was leisurely munching another grape.

"We do dash ahead, Sir," Denny said. "Maybe it took courage to climb down the ice wall of the crevasse. But it had to be a couple of fools who would hike deeper and deeper into a break in a glacier. We got through, but it wasn't courage. It was luck."

"The man Smith had another word. Fate. He used it often. Perhaps it was fate that brought you through. Not only your fate, but ours."

I hadn't thought of that. But look at the impact Smith had made. We knew things he never knew, and there were two of us. The Primate did have things to think about. I could see that. I knew Denny well enough to know that he could see it too.

"Would you say, Sir," I said slowly, "that the coming of Smith was a bad thing? Did it change the lives of the people in harmful ways? Did he bring thoughts or learnings that you wish he had left behind?"

I think the Primate liked it, my coming to the point like that. His expression was approving, if I read his face rightly.

"I have thought on this," he said. "I can see no harm and more than a little good. Smith did not try to impress us with wisdom. He cared not whether we changed our habits or our thoughts. He was a lost and a lonely man, and his only hope was to go back whence he came."

"Did he try?"

"From his telling he was one of three, and they sought to climb a great peak in a snow blizzard. His companions died, frozen, and he left them for the snow to cover. His food was gone. He thought he would die as well. But he was a strong man, and somehow he descended. He wandered, not knowing where he was, and hunters found him, almost starved and blind from the snow and wind. Men from Chan-Cho-Pan, they were."

"My father," Elg said proudly.

"Your father, Elg," the sage confirmed, "and three others. It was in well-known hunting range, and they wondered much whence he came. They brought him back to the garn. He was fed and tended, and his eyes could see again. But it was long before anyone could understand his speech. Men did go back and follow his trail in the snow, but it went deeper and deeper into the ranges until finally the winds had filled and destroyed it for even the best of trackers."

The Primate's deep voice trailed into silence. He looked away out the wide window, his craggy face pensive, as though he were sharing the homesick despair of the man

Smith. As though it were willing its own behavior, his big right hand reached for a grape, his mouth received it, and he chewed, reflectively. Then he came back to us.

"He learned our speech. He told us as I have told you, but in many more words. He, as have you, said that he came from beyond the snow.

"Men made long trips, long climbs, and took him far in the direction he pointed out. But always mountains were strange, and he recognized no land. None were surprised, for nothing lives in the ice fields.

"And finally he knew that he could not go back. He taught us all his speech, and how things are written, with symbols he called letters. He made paper from wood and drew silk from insects and taught us a simple music called jazz. He spoke of a thousand things, and his face would glow when he spoke, and often his eyes had tears. For many seasons and cycles of seasons he lived and worked and hunted, and had pleasure of a sort.

"But more and more he sat and looked at the snow peaks, as though his mind and his memory and all his being except his body reached on beyond the range. And so he sat, and grew weak and enfeebled before our eyes. His skin wrinkled and yellowed, his hair became thin and white. It was a strange thing to see."

"Maybe," I ventured, "maybe he was just old."

"This was considered. But it could not have been. He withered and ate less and less, and finally, one day in his chair, life left him. Yet he was not old. Never did he begin to grow small."

It was that unexpected. I'm pretty sure my mouth must have dropped open. Denny sat with a stunned, set look on his baby face, and I know the Primate wondered. He couldn't, though, possibly have imagined how he had hit us. He had spoken of something that all men knew. He couldn't divine how strange his words were to us. He was only a man, after all.

The White Cliffs, where all men go, but where prying outsiders cannot explore. . . . The midget coffin and tiny bones still tucked away in my packsack in the guest house at Chan-Cho-Pan. . . . I had an inkling. But what I thought was simpler than the truth.

Yet I couldn't ask. I don't know why. And when I had my cool again, and told of my share of our trip from the land beyond, I did not mention the coffin and the unbelievable bones. The time would come when I'd regret it, but these things you don't know in advance.

The little break passed, and while it was pretty certain that Elg and the Primate saw and wondered, it didn't change the flavor, the *feel* of our talking. It was the most instructive day I ever spent.

We broke the sitting by walking. First, around in the big sleeping hall; later, after a lunch of steamed small crayfish and peaches and grapes, out of the great door and down through the vineyards and orchards to the river. But the talk never stopped. We finished our adventure tale and went on to the world of 1976, until we began to realize that what we told would make even our hike account less believable. It didn't, though.

Once the Primate said, "These are wonders. They tax the grasp of man. But no one could invent them. I sense that they are real, these incredible things you speak of. Somewhere, they exist."

I chuckled to myself over that one. He didn't doubt the possibility of our lying. He simply doubted our capacity.

We didn't do all the informing. In between the bits of our own story we learned more of the land and the people around us. The facts were mostly simpler, but we had as hard a time believing.

And one thing we came back to, again and again. They thought our accounts of our world marvelous. The stories of Smith must have been as strange, for he was the first alien even their legends mentioned. But there seemed to me to be a lack, something missing, in the way they responded to those tales of our land, somewhere.

I said to the Primate, "Elg and Orb and every man we have met are strong and tough. We rarely have seen such men. Surely they have climbed much into the snow peaks to the east. I'd think they'd never quit. Aren't you, aren't you all, curious about what lies beyond?"

The Primate knew what I meant.

"We have explored," he said gravely. "Staying far from the River of Bones, men from every garn have climbed far. From the highest peaks, reached by utmost toil, nothing can be seen but ice and snow. When I had few years I myself climbed there. There is no life there, and the snows and the bitter winds go on to the edge of the world."

I bit into a peach, mellow and sweet, that I had just picked from a skillfully pruned tree. Peaches do not grow in the Arctic.

"Then where," I asked, "did we come from?"

"You know what you know," the sage said. "For me, I have much to think on. You may go among the garns, and teach and learn any things you believe good. And," with a twinkle of disbelief in his grave eyes, "if your aircraft comes, I must be informed."

There was more, but this was the real end. The Primate had disposed.

We ate again, roast rabbits with a kind of steamed turnip piled about them, more new corn, and milk. We bathed again in the pool and slept again on the wide, comfortable couches.

"Now that you are with us, use your wisdom for good."

Those were the Primate's last words as we left in the earliest morning light. The sun found us well on our way, behind the tireless Elg.

Chapter 7

It was a different journey back. Oh, we ached and gasped for breath as before, following perhaps the best trail man I'll ever see. That's not what I mean. What made it different was the fixing of our status here, the Primate's calm certainty that we never would be able to leave.

Chan-Cho-Pan seemed familiar, friendly, almost like home. We were glad to be back at the guest house of the White Pines. The door stood ajar, as always, and our big pack frames and our climbing gear lay where we had dropped them. Even the brutal cold of the dipped and poured shower water was not as shocking as we remembered. And when Oo-ah, her long eyes shining, came in with a big fragrant tray, that completed it. She was *glad* to see us!

Her bright orange blouse and short skirt were crisp and fresh. New, ornamented moccasins were on her small feet.

The rope of glossy black hair was arranged in a strange coil almost Japanese in effect, and she brought a warm, pleasant perfume with her. She had looked forward to our return! She had missed us!

I realized that I was repeating these things again and again in my mind, and of course I knew what I really meant. I had missed her!

"Oo-ah, you are the most beautiful woman in the world!" Denny was laughing as he clasped his hands and bowed.

And she: "Be refreshed! Am I even more beautiful than the food?"

"Take it away and I'll still be happy, as long as you are here!"

She took the cloth from the tray.

"One does not doubt the spoken word of a guest," she smiled, "but it would not be courteous to test you. Come, eat."

I had bowed silently, and silently I took my seat. It wasn't like me. I think of plenty to say, as a rule.

But I hadn't spoken much on the trail back. It seemed almost as if I had withdrawn from myself and now stood aside, watching as an outsider would while two men tried to realize and to fit themselves into a new life frame, a completely unexpected fate. The Primate believed that for us our world was gone. In one sense I didn't follow him at all. I knew we'd try to get out. To do it we'd have to go back up the River of Bones, and *that* a whole world of people would try to prevent.

And Oo-ah! I've known girls. Plenty of times I had had my company in the perfumed night, when the moon was a body in the sky that gave soft light and was not just a rocket target. And those girls were fine, in those moments and in their ways. But they blurred into each other in my memory.

When it hits you, you know it, I suppose. I knew this girl would never blur, never fade. So I sat silently and ate warm roast slices of luscious sweet meat (later it was told that Orb had slain a bear) garnished with slices of boiled eggs, a great mound of steamed cabbages, the whole pungent with herbs. I drank the cold milk from the wooden goblet, and it was Denny who laughed and joked with Oo-ah.

I give them both this. They respected my silence. They were sensitive enough not to comment or inquire. There was no strain. And when we were stuffed, and before she lifted the tray of scraps and remnants, Oo-ah clasped her hands, bowed her fine head, and said, "Have comfort! You are home!"

Of course she spoke to us both, but I thought it was at me she looked.

Where before our audience with the Primate we had been eager to travel, to explore, to visit among the garns, now it didn't seem so urgent. Without saying anything, we put it off. I think we felt the probable similarity of life in the other societies, and, without consciously resolving it, we chose to stay and live among our friends.

Sure, we intended to go later. And the curiosity wasn't one-sided, anyhow. Men came from afar to see us. The guest houses of Chan-Cho-Pan had not been so used in living memory.

It seemed polite to be devious about it. No man ever said he came only to see us. Each was simply a traveler, a hunter, a runner, far from his garn. It was courtesy, it was tradition, that he be given rest and food and the news of happenings. That was what guest houses were for.

Orb's ten-sun as greeter of guests had finished. His replacement was Dor. Big, a little slower, a little more silent, Dor was cast from the same mold as Elg and Orb. He it was who first said to us, "Live and enjoy!" instead of the usual, "You are guests!" He didn't explain when he moved us from the guest house of the White Pines to a much smaller dwelling. He didn't need to. We knew it to be a house for men who have no women and therefore have less need for much space. A bachelor house. We were no longer transients.

"This is the house of the Lindens," Dor said. "Now it is your house. It turns the rain, the place for fire does not smoke, water is near. Live and enjoy!

"You may take food wherever there is plenty. When you hunt, share meat with those who have none. When a man needs help with a task, help him. When you have something to lift that is more than your strength, someone will pass by."

And that, we found, was just the way it was.

"It doesn't make sense," Denny said. "It's completely random. Nobody runs the blasted town at all!"

"I've never seen a neater community in my life," I said. "Everything's clean, everybody eats, everything's in repair. Even the trees are pruned to this week. Seems to work."

Denny shook his head. "I don't see how. Who coordinates? Who starts things? Who decides what needs doing?"

"Dor says that if it's undone, it needs doing. If a man does a task, then others need not do it and may do something else."

"Double-talk!" Denny said.

"I wonder. Quoting Dor again, if no one feels a need to do a task, then it follows that it doesn't need to be done, for no one requires it. If it is necessary, someone will do it."

"And what about the character who never does anything, and so leaves other people to do everything?"

I grinned at him. "That, I guess, is the catch. He doesn't exist. With these people, every man's sense of responsibility is as basic as his hunger. He wouldn't understand the delightful possibilities offered by being a bum."

"Incredible!" Denny said.

"No more incredible than our being here at all," I reminded him.

"There, my friend, you have a point. You do indeed have a point."

Old camp cooks like Denny and me naturally wouldn't suffer by having to fix our own chow. For nobody brought meals to a bachelor house. Bad form, apparently. We learned where the fields were, out in the varied countryside beyond the town. We took what we wanted, beans, potatoes, corn, squash, a meal at a time. When we found a man working in a field, we pitched in and put in the day helping.

A hunter would stop by with a carcass on his shoulder.

"Have you meat?" he'd say, and if we hadn't, he'd cut us off a chunk.

We got invited out a lot, too. More than most bachelors, I suppose. Nothing formal, though. It was all on the spur of the moment, or so the impression was.

"We have prepared a large amount. Sit with us."

"The corn will soon be too hard to roast. Enjoy it with us."

And, also just by chance, more likely than not there would be a girl, or maybe two, sturdy, graceful, bright-eyed young women with hard-to-remember names always of two liquid vowel-sounding syllables. We had learned Oo-ah at the beginning. There were many reasons why her name was not strange. But Ee-oh, and Aa-ey, and Ei-oo. . . . Try to remember twenty such. The numbers of possible combinations didn't figure to be large, but they were all different. The Elkans had no trouble. We stayed confused. Fortunately, they expected no better of us. We were the laughing despair of the girls, and they corrected us again and again.

So some weeks passed. By my reckoning July was coming up soon. I tried to figure the date exactly, and found that I had truly lost count. The Elkans kept time after a fashion of their own, but they saw no point to specific dates. There were certain exceptions, as we found. Seasons, times when things occurred, blossoming time of plants, the calving of the elk, these were meaningful and served well enough for reference points. In spite of the man Smith and his making of paper, I could find no evidence that they wrote down anything, or even bothered to remember the letters he had tried to teach. The spoken language they had seized upon. With excellent mimicry and memory they used it more and more.

Some customs made no sense to us. Others, though, were familiar.

On a sunny afternoon, Orb looked into our door.

"On this evening Oo-ah, the girl-child of Arn the Artisan, will have lived eighteen cycles of seasons. There will be appropriate recognition of this fact."

"Now there sure ought to be!" Denny was fervent. " 'Girl-child,' ha! She's a doll, that girl. She could have me, anytime!"

I was surprised at how that didn't go over.

"You are a guest, not a suitor," Orb said with polite directness. "It would be well to remember this."

We hadn't seen Oo-ah much since we left the guest house. Twice we had had those offhand invitations to dinner at the home of Arn, and he had shown us his shop and the puzzling things he made in it. The meals had been as only Oo-ah could prepare them, and she had seemed delighted to talk with both of us. We hadn't yet learned the proper form for returning such hospitality.

Apparently Orb was inviting us again, this time to a party, but he was telling us our place, too.

Knowing Denny, I answered in a hurry.

"We will be guests to honor Oo-ah, but we are no longer guests in this garn, else we would occupy a guest house. Is this not true?"

The big fellow looked at me gravely for a moment, then suddenly flashed his hypnotic smile.

"You have truth. I spoke with haste. I admire you each, but perhaps I spoke what I wished," he added honestly.

Denny chuckled.

"You saw her first," he said. "If I remember, after eighteen a girl can take a husband. You'd like to be it, I gather. Well, tell her so, boy, tell her so!"

Orb looked at us both with puzzlement.

"You are strange men," he said. "Often I cannot tell how you think."

I was glad Denny had spoken. My silence gave consent, I suppose, but I couldn't have said it. I had made no move to show how I felt about this golden-eyed daughter of this land that didn't exist. When we three were together, it was Denny and she who did most of the talking, most of the joking and laughing. Often I sat quietly, watching, thinking, not being sure I believed what I saw, what I felt. And groping, groping, for the right thing to do about it. Probably, and rightly, this mighty young man with the Hollywood smile was the proper answer. But I hadn't yet faced it.

Chapter 8

No dwelling could have held the gathering to honor Oo-ah's coming of age, so at dusk they came swarming into the park. Flaring torches were set in stone receptacles. A big fire burned in a stone-rimmed pit. Long tables were brought from nearby dwellings, massive wooden tables that I could scarcely have lifted, but carried like bags of feathers above the heads of laughing young men. And food came from everywhere to fill the tables.

I suspected that most such parties were considerably more modest than this. Apparently, Oo-ah was special in other ways and to other people besides Orb and Denny and me. Also, she was the daughter of Arn the Artisan, and Arn's service to the garn was different and unique. We, Denny and

I, still didn't quite understand, but it was beginning to filter through. It simply was outside our frame of thinking.

We knew that Arn hunted only when he needed recreation and change. He worked occasionally in the fields or lent a hand at rebuilding a dwelling, but only enough to keep his body strong. Meat was left on his table, vegetables in his bins, fruit in his baskets. If the poles and sod of his roof needed repairing, it was done. Even the four trees of his home plot, four great maples, were pruned and tended as they required. And no one spoke of these things; no one directed. They were just done.

For the most part, Arn worked in his workshop and at his benches. He worked with wood and with metal, and with a craftsmanship that would have been remarkable anywhere. He built furniture: chairs, tables, benches, couches, cabinets. The wood was delicately finished, the metal of hinges and fasteners finely worked. He had showed it all to Denny and me on our first visit.

Denny especially had been delighted. He's clever at carving with those big fingers of his. I remember him picking up a chair and holding it to the light to examine it.

"Perfect!" he enthused. "Any kid would love stuff like this!"

"Kid?" The Artisan puckered his brows.

"I'm sorry. Child. I forget we don't speak as you do."

"Child?" Arn was even more puzzled. And in me something rang a bell.

Six-inch chairs. Foot-long couches. Tables I could span with the palm of my hand. . . . On a shelf I had a glimpse of tiny chests, sitting on carved wooden feet infinitely small. I had seen something like them before. There was one in my packsack.

"Denny just means," I said, "that in our land children love small models of the furniture they use themselves. We know that here it is not so."

Denny caught wise, and we got out of it. Later the two of us talked and talked, and the more we talked the less the whole thing made sense.

But the bright fire and the abundant food and the many people at Oo-ah's birthday party just re-emphasized the fact that Arn, as well as his daughter, filled a special niche in the garn Chan-Cho-Pan.

It would have been just a party, though, even if a big and

busy one, if the guests hadn't varied the program. Maybe guests is not quite the right word, for Denny and I were technically residents, well known, but certainly we were alien. The third guest also was known to all. Who doesn't know Muhammad Ali, Brooks Robinson, the great Johnny Unitas?

"This is Apt," Arn said to us. The man before us bowed a head that was fully seven feet above the grass he stood on, clasped hands that could have throttled an ox.

"Live and enjoy," the giant said. His deep voice was smooth, his execution of the form polite. But when he raised his head we could see that his eyes were pale and strange.

Denny and I went through the ritual.

"You are kind," I said. "We thank you."

Apt studied us with a speculative interest.

"That is not correct," he said at last. "I am not kind. But I can kill a bear with the short club, and the man doesn't live who can overcome me at wrestling. For three cycles of seasons I have held the token from the Games. No man is my master."

Like everyone else, he seemed to have no trouble finding the English words he needed. He spoke slowly. The belligerent, little-boy speech came strangely in that stilted British accent. The boast was the first we had heard from any man here. It was easy to see that Apt was not like other men.

"Apt visits from Che-Chan-Da," Arn said. "He gives honor to his garn with his hunting and his wrestling."

The giant disregarded him. He also ignored me, presumably as a midget not worth considering. But he looked at Denny's big frame and barrel chest hopefully.

"In this land from whence you came, perhaps they wrestle?"

"Some," Denny admitted. "But, as you can see, we are little men."

"*He* was not fed." Apt jerked his head at me. "But you are well grown. Perhaps you would like to test me?"

Denny hesitated. I watched the cherubic, happy grin, the dancing eyes, the pleased look of the enormous baby that with Denny always mean trouble. I started forward, but Arn was before me.

"Not this night, Apt," he said, and somehow authority spoke. "We gather to honor Oo-ah. All else waits."

The giant paused for just a breath, then sighed and shrugged.

"You have truth," he said graciously. "Tonight the firelight falls on Oo-ah. And when the songs are over and the food eaten, I will speak for her to grace my home plot. Where could she find a better man?"

"Later, Apt," Arn repeated. "Tonight we but laugh, talk, and eat."

And so we did, not necessarily in that order. There were seven kinds of meat, and I sampled them all. For the first time I saw long slender loaves of mixed barley and wheat flour, just baked, and as delicious as any cake. There were potatoes and squashes and late corn, things that could be roasted and eaten in hand, to smear your face and get in your ears. Fruits were mounded on the tables. The evening was fragrant with ripe grapes, peaches, plums, and small yellow apples. The big fire in the stone-rimmed pit licked high over the oak logs. Truly the firelight did fall on Oo-ah.

And what a picture she made! She sat like a queen on one of the usual four-legged stools, surrounded by a swarm of girls and young women, all in bright blouses and brief skirts and moccasins, all with ropes of black hair coiled high on well-shaped heads. They had crowned her with a wreath of wild pink roses, and she did not reach for her food. It was brought to her by her friends, in their hands, and they all laughed and chattered as they ate, like a tree full of mockingbirds.

Men and women milled in and out of the firelight. For the first time I saw them together in numbers, and I marveled at what a noble race it was. Tall, clean-limbed, mighty were the men; sturdy, shapely, graceful were the women. And none seemed old.

This last was not just chance. The important men and women of the garn were here. Arn himself was known to be of the Primate's age. Yet neither would have been judged to be more than forty or so. The incredible evidence was piling up. When these people were old, they were different. They underwent metamorphosis. They became tiny. Under the protective barrier of the White Cliffs they lived in old age, lived another life in doll-sized houses, and were buried at last in coffins a normal man could put in his pocket!

I ate, and arranged my facts, and realized dimly how completely we had left the world we knew, Denny and I. Going back would not be a simple matter of distance. We hadn't just come under the glacier, under a mountain range. What we had done, I didn't know. I felt strange and numb.

"Ah!" Orb stood beside me. "Here is Val!"

"Ah-h-h!" Everybody took it up.

Val was sure of his welcome. He grinned happily as he strode into the firelight. He was stripped to a single curl of elkhide around his middle. His feet were bare. His black hair fell to his shoulders. He moved around the firelit circle with the fluid grace of a sumo wrestler, in a half crouch, and his big arms tenderly cradled a guitar!

"That is the instrument of the man Smith," Orb whispered. "It was long in the making, and with it he taught the people jazz. Many can make it sing, but Val is best."

The musician finally stood before Oo-ah and her lovely court. He drew his fingers slowly across the guitar strings, producing mellow chords. The firelight played on his finely muscled body. His face became intent, absorbed.

"Each man has a thing he loves best," Orb observed. "For Val, there is nothing like the sounds he can make with those strings. For them he will forget food; forget the girls are smiling."

Val swayed, the guitar murmured, and gradually a tune took shape. It had been changed and it was better, but I recognized it. Val did not sing. The guitar, though, almost spoke words. I found myself swaying like everyone else, and I was humming under my breath.

"*Daisy, Daisy, give me your answer, do!*"

That's what it was.

Whatever the man Smith had been, he was no musician. He had been a craftsman who could build a fine guitar. Then all he could produce with it was a hodgepodge of fragments. *Daisy* was followed by other old popular trivia, folk-tune artifacts, and a stretch that surely had had its origin as the Toreador song from *Carmen*. None of it was sung. It was just played. And because Val was a man who felt music, much of it had fineness that the originals must have lacked. Especially Smith's rendition of them. He must have been a literal man. Jazz, ha! Very little of what the naked musician played could properly be called that.

"Only one thing missing," Denny growled in my ear. "*Turkey in the Straw*. Think he doesn't know it?"

"Smith was an Englishman," I said. "I'm surprised he knew some of this stuff. But I *have* been waiting for *Alouette*."

"Well, I know them both," Denny said. "Watch!"

He pushed out into the firelight when Val reached a pause in his playing. He pounded his big palms together in applause. I joined him. Everyone looked on in puzzlement, then caught on. We were appreciating. Tentatively at first, then with rolling vigor, they gave Val what must have been the first round of hand clapping ever heard in this land.

"Guitar music!" Denny said. "Now this is a surprise! In our land many people pick and sing. Not many as well as you, though," he told the flattered Val.

"They are sounds remembered from the man Smith," Val said. "He was before my years, and perhaps they are changed by many memories." He studied Denny speculatively. Then suddenly he extended the guitar.

"You know this instrument," he stated. "My eyes tell me. Doubtless you can make it sing."

Back at Kluane Denny had a battered old git-fiddle he loved to strum. His voice was nothing much, but it was fairly true and loud. Probably Smith hadn't been able to sing at all, so only the tunes had come down in this land. In fifteen minutes Denny changed all that.

The big fellow examined the guitar. Anyone could see that he was greeting a friend. He plucked each string, got back a true sound. Each was properly tuned. Then he settled the instrument, glanced around the circle, and slid into *Turkey in the Straw*.

I could hear the muffled "Ah-hs," the caught breaths. The second time around he sang the words. He motioned to me and I picked it up. Like the ice work, the trail work, and the climbing, we had done this together too.

It wasn't much of a performance. It didn't have to be. The idea that words went with the tunes was as new as anything we had brought to this land. It was unbelievable that a people as happy as these had never had song. But they hadn't. And from Smith they only had the word.

Denny sang *Alouette*, and the French was a sensation. I stood between Orb and Val, dwarfed by the height and breadth of them. When it was clear that the words he sang were not English, not the Elkan tongue, they turned to me.

"This is most strange," Val said. "What is this he speaks, while the instrument sings?"

"In our land," I explained, "we have many kinds of

speech. This song is sung in a tongue called French. It is the speech of the people of a large garn called France."

"We learn from you." Orb used a standard comment. "English is a good tongue. Why would they need another?"

"Each garn feels that its own speech is best," I explained. "France long was ruled by a very old man, tall as you are tall, who insisted that all things French were best. He is gone, but his thoughts remain. The French love their speech."

Orb nodded knowingly.

"To have pride in one's garn is good, but not beyond truth. Now that this ruler has gone to the White Cliffs, perhaps the people may choose more wisely and use English for their speech."

It was a point of view. I chuckled inside when I imagined what Denny would think of it. He finished his song and got another round of hand-clapping applause. The Elkans loved this new way of appreciating.

We broke it off, then. Val was given the guitar again, and I marveled once more at these people. We had taken away Val's spotlight, but there was no resentment, no envy, only interest and delight.

"When there is sunlight, I will visit your home plot," he told Denny. "Perhaps I may learn from you the speaking while the instrument sings."

"You'll be good," Denny assured him. "I know the words, but you've got the talent. In a week you could pick and sing on TV—if there were any TV," he added.

The big musician looked puzzled. Then he smiled and shrugged his naked shoulders.

"There is also much of English I may learn," he said. "You often speak words never told of the man Smith."

It was growing late. Arn the Artisan strode out into the firelight, an imposing figure of a man. He raised his hand.

"As the parent of Oo-ah, I speak my happiness at the many persons here to give her pleasure. To Vin and to Denny, who may not understand, I explain that among our customs is the habit of recognizing the recurrence of the time of birth of each person. It is trivial, perhaps, but beneficial. Each man and woman and child needs to feel sometimes that all the garn regards him or her with favor. We suspect that this is a need of every creature."

" 'Every man needs to be looked up to his share of times,' " I mused. "Now where did I hear that?"

"For Oo-ah there have been ten and eight of these meetings. To the next one she may bring a man of her choosing, if she wills. Perhaps before that I go to the White Cliffs. I have had signs. So I speak now, and thank you."

Elg struck his palms together, and Orb, and Val, and the sound grew from a ripple to a steady, waterfall roar. Neither Val nor Denny had got such a hand, for this had in it not just appreciation, but affection and respect as well. Oo-ah ran out and stood on her toes to kiss him—and the applause built again.

The girl turned her glowing face to the crowd.

"I, Oo-ah, thank you also. Never will I have a day of birth more fine. What more could any woman have? Can anyone say?" She sparkled happily at the faces around her. "Come, speak!" she challenged.

I had almost forgotten the giant Apt, but when I saw him move forward I knew what was on his mind—again. He could spoil the fun; ruin the party—and he intended to. I acted in desperation, swiftly.

"I will speak," I said loudly. I was smiling, and I kept it light. Oo-ah smiled too, and I fancied, or perhaps I hoped, that there was a special interest there.

"Birthdays are not strange to Denny and to me. In our land they also are a custom. At such times we give gifts to the one whose birthday it is. So, I will give Oo-ah a gift."

I paused. The audience seemed to be hooked. Apt was stymied. He looked baffled.

"I cannot give something she may hold in her hands. But you know well how both Denny and I confuse all the women's and girl's names. Why may I not give her a name from my land, so that you may at least know without doubt that we speak of her?"

I could see the idea take hold. I followed up.

"Oo-ah is now a woman. From this day, to me she will be Marya, a name much used and loved in the world from which we come."

"Marya." The girl turned the name softly on her tongue. "Marya. It has a pleasant sound. I do not mind. Perhaps it is a good thing. Very well. To you and to Denny, I am Marya."

Then promptly all the girls crowded around me.

"We, too, wish names!"

"Never do you know what I am called!"

And one small beauty with flashing eyes: "Give me a great name—one that takes long to speak!"

Denny's laugh rumbled. "I know you," he cried. "You are Hildegarde!"

And: "Betty! Sandra! Susan! Peggy! Barbie! Leslie! Judy! Jenny! . . ."

They were simple names, off the tops of our heads and all in fun, but we had started something. We didn't know it, but every woman in the garn would want a name. It would cause mixed feelings, like the jazz of the man Smith.

Later, as we left, I heard one girl murmur, "A second naming! Will our mothers smile or weep?"

That party did several things for Denny and for me. It showed us all too clearly that we were of the people now. We were adopted residents of Chan-Cho-Pan, and it was fully expected that we would stay. And we were, with our different skills and knowledge, the successors of the man Smith.

For me, it was another thing. When Oo-ah became Marya, it was the end of my silence, of my sitting quietly while she laughed with Denny. I couldn't do it any longer. She might perfer him, or Orb, or even the giant Apt, but she was going to have the opportunity to include me in her choosing.

Chapter 9

I took on more than my share of the hunting. I hunted alone, practicing endlessly with the short cedar bow and the long slender arrows Arn had helped me to make. Each arrow was tipped with a small head of tempered steel, sharpened to a bright point. With a quiver of these, my thin Elkan knife in its sheath at my left hip, and the four-foot Elkan hunting club in my hands, I ranged the hills, skulked through the heavy timber, skirted the marshes for miles. I lost a lot of arrows, then suddenly I got the knack of it.

As I trained into a condition I'd never known before, I

found that I could pin a squirrel to a tree, pluck a duck out of the air. It was more than a skill. It was a talent. I could have practiced forever and never become the bowman I was without that little special something. I could outshoot Orb, who was far bigger, stronger, with better coordination, and he had know the bow all his years. I think it delighted him, even when it exasperated him.

"You do not aim!" he'd cry. "Yet the arrow goes true! A strange place must be this land of yours, where each man is remarkable!"

There was no way I could tell him how wrong he was, but I didn't think it mattered, anyway. I was almost convinced that we were here to stay; that, like the man Smith, we would never find a way to return to our own land, our own world.

And the thing that would have seemed to the Elkans most remarkable of all I never revealed. I carried my bow, my quiver, my knife, and my club, I made some good kills and I had some close calls, and all the while, strapped down to my right thigh, buttoned tight in its holster, I carried the .357 magnum. When I knew I was alone I cleaned it, checked beginning rust with bear fat, tested its action. It rode on my leg fully loaded, but I never fired it. I wasn't sure why. It just didn't seem the thing to do.

Often I remembered the Primate's words about fate. Long before my gift with the bow came to me, I had another reason to hunt alone in the wild country. I hadn't before known it, but Marya, too, loved to roam the hills. She owned a shaggy bear dog the size of a small pony. With this imposing brute, a light club, and a thin knife she wandered far and wide.

I met her first afield when I was still new with the bow and was stumbling back from a day of futile practice. I was discouraged. She was prone in the matted needles under a huge old pine tree, a spot I later knew to be one of her favorites. I would have passed her by but for the low rumble of the bear dog.

"This is not how a hunter is alert," she informed me. "I might have been a bear. Easily I could have been the big mountain cat, which can creep like a shadow."

"I know," I told her. "And he could have taken this thing from me and shot me with it. I'm afraid I'm no hunter with the bow, Marya."

She patted the spongy brown needles beside her.

"Sit," she invited. "Have comfort."

I hastened to accept. The bear dog took a step, his lip lifted, his yellow canines frightening.

"Tor! Be silent! It is—it is *okay*!"

And it was.

On later trips afield I'd usually come back by the hill with the big pine. Often enough, she'd be there. We'd sit, and perhaps share food, and there never seemed time for all the talking we wanted to do. She rejoiced with me when the bow began to behave. She marveled at the first deer I brought in on my shoulder, just as though we both didn't know that any man in the garn could have done it with less effort. And when my arrows finally flew to any target as though they were magnetized, I knew she was really proud. Yet in all those weeks I never so much as touched her hand.

"I have sadness for my father," she said one day. We sat on the grass near the old pine. The long slope lay beyond us. A stream curved away in the distance. The girl was silent for a space, then added, "His journey has begun."

There was no surprise in her manner, no acute sorrow. Just, as she had said, a sadness.

"Marya," I said finally, "I think I know what you mean. It is strange to me, the strangest thing in this strange land. For it does not happen to us."

She nodded. She was not looking at me. She gazed into distance, and her fine, strong profile showed a maturity she had not had when two strangers blundered out into the River of Bones.

"So it was said of the man Smith. He did not grow small."

I waited. Finally I asked, "How long will it take, Marya?"

"Perhaps three tens of sun-spans; perhaps even four. Arn the Artisan is a strong man, even though he has many years. For him it will be slow."

"You are young to be his daughter," I ventured. "His children should be older."

She turned on the grass to look at me with those amazingly long, almost golden eyes, a beauty different even in her society.

"Arn the Artisan had his art. He had no need of woman until my mother came. By then he had many years, and she was no longer very young. But they loved, and no one thought it strange. And I am the result." She smiled almost dreamily. "I remember her only dimly. But she was happy. None could laugh as she did."

"Yet she died? How, Marya?"

"She did not go to the White Cliffs. Her coffin was never made. She loved to roam the hills and forests, as I do. And one day she did not return. Hunters from the ten garns searched, together and separately. There was never a trace. It was said that a bear destroyed her, so my father has ruled that I always take the dog with me. But I do not believe. Nothing was found. Nothing!"

I had a thought.

"Perhaps she went—to my land. Have you thought of that?"

Marya nodded slowly. "I have thought. That is one of the reasons you interest me. Only one!" she added hastily, and with red staining her high cheeks.

I could have spoken then but I did not. I didn't know.

But as soon as we could make an excuse, Denny and I went to see Arn.

He seemed as usual. We had always interested him, and he welcomed us.

"I am told that the arrows fly always straighter," he greeted me. "I am proud to have helped with the bow."

"Without you there would have been no bow." It's funny how easily you can learn to be gracious.

"I had no hand in Denny's art," the Artisan said, "yet I am told that no man in the garn can stand against him in the wrestling."

"From my father I got thick arms and a hard head," Denny grinned. "From my mother yellow hair, laughter, and indolence, which she was pleased to call a sense of leisure. I wrestle to avoid work."

The Artisan chuckled.

"It was a happy blending," he said. "The garn laughs with you. Also many believe you can overcome even Apt at the Games."

"If he doesn't," I said drily, "he'll need his sense of humor. Apt would gladly break his ribs."

Arn became grave.

"You have truth," he said. "He is not as other young men. Because of Oo-ah, whom you call now Marya, he causes me to think."

"We'll help you," I said. "Think, that is. I've got a feeling that what that boy needs is a good head-shrinker."

"Head-shrinker? This surely has one of your strange meanings."

"It does," Denny assured the Artisan. "Don't mind him. His English is terrible."

The tall man, whom we now knew to be very old, stood looking at us with what seemed like an almost fatherly fondness.

"A benevolent fate sent you both to this land," he said. "You laugh much, but you are men."

We were standing before the door to his dwelling. He pushed it wide. The sun was low.

"Sit with us," he invited. "There is much prepared of the mixture that is Denny's favorite, that which he has taught to Oo-ah, the mixture called stew."

So we stayed to mutton stew with pungent herbs, potatoes, and carrots. That, with plenty of cool elk milk and corn cakes, will make men out of boys. And it'll keep men from backsliding, too.

We had heard much of the Games. They were mentioned in conversation whenever a man was outstanding in any physical exercises or arts. The fast runner, the man who could lift, the swift climber, the powerful wrestler, the skillful bowman, each was mentioned to compete in the Games. Early I had envisioned a sort of Elkan Olympics, with work and preparations and pageantry, with champions in each activity from every garn fighting it out for grand championships. I even looked for ornate or valuable prizes, Olympic medals of each sort.

I was sure that somewhere there was a stadium, a meeting place where the Games could be held in the combined sight of the assembled garns. There obviously had to be committees planning, coordinators doing whatever it is coordinators do. Somewhere, somehow, records must be kept. It seemed reasonable enough that much of tradition would at first be kept from us, the outlanders, adopted and welcome though we were.

Thus, as usual, I speculated in terms of the customs of my world. And, also as usual, I was wrong.

"The last rains have swept the hills," Elg observed casually to us on a dew-wet morning. "For a five-sun there will be no clouds." We were turning melons in a field and putting straw under them, so that they wouldn't settle into the rain-soft ground.

"Every farmer thinks he's a weather prophet," Denny said. "But if it's bright tomorrow I'm going to do some roofing. That last rain dripped right through on my face as I slept."

"A task will keep," Elg said. "In two sun-spans there will be the Games."

I straightened my back and stared at him. I was just a little irritated.

"Nice of you to mention it," I said grumpily. "We might have overlooked going entirely."

Elg was tranquil.

"It was not before known," he said. "The weather disposes. Only this day came runners from Che-Chan-Da, from Da-Ma-Ten, and from the Primate. The Games are agreed."

"We've been in this field since dawn," Denny said. "How do you know?"

Elg's amusement showed on his face, just as it had on that first day, when we couldn't follow his pace.

"Your seeing is improved since you began to dwell in this land, but blindness still afflicts you," he laughed. "Each runner has crossed the hills before you, carrying the small staff with the red pennant that means the Games. Soon will go our runners to Char-Che-Po and to the garns southward. Watch, and you will see."

"The Fiery Cross?" I muttered. "I don't believe it."

But within the hour Elg pointed them out, three small figures each headed for a different point of the compass, their bits of red flashing. Each man traveled at a fluid lope that would have run down a wolf in the open. They vanished over the hills in minutes.

"And back home they're jogging for health," Denny chuckled. "What price 'civilization'?"

Like parties and hunts and invitations to dinner, the Games occurred casually, almost on the spur of the moment. There was no training of athletes. It would have been silly. Each did the thing he was best at, and every man was always in the best possible condition anyway.

There were no formal entries, no garn champions, no records. If a man thought well of himself at anything he issued a challenge. Generally he had takers, and they had at it then and there. There were no teams. Everything was individual prowess. There were no weight, age, or any other classes. You did or you didn't. You won or you lost. When you come to it, classifying is alibiing of a sort. And among these people there were no alibis. Then, and now in retrospect, it made simple and amazingly good sense.

Of course, we gathered these facts piecemeal, the rest of that day from Elg, and later from Orb and Val.

"You will win over all with the bow," Orb said to me. "Your arrows have eyes. Many hunters will come only to see you shoot."

"Orb lifts weights no other man can support," Val said. "Chan-Cho-Pan will have much honor at these Games."

"Apt will seek Denny to test him in the wrestling," Elg contributed. "It is not usually done thus, but Apt is a strange man. He wishes to hurt."

"This is not a good thing," Val said. "Apt dislikes without reason. As Vin has said, perhaps he requires the services of one who cures wrong heads. But," he added, "in this land there are none such."

"You're just as well off," I said drily. "You don't need vultures where carrion is scarce."

Elg liked that.

"Another of your strange sayings that have meaning other than what is said. I am arranging them all in my mind. I give them thought as I work in the fields and orchards. They are often both clever and wise."

"That's all I need," I growled. "Little Vin has become a philosopher!"

I made a playful pass at Elg's chin with a clenched fist. He picked it off with a movement too fast to see, and the next moment was holding me at arm's length over his head as though I were a sheaf of wheat.

"At least," he said laughing, "*you* will cause no fears at the wrestling!"

Chapter 10

With the next sun we traveled to the place appointed for the Games. We were fortunate. It lay this year between us and Che-Chan-Da, hardly more than a half day distant. The location rotated, so that in turn all garns would be close. That meant, in effect, that the closer garns were in charge of arrangements, so to say, since they would arrive earlier. There was no other planning that we could detect.

Denny and I traveled with Orb and Val and Wil, a slender young fellow from Che-Chan-Da, one of the runners of the previous day. He could run like a questing hound and was one of the favorites to take the running token. We were all bachelors together. I missed Elg, but he traveled with his wife and two small sons.

The vast escarpment of the White Cliffs blazed at us as we surmounted hill after hill, striding steadily northwest. We covered six to eight miles each hour, even though we stopped appreciatively when the view was good and listened to a travelog from Orb or Wil. I grinned to myself when I thought of what this pace would have done to me two months before. Now, no problem. My lungs provided oxygen to spare. My legs were never tired. I felt as good at nightfall as at dawn, and a half-day trip across rough country was nothing.

At levels lower than the hillslopes that we climbed out of sheer well-being we could see families moving along the trails. There were occasional elk carts, each drawn by a single bull and usually with a small boy driver. These, we knew, carried food.

They were not the only food source, though. The bands of bachelors such as ourselves hunted as they traveled. Even large carcasses were carried entire, shifted from set to set of wide shoulders so that no man would be inconvenienced for long. Girls stopped by streams long enough to snare strings of brook trout and rainbows and grayling. Orchards on slopes and benches were levied upon, but sensibly, leaving plenty.

"Others are before us," Orb said.

Blue threads of smoke from perhaps a dozen cook fires already were spindling upward into the noon sky. Little groups were thinly scattered along a wide, grassy bench that broke and sloped away steeply to a small, clear stream. Beyond lay an open valley, miles of rolling meadows partly divided and partitioned by strips and reaching fingers of woodland. There were no buildings, no pavilions, no stands or tracks or appointments of any sort. Just a wide, beautiful natural setting into which almost the entire population of the ten garns were already beginning to pour.

"We will share our meat," Orb said. "Since we each will try in the Games, we need not prepare it. Others will invite us to sit."

He shouldered the deer I had shot some miles back. He and Denny had shifted it back and forth between them. I carried my bow and four quivers of arrows. Across Val's broad back was carefully strapped the guitar of the man Smith, and Wil carried extra blanket rolls.

All the sunny afternoon and into the moonlit evening the endless drift of people continued. The stars brightened as the moon sank, and the twinkle of a thousand fires joined them at the horizon. As I had been since the day I arrived in this land, I was impressed once more by the *quietness* of the people. By the night's end forty thousand were camped within two or three miles, yet all we could hear was a soft murmur. Not once a shout, a yell, a raucous laugh. It was as unbelievable as it was pleasant.

During the time of assembling, a few simple preparations were made. Elg and Orb showed us.

"Here will be the trials with the bow," Elg explained. "There is distance to thirty tens of paces. The slope behind is soft, and gathers the arrows without harm. There will be need for many targets."

So, since there was need, we made them then and there. Orb and I cut bundles of straight, green sticks, the thickness of a thumb and the height of a man, each sharpened for pushing or driving into the ground. Denny and Elg cut squares from a dry, stiff elkhide, a handspan across, until they had a stack of them. Elg cut clusters of the branched thorns of a tree that looked like honey locust, then separated them into wicked-looking pins a finger-joint in length. A stake was pushed into the ground, then a square of hide was pinned to the top of it with a thorn. At even a hundred paces you could scarcely see it, much less hit it. But that was the bow target.

The rolling meadows of the valley were green and fine, but one small area made an interesting contrast. Although no rock outcrops showed, a space of perhaps an acre was a scattered jumble of surface rocks and small boulders. All were shiny and weathered, some brightly colored, every shape you can imagine.

"The stones for lifting," Orb explained. "They have been brought here from far, some a thousand life spans ago. Some no man can lift, others are practice for boys of ten cycles of seasons."

I picked a medium-sized chunk of quartz, tried to rock it loose. I might as well have tried to move a nearby hill.

Orb tore it free, got his great fingers under it, and slowly pressed it above his head. Then he tossed it from him with a crash.

"Size is not all," he laughed. "You chose one with weight. Always I lift that one, to make my arms loose for the larger lifts."

"Bow targets that can't be seen, weights that only giants can lift. What else?" I asked.

They pointed out what else.

"There will the runners go. Along the stream, crossing at the shallows, then through the woodland, over yonder hill, and beyond to a great tree that all know. Then back around the far slope and across the meadow to a rope that will be stretched here."

I estimated a course of about four miles, with plenty of hazards. There were no dashes. These would have been trivial. They ran the whole course at top speed.

"Yonder, where the stream turns hard against the hill, is the cliff for climbing. Since climbing it is no difficult thing, speed is the concern. He who first reaches the top gains the token."

Later, when we got closer, we found a sheer, raw granite face at least three hundred feet high, with only an occasional crack and weathering check for handholds. It would have taken me two hours with pitons and hammer to make that climb. Yet I was to see almost naked young men go up it like flies up a wall.

"There, where the grass grows deeply and the soil is fine and soft, there is where Apt will strive to break your bones." Elg spoke to Denny, and he was smiling, but his blue eyes were serious. "That is the place of the wrestling. On the slope above many can sit to watch. The wrestling interests all. Sometimes five tens of contests go on at once in this space. Many young men think well of themselves."

Fifty matches at once! It didn't sound credible, but we saw it happen.

There were other, lesser contests. These, though, were the features. No swimming, though I knew all swam like seals. No teams or team sports. They used the word Games, but those were exactly what did not occur. The whole was closest, I suppose, to a big country field meet, and every effort was an individual matter. If records had been kept, Olympic marks would have been puling by comparison.

As I've said, people continued to arrive all through the short summer night. When the sun was an hour high, the Games began.

At breakfast Denny and I sat with Elg and his slender wife, a happy young woman with the easily forgotten name of Ee-aa. We called her Bess, and it worked out fine. The two small boys sat, one by each of us, marveling at the meat and corn cakes and fruit and milk we put away. They were called Erg and Wat, and I don't care what you're thinking. Those were their names.

"If you eat much, will you overcome Apt?" Wat looked very small by Denny.

Denny pushed the small nose with a large finger.

"At least I'll not be hungry when I try," he said.

"Apt is very great," the little boy said seriously. "Perhaps you should have another cake."

"Don't remind him," I said. "He can think of things like that by himself."

But Denny rose and stretched and grinned. I guess I'd not particularly thought of it before, but he was pretty great himself. Always a fellow who didn't know his own strength, these last months had done the final tempering job. Except for his good-humored face, he no longer looked like an enormous baby. He looked like a man, a tremendous man. He was built on Elkan scale, but with a chest even wider, arms thicker. By the huge Apt he would still look small. There were signs, though, that a bet on Denny wouldn't be as foolish as you might think. I realized that behind that grin he was keyed high. Denny had been thinking. Denny was *up*. His eyes were glinting with that wild, little-boy recklessness. I knew that what was to happen would become legend.

"A few are already trying the targets," Elg said to me. "All who wish to challenge with the bow will do so early. Before the sun is high you will wear the token."

"If all were as confident as you, I needn't have come at all," I grinned. "It could have been sent to me in the mail."

"In the mail . . . ?" Elg began.

"By runner," I amended hastily.

"Would it bug you if I watch?" Denny asked. "I won't go near the wrestling until the crowd thins out. Maybe," he added, "they'll have to send for me."

Elg looked puzzled and disturbed.

"This is not done," he said.

"Apt would do it," Denny said. "I've become his problem, even though I've never said a word. He won't be content until he has slammed me into the sod."

"This, I suddenly feel, will not be an easy thing. Let us all watch the tests with the bow. These small men must see how hunters shoot." Elg marshalled his little family, and Denny went with them.

I checked my bow and strings once more, reselected the arrows I would use. That made about the fifth time. I felt strange and uneasy when I first came down on the line, meeting the open, interested scrutiny of the best bowmen of the ten garns. All, of course, had heard of me. Most were seeing me for the first time. We all clasped hands and bowed. A hundred men named names at once. It was a form, and it didn't matter that the names could not be understood.

The targets were as small and hard to see as they had been when we made them. We started at a hundred paces. I almost had stage fright, almost panicked as I loosed my first arrow. I barely nicked my target, and that was luck. The feel wasn't there. But half the men missed completely. It didn't seem to bother them, though. They smiled and chatted with each other, commenting on the shots, analyzing what was wrong.

With my next arrow the feel came back. My shot took away the square of hide and left the green withe vibrating. From the watching thousands came the first soft "Ah-h!"

After that I couldn't miss. Two hundred, two hundred fifty paces. We were launching arrows on a high arc, dropping them on the targets. One by one the contestants unstrung their bows and bowed, laughing. They enjoyed every good shot, whether they could have made it or not.

I drove home three arrows at three hundred paces. My last opponent, a steady-eyed giant from Da-Ma-Ten, could manage but two. He slipped his bow string, grasped his hands, and bowed.

"The token is yours," he said. "Your arrows have eyes. Never have the Games seen better shooting."

Chance, fool luck, these have been the story of my life. And once again it happened. As I bowed in acknowledgment, my eye picked up darting movements along the stream bank, off in the direction of the running course. Four dogs had flushed out a coyote, and the noisy, pell-mell chase literally split the Games apart. The little yellow wolf was running as only he could, but the dogs were big and fast. I could hear the growing murmur from the long slope as more and more spectators watched the chase rather than the contests.

The coyote passed a hundred paces from us and sped along the stream, quartering away. The dogs were gaining. The coyote's doom was sealed. I whipped out the last arrow in my quiver, notched it as I brought up the bow. There it was, a moving, twisting target, now a hundred and fifty paces, drawing away.

I didn't think. It was the talent, the instinct, the something extra that aimed and drew and launched that arrow. It wasn't a reasonable shot. It was a foolish, a stupid, a bragging shot. The bow whipped. The next instant the "Ah-h-h's" swept along the slopes like a wind. I had hit a running coyote at nearly two hundred paces, hit it fair and true just behind the shoulders. A kill shot. A hunting people knew it.

"Always," said the hunter from Da-Ma-Ten, "always this shooting will be remembered."

So I had my moment of glory.

Chapter 11

For hours more the finest athletes the face of Earth has seen, if Elkan is of Earth, ran and leaped and climbed and lifted. For miles along the slope women and children and men who made no challenges watched the things they liked best. Nor did they stay on the slopes. They thronged the valley, crowded near events hard to see, mingled with the contestants in a confusion that was actually more apparent than real. Somehow, there was order, and events went off in good time.

I suppose it was consistent that there were no timers, no starters, no referees. The contestants themselves decided the winners, did it with a fairness that hardly seemed human to me. A beaten man seemed always really to admire the performance that defeated him.

As we had hoped, for we liked him, Wil took the running token. None could match Orb's final lift. Two mighty youngsters from Char-Che-Po climbed the cliff so nearly together that a winner could not be named. So they cheerfully went back to the starting point, back to the cliff base, and *climbed it again*!

Once up that cliff in racing time and any believable man would have had it for the day. These, though, were not believable men. Of all the performances I saw that day, I think that final cliff climb stands out. It was an incredible thing, a miracle of timing and balance and judgment and speed. One slip, one missed fingertip hold, and they would have gone crashing to their deaths. Yet the way they did it was like a poem.

It was simple justice, too, that they bounded over the cliff edge again as one man. Another dead heat. They had come by different routes, had different decisions to make, solved different problems, but there was no difference in the result. The thronging spectators decreed the answer: "Two tokens!"

It was a deep-toned murmur following the "Ah-hs" of appreciation. There was no other possible solution. Co-champions. In the Olympics I remembered, two gold medals.

I was standing at the cliff edge when the two contestants, sweat pouring from their sleek, nearly naked bodies, their mighty chests heaving, faced each other, clasped great hands with ripped and bleeding fingers, and courteously saluted each other with bowed heads. And I did a double-take. Each was the image of the other! They were brothers. Identical twins! And identical performances no other man in all the ten garns could match. You know, there may be something to this heredity business after all. Mendel could be right!

I wandered, mingled with the crowds, enjoyed the feelings of honesty, of cleanliness, of courtesy, and of vital well-being that no other gathering of people had ever projected. They all knew me. I bowed numberless times. The children would touch me as I went by.

There was a smooth slab of granite, of the right height for comfortable sitting, under a spreading oak tree by the stream. Here the Primate sat and talked with Arn the Artisan. I bowed before them.

"You have traveled a long trail since last we spoke," the Primate greeted me. He seemed unchanged; still a big farmer with craggy features and deep, wise eyes. "I saw your last shot. No other could have made it."

"There is a thing called chance," I replied. "It was with me on that shot. I should never have tried it."

The Primate laughed. He knew that what I said was the simple truth. And he liked it.

"That you know it is enough," he said. "A man who never courts chance is safe, but he is a poor thing for all that. Your token is here. A better bowman has not worn it."

I took it from his big, calloused fingers, a flat, worn silver disc, the back fitted with a pin and catch. On the front the outline of a bow was etched simply.

We had learned that, when the Games began, all who held tokens returned them to the Primate. Then, when each contest ended, the new winner stopped by the Primate's seat and received the disc, as I had just done. It was carried through with complete casualness. There was no hint of ceremony. Everyone knew who had taken the token, would have known quite as well if no disc had existed. But to wear the token brought honor to one's garn, so men wore them. Their friends were proud.

"My hands fashioned that token," Arn said with a smile. "The one before it was lost when my years were few. I will not see another wear it. It pleases me that it lies now in your hand."

Arn seemed thinner than when I had seen him last. There were lines from his mouth, his eyes sunken. There was something else, something I couldn't put my finger on until he stood to bow when I withdrew. Arn, whose height had topped Denny, was not now so tall as I!

It had been explained to me, I had accepted it, but it stunned me just the same. A man does not shrink to a fraction of his greatest size! It is physiologically impossible. But there before me, in a man I knew well, it was beginning. I wandered across the valley in a half daze, weaving among the crowd, yet so alone that I didn't see or acknowledge the bows as I passed. Slowly I adjusted.

I was at the base of the slope. Thousands of people sat above me, and I realized that I was at the edge of the wrestling field. For hours dozens of young men had tested each other here, tremendous fellows who could have toyed with our heavyweight champions. The lush grass was now trampled and flattened. A number of matches were still going on. Occasionally a soft "Ah-h!" swept the slope as a good fall was made.

The people were waiting, though. I could feel it. These were, after all, just prelims. The big match was still coming up.

I climbed the slope, looking for a good spot where I could sit and view the action. There was no indication of where it would be, but I guessed that the middle of the strip would be appropriate. Center stage. From a small ledge up ahead a big arm beckoned. Orb and Val were reserving a seat for me. Orb wore his lifting token.

"That I may sit with two tokens is an honor," Val said. I grinned, thinking it a part of the joking and kidding we carried on most of the time. Then I realized that the musician was not smiling. He was respectful, completely serious. He meant what he said, exactly.

"If there were a token for music, you would wear it," I said. "To each his own gift."

"I thank you," Val said. "You are kind. When the contests

are finished, after the last meal, I will make the guitar sing for all the garns. They will enjoy it, I think."

Again, no smugness. Just a simple statement of what he felt to be fact. And he was right, of course. He could provide a fitting end to the Games.

From the end of the field, along the base of the slope, Denny came striding, shoulder to shoulder with Elg. Each was stripped to the breechclout of the wrestler. Wrestler's moccasins, snugly held by thongs crisscrossed at the ankles, were on their feet. Elg was an imposing figure of a man, his tanned naked body lithe and perfect. But Denny looked mightier still. His arms were heavier, his chest thicker. His long, yellow hair blew as he walked with the gliding Elkan stride. Like many blond men, his skin did not tan deeply and he showed pale against the shifting backdrop of weather-darkened young men.

There was a level, grassy patch almost directly below us which had been untouched by the trampling feet of the wrestlers. I realized that it must have been deliberately avoided. It was the best, the most visible spot, and they had saved it for the headliner.

Elg and Denny wasted no time. They faced each other, clasped hands, and bowed. Then they came together like a couple of bulls, head against head, arms wrapped, shoulder against shoulder. Big legs flexed as they pushed and shoved each other. I was astonished. Orb saw it and smiled.

"It is ritual," he explained. "They will not wrestle. Elg loosens Denny's muscles, then he will pretend defeat. Denny will stand, a victor, to be tested by any who wish. And Apt will come."

So it was. After several minutes the two big bodies began to shine with sweat. Suddenly Elg broke away, turned his back, and strode to the edge of the grass patch. He stood for a moment, his head hanging, the picture of dejection. Then he faced Denny, clasped left hand with right, and bowed. Denny returned the courtesy. Elg turned and walked slowly away, and Denny stood alone in the center of the grass patch. All other matches were finished. From the slope thousands of pairs of eyes looked down on him. He was in the middle of the spotlight, center stage. And you know, I think he liked it.

He faced the slope and flung back his yellow hair. The wild, reckless little-boy grin was on his face. We were too far to see, but I could imagine the flickering, challenging dance of his blue eyes. We could feel the tension build.

Apt had been waiting. He came promptly. He strode alone along the base of the slope, a man so big you didn't comprehend it until he passed other men, dwarfing them in passing. For, like most Elkans, he was perfectly proportioned. He moved with the grace of his race, his breechclout and moccasins were like all others, his black hair flowed and was cut at the shoulders like that of most other men. Yet when he paced onto the grass patch Denny literally seemed to shrink in size.

Five strides from Denny, Apt halted. He grasped one tremendous hand with the other, bowed his head. His deep voice came to us clearly.

"I will test you," Apt said.

Denny grasped hands and bowed. "I will welcome it," he said. I suppose Elg had briefed him on form.

"Three times Apt has wrestled today," Val said. "Each time the man who tested him was injured. This is not a good thing."

"It is not a necessary thing," Orb almost growled, the first time I ever saw him in such a mood. I could feel his great muscles tense as he leaned forward beside me. "If Denny has hurt, perhaps I will see if Apt can be lifted."

I smothered my chuckle, for Orb was not clowning. An angry Elkan was something I had never experienced. I could imagine, just barely, what Orb without the restraint of courtesy and kindness might be like.

Apt moved forward, Denny met him. Head to head, arms wrapped, they strained in place, almost motionless. My muscles ached and cracked in sympathy. No ordinary man could have stood that pressure for an instant, I knew.

Then they broke. Apt flexed his great fingers, moved forward again. Denny wheeled out of reach, circled the giant, feinted in and out. Apt's face was expressionless, but Denny's view of his strange eyes must have been unnerving.

Apt leaped forward like an agile bear, great clutching hands before him. Denny ducked and spun to the side and almost evaded the rush. Almost. He flung up his left arm for balance and the giant's fingers closed on his wrist. Apt pivoted, trying to better his hold, and Denny swung with him. His weight broke the hold, but Apt's whirling body flung him a dozen feet away, prone and rolling in the long grass.

The giant followed at terrifying speed. His big moccasins

thudded into the sod just as Denny's body left it. There was no doubt of what he had tried to do. Stomp. Break ribs. Orb's breath hissed in my ear as Denny bounded to his feet again. Along the slope the sighing "Ah-h-h!" was one of relief, I felt sure.

One thing was plain. This was not to be a wrestling match. Two men were not matching strength and skill in a friendly contest for a token. Apt's strange obsession had taken over completely. He was not trying for a fall. He meant to hurt, to maim.

Denny must have realized it as soon as did we, the watchers. And any restraint he may have felt probably vanished when Apt attempted his stomp. I saw the excitement leave his face, replaced by the cold, workmanlike mask of an executioner. Denny knew what he had to do. He had to survive. Anything was legal.

As I look back, I know that in conventional Elkan wrestling Apt would have retained his token. He was bigger, stronger, and almost as fast as Denny. But Elkan wrestling is simple. They know a few holds. The rest is agility and strength. Denny knew more. He needed it all, though, against Apt's singleminded attack and unbelievable stamina.

He turned the match around at Apt's next rush. As he ducked under the giant's arms the outer edge of his right hand chopped across Apt's solar plexus. It was a karate swing from position. We heard it as a solid thud from our seat on the slope. It would have killed me. Apt's mouth sagged, he staggered, then whirled like a cat and Denny barely evaded his rush again.

But Denny had made up his mind. As the giant spun from the rush he was met by the first flying dropkick ever seen by these people. Denny's moccasins thudded fairly against his jaw and the side of his face. Apt dropped to a knee, shaking his great head, then came back to his feet. Denny was ready. Again he launched himself like a projectile, flinging his two hundred sixty pounds, moccasins first, against the side of Apt's head. The giant staggered once more. Denny was on him faster than I've ever seen a big man move. He clamped an outside armlock on Apt's left arm, threw all his weight behind it. There could be but one result. Apt fell backward with a stunning crash.

Denny released him as he fell, then dropped on him and pinned out each huge arm with a knee. For a moment he sat on the great chest, then sprang away and stood, alert and ready.

For half a minute Apt lay there, not moving. There were thirty thousand people along the slope, and from them all there was not a sound. Then Apt rose to his feet, steadily and easily, completely recovered. He looked along the crowded benches, his face expressionless as always. He faced Denny, clasped his huge hands, bowed his head.

"The token is yours," he said clearly. "You are a very strong man."

He waited for no response, but turned his back and strode easily away across the meadow. Only then came the soft, almost hushed "Ah-h-h!" of the people. The awe in it was apparent and understandable. There had never been a match like this in the history or the legends of the Games.

Beside me Orb's big body sagged back on the grass in relief. Val flexed the fingers that soon were to make the guitar sing. His fists had been clenched tight. I knew how he felt. So had mine.

"This is not how men wrestle," Val said, "but it was not a bad thing. It was a thing that had to be done, I think."

"You have truth," Orb agreed, "and only Denny could have done it. I will learn that fashion of holding the arms. As Vin sometimes speaks, it *works*!"

The Games were over. On the slope, the meadows, the woods, all along the stream, crowds of people shifted and blended and moved. Cook-fire smoke thickened. People would eat this last meal in larger groups. Friends would visit with friends from other garns. There would be much talk of all the contests, and the group that entertained a token-wearer would be proud. So we each sat with a different group. It was custom. I sat with families from Da-Ma-Ten, and we spoke of the hunting of the great white bears that come from the north along the seacoast when the ice floes form. These were the farthest ranging of the hunters, these men of Da-Ma-Ten. They couldn't say enough about my way with the bow.

"The guest houses of Da-Ma-Ten will be proud," they told me. "Come when the first snows fall, and we will show you ice hunting. Your bow will take a fine, white robe."

"I'll come," I promised.

It was sunset. Forty thousand people had eaten and talked

and savored the last hour of this most anticipated of Elkan gatherings. It was time for Val and his guitar. He did not disappoint.

From Denny he had learned, as he said, "the speaking while the instrument sang." He had memorized *Turkey in the Straw* and *Alouette*. The English of the one probably made no more sense to him than the French of the other, but he sang them in a true, clear baritone that seemed to flood the slope from the high point where he stood, his big form shadowy against the evening sky.

Everyone listened. To the garns other than Chan-Cho-Pan the guitar was still a rare and a strange thing. Many had heard it before only at the Games. The singing was a surprise even to me. And even while I admired I had to choke back the laughter when Val sang his concluding number. Denny had had his private joke. With earnestness and vigor and surprising art the musician belted out his finale, singing of things he could not possibly imagine or envision. He sang *The Wabash Cannonball*, and the "Ah-h-hs" that sighed along the slope when he finished must have made him feel that he had, in his way, really taken a token.

Chapter 12

You might have thought that, after the Games, things would have seemed anticlimactic for a while. Actually, after a couple of days, I had almost forgotten them. I wore my token, but I didn't look back.

We had another concern, Denny and I. The whole garn had it as well, and we understood this, but it was different with us. To the Elkans, it was the way things were. To us, it was still not believable.

Day by day we watched it, the slow shrinking of the body of Arn the Artisan. He had ceased to eat. He sat all day in his workshop, slowly and lovingly putting finishing touches on a whole set of tiny furniture. He welcomed our brief visits but would not notice us for long, his attention going back to the careful carving and polishing.

"He will remember us less and less," Marya said. "His thoughts already go forward to the life he will live there under the White Cliffs. He makes his furnishings ready. There will be a house, and those who have gone before will welcome him."

We couldn't question Marya further about these things so close to her life, so, as we had done on many occasions before, we went to Elg.

"We watch Arn grow small," I explained to him. "We understand, of course, that here all men do this. We have said that in our world this does not happen, and it was seen in the case of the man Smith that it did not. We call this change metamorphosis—and there is a word for your memory! Many insects change from one form to another; it is a common thing among the frogs and their relatives. But even they rarely grow smaller.

"We live here now. Perhaps we will die here. We would like to know more of this thing. As Elkans, we should know more. Then, perhaps, we will understand a little better. Please tell us."

Elg had unloaded a large pile of yellow pumpkins in his dooryard. He was sorting and stacking them neatly in small pyramids according to size and depth of color. Then anyone who wished a pumpkin could select what pleased him without trouble. Anyone who passed by would be welcome.

"You have right," Elg agreed. We had pitched in automatically, and the three of us stacked the pumpkins in short order. "You should know. It will disappoint you, I think, that there is little more to tell."

Simply, he filled in the gaps in our knowledge. He told of the sheltered country under the White Cliffs, where it is warmest, where the winds are screened, the rains gentle. Rarely does the snow fall there. The White Cliffs, like giant reflectors, mellow the climate along their bases.

"Here men live more years, live them as tiny people. How long we do not know. They make houses, grow plants, hunt small beasts. But at last they die and are buried by their fellows. Each man, each woman, takes along the furnishings that have been made; these, and a coffin. Each carves and decorates his coffin after going beyond the wall."

"That is another thing we don't understand," Denny said. "What means 'going beyond the wall'?"

Elg smiled. "We have, in truth, kept you away from the lands along the White Cliffs. When you have hunted, you have respected our telling. You have not tried to go near the Cliffs. But had you gone closer, you would have come upon the wall.

"It is not a great thing. Easily you might step over it. It is made of the stones from the fields, firmly stacked together, as men always build walls. For many sun-spans of travel it runs, from the icy lands from whence you came to where the great water begins. Not even legend tells when it was built. By beyond it lies the land of the Little People, the land where life *ends*. No man goes beyond the wall until he is ready to dwell there."

"A dry wall," I said. "Like around a New England sheep pasture. It should have crumbled to ruins long ago."

"Men may go *to* the wall," Elg explained. "It is even usual to approach it and travel along it for a time. If stones have become displaced, he who passes by will set the break in order again. So the wall is ever new."

I looked at Denny. I think we both shook our heads. Universal assumption of responsibility! It was still a hard thing to grasp.

"The wall, then, is just a boundary," Denny said. "It doesn't keep anything out."

"This is not truly known," Elg said gravely, "but I will tell you what men say. It is said that the bear will not cross the wall, nor the wolf. I have myself seen elk run alongside it; hunted elk, in panic. They might have cleared it at a stride, but never have I seen one do it."

What Elg believed was open and clear. And we had seen too much that was different in these past months to scoff or to deny. We accepted it, and let the subject drop. But if I thought of hunting toward the wall, and of making sure I had my field glasses, do you blame me?

As her father grew smaller day by day, Marya's life was, I knew, approaching a crossroad. I could, I think, have helped to solve it, but my old diffidence was back again, and I waited. It seemed to me that Marya should think her own thoughts, make her own decision. To you it may not appear a great thing, this problem of Marya's. But Elkans face it only once.

On a day that I thought must be early September we sat again on the hill under the big pine. Marya had brought apples, and we ate as we sat and shared companionship. And I felt at ease, at peace with this golden-eyed girl as I never had with another human being. Her strong, perfect teeth sheared bites from the apple in her brown hand. She smiled at me with lips moist with the sweet juice of the fruit. It was an honest satisfying of a forthright hunger. In the same fashion Marya would satisfy all the hungers she would ever know. She was no longer a girl. She was a rare and lovely woman, and that, simply enough, was her problem.

"Soon," she said, "very soon now, my father goes beyond the wall to the White Cliffs. He will think of me only dimly, as a dream he once had. But he must be happy about me when he goes, or his time under the Cliffs will not be peaceful, will not be pleasant. So—I must choose a man—and I cannot."

Things had happened during the last five-suns. I knew of them. I knew, too, that she was finally asking me for help.

Orb had spoken, plainly and simply. Of all women, he preferred her. He wished to lie beside her, and to stand always with her before the garns. He would be proud.

Apt had come visiting again from Che-Chan-Da. With Arn no longer to be considered, he too spoke plainly, not to Marya, but to the men of Chan-Cho-Pan.

"If another man seeks Oo-ah," Apt announced, "he first must overcome me at the wrestling. I do not wear a token but I stand between all men and this woman. Let the garn know it."

"As you well know, this is not done," Elg reminded him. "Many lifespans ago the Primate disposed. The woman chooses."

"The Primate is a man who lives outside a society," the giant said. "I am Apt. I will decide what is best for me. If necessary, I will take Oo-ah and live outside a society also. But take her I will, soon or late."

"As long as only words are spoken, you are a guest," Elg said. "The Primate will be informed. He will again dispose. You will wait for that."

These things I had only heard. It was known that a special runner had gone to the Primate. Orb stayed near his home plot, doing tasks that were not necessary. From his door he could see the house of the Maples, where Arn the Artisan was spending his last days in the garn. The men of Chan-Cho-Pan were much in the streets, prowling with a gliding restlessness on errands they could not have described. For the first time I felt tension in this land.

Apt knew. He had left the guest house of the Hemlocks and gone on a solitary hunt. He had returned with the carcass of a huge bear on his shoulders, its skull crushed by his hunting club. From homeplot to homeplot he had gone, cutting for all who needed until only the hide was left.

"I am grateful to be a guest in this garn," he told each man or woman. "Here is meat for your table."

It was a thing a guest would do, an appropriate gesture from a great hunter. Each family that needed meat accepted it with proper courtesy.

I had been wandering far with my bow, shooting nothing, and had finally come back to the big pine. Marya was there, guarded by the shaggy bulk and yellow fangs of the bear dog Tor. But he wagged his tail at me. So we shared apples, and Marya asked for help. She opened the door. The thing that had bothered me, deep inside, finally came out.

"Many men want you," I said. "Men who are strong and would stand with you proudly. Many have spoken. But I think you have chosen, and the man has said no word. Do I have truth?"

She looked at me steadily, her long eyes grave and honest.

"You have truth," she said.

It was a rough deal, but I played it out. Give me credit.

"Then let me speak for him," I said. "You know as well as I how Denny feels about you. He is big, as Elkan men are big, perhaps the mightiest man in the world. He fears no man and no beast. But suddenly I know one thing he does fear. He will not speak to you. Yet when you are present he looks at no one else."

The girl's eyes wavered, then she looked away, out over the rolling country beneath us. She reached out a hand and gently tousled the bear dog's shaggy, ugly head. Her voice came softly: "Denny is a great laughing boy, and always I'll love him. But—*you* are a man. To me, at least, there is a difference. And Denny does not speak because Denny knows. He is not afraid of a woman."

It shouldn't be said that I was the last to know. It just didn't make sense. I know that size is more than height and weight, but Marya had grown up surrounded by impressive men. Arn the Artisan had been the standard by whom she measured. I knew well enough that I could turn in his moccasins without moving them. But his daughter reached her brown hand to me, the apple juice still glistening on her red lips, a slow smile starting. And I picked her up as though she were a small child, and held her tight. After all, I am not completely puny.

As I've said before, chance, coincidence, these make up the story of my life. The Fates pick on me. And this time they were on the ball as usual. The warmth and softness and fragrance of the girl in my arms were still scarcely real when the bear dog rumbled deep in his throat. Marya looked over my shoulder. She pushed me away gently.

"Apt comes," she whispered.

We knew that the giant had seen. Even though I intended to shout the news wherever Elkan ears could hear, it was bound to be a little tricky to break it to Apt first of all. I had a feeling he wasn't going to congratulate me.

But the customs fixed and practiced by a thousand generations were not easily ignored, even by Apt. His strange eyes were leaping wildly, yet he paused three strides from us, clasped his huge hands, slightly bowed his head. His deep voice was smooth and untroubled.

"Oo-ah! Vin! Live and enjoy!"

We returned the courtesy.

"Thank you," I said. "It was what we had in mind. It is pleasant to hear you speak it."

Apt stared at me steadily.

"Your tongue," he said, "is faster than mine, but you are a small man. Your tongue will not help you in the wrestling. And you know that the man who has Oo-ah first must overcome me."

Again big Tor rumbled. Marya dropped a hand on his great head, soothing him. Apt ignored them both.

"Have you thought," I asked, "that another man might offer Marya that which even you cannot? Only she can know. That is why, as you well understand, the woman has always chosen."

I was ready for anything, or so I thought. Apt fooled me. His pale eyes slid past mine, darted from girl to dog to the landscape around. Then they focused.

My small rucksack lay where I had tossed it on the grass. With one great stride Apt had it.

"Let us see," he said, "what a small man would have to offer as the husband of the daughter of Arn."

It was a childish thing, deliberately challenging and insulting. Apt dumped the sack. A hodgepodge of stuff spilled out: a couple of packages of iron rations, a small first-aid kit, cartridges for the .357, a roll of wool socks, a plastic poncho wrapped around a loaf-like object. Apt shook the poncho—and the little coffin rolled out on the grass. I had even forgotten it was there. The rotten rubber bands snapped, the lid popped open, and the tiny skull tumbled past the crumpled paper I had placed there months before.

I heard Marya's soft gasp. Even the giant was horrified.

"A *desecrater*!"

The bear dog pressed close against Marya, his lip curled. And she, my girl, my woman, was looking at me as she had never looked before.

Apt spoke in a shaken voice: "This is something no one has *ever* done! The Primate must dispose. I will take him there myself, now. For this there can be no pardon."

For a moment I faced them: the pale girl, the puzzled, alert dog, the stern giant. Then I tried: "Marya," I said, "we found that on the trail when we came up from the River of Bones. Only recently, as you know, have we even understood what it was. You must believe me when I say that I have not descrated. It was in my mind to speak to Elg of this thing, but the time never seemed right. It was hard to speak, for nowhere else in the world do people grow small."

"You will go with Apt," the girl said. The life had gone out of her voice. "The Primate will dispose."

I considered. Suddenly I seemed to have no emotional involvement in the situation at all. It was just a problem. The giant stood with an inherent dignity, but his triumph glowed in his eyes. And I decided.

"I don't think this is something the Primate can dispose. He won't have all the information. He would not understand, as you don't. So I think I won't recognize citizen's arrest this time. I won't go with Apt."

The giant grinned, flexed his fingers, shrugged his huge shoulders.

"You have no choice. You can neither overcome me nor run away. No man is the master of Apt."

It was my turn to grin. "Denny?" I inquired wickedly.

Apt's grin faded. His pale eyes flickered.

"It was a trick," he said sullenly. "*You* go to the Primate, nonetheless."

"No," I said. I slipped the magnum from its holster and held it lightly in my hand. "You are a just people, but there are many things you do not understand. This," I waved the gun, "is one. Observe!"

A woodchuck was feeding in the grass a score of paces down the hill. I leveled the weapon. I was careful. This was no bow, but I was good with it. Both people and dog started back from the flat, deadly sound it made. Down the slope the big rodent leaped convulsively, then lay kicking. In a moment it was dead.

Moving slowly, I turned and repacked my rucksack, holding the gun ready. I didn't touch the little coffin.

"I wouldn't like to serve you so," I told the still giant, "but I can. With this I could stop the dog in mid-leap. There is no way to tell you that I am not a desecrater, because there is the coffin, and in it are the, to me, unbelievable bones of a man. So you're right. I have no choice. I must go back up the River of Bones, strive to find the trail into the ice wall, go back, if I can, where I came from. Tell Denny. He has desecrated nothing, but he may wish to come."

I looked sadly at my girl. All I really felt was a sort of numbness. Things had happened too fast.

"Marya, good-bye. I love you, but that wouldn't be enough now. Orb is a good man. You can be happy with him."

I shrugged into the pack, then backed away a few steps, the gun still ready in my hand.

"Make no attempt to be reckless," I said to Apt. "It will cause tragedy. You have seen, and you have my word."

I turned and strode away, falling naturally into the gliding pace of the Elkan hunter I had become. I wasn't followed. But I heard, or fancied that I heard, a little choking sob from Marya and an anxious whine from the bear dog.

Chapter 13

It was midafternoon. I had been on the trail for an hour or so. I strode it openly, without haste, six miles to the hour. The trail was easier than cross country, and anyway, I didn't fool myself. I knew that something would be done. What, I hadn't much idea, but if they wanted to catch me, they could.

I remembered that there were ways, emergency ways, of communicating with the Primate. I'd never seen them used; didn't know how they worked. Smoke? Man-to-man calls? In a land where nobody shouted, the first sounded more reasonable. But it was just something for my mind to chew on as I kept steadily to the trail.

I did know, of course, that what they thought I had done would be equally of concern to every society. The settlements of tiny people under the White Cliffs were where man's life ended. They were the responsibility and the sacred trust of all.

The head of that fissure in the rock wall, with its narrow trail leading down into the gorge of the River of Bones, was reasonably distant. I estimated twenty miles. I could easily make it by sunset. I did, though, think with some regret of that pot of stew Denny planned to have, back at the house of the Lindens. A couple of apples were all I'd had since morning.

The sun was sinking into the far marshes and the moon was just coming into view in a notch of the distant snow ranges when I came finally to the beginning of the fissure. And I became wary. Men could easily have come ahead of me. I was now a good man on the trail, but I'd never approach the traveling ability of an Elg or an Orb, for instance. There could be men in the fissure, waiting around a turn or on a ledge above the trail. I studied the whole setup carefully. There was no sign.

The coolness of the wind off the snow ranges reminded me

of another thing. I wasn't equipped for the River of Bones. Even less for the ice tunnel. My parka, my thermal breeches and underwear, my snow boots, my very gloves, all were back in the little dwelling where Denny was, perhaps, still keeping the stew kettle hot. Would it be possible to ascend the river, go back through the corridor, climb out of a crevasse onto Seward Glacier in September? All this without ropes, ice axe, crampons? My common sense said no. But what else could I do? Choice appeared to be pretty limited, since I had rejected disposal by the Primate. In effect, I had renounced this world. I guess my subconscious was hoping that there would be no problem after all; was hoping that there would be no tunnel.

I studied the area around the fissure again. Then I decided. The slope beyond, eastward toward the snow country, was a jumble of great boulders for miles. I skulked into them, worked my way into a sheltered spot where I could watch the fissure from half a mile away. With my small field glass I could cover the fissure mouth, the trail, the country sloping away, the same landscape that had so pleased Denny and me, back a thousand years before—or so it seemed.

The sun was gone. The moon rose high. I watched and dozed and waked again. What I would do when men came, I don't think I knew. The magnum lay on a flat rock in front of me. I was sure, though, that I wouldn't use it on a man, not even Apt.

The sun rose again. I munched iron rations, sat quietly in my lookout. I was weighing the idea of slipping down to a trickle of water I could see below when I heard my first unusual sound. It came from behind me. It was a stealthy sound, like the faint whisper of the passage of a stalking animal. I crouched low in my hiding place, suddenly tense, watching. Involuntarily my hand went to the magnum.

Marya glided into view, Marya hooded, cloaked, and high-booted, Marya with my pack frame fully packed and riding high above her sturdy shoulders. She paused, carefully studying the terrain down toward the fissure. I whistled softly.

Slowly she turned toward the sound of the whistle, the alertness of the wild thing in every line of her body. The look of incredulous joy that flowed into her face as she saw me told all I needed to know. Desecrater, villain, destroyer of tradition—whatever I was she was my woman. Yet she came to me with dignity and restraint. Swiftly she shrugged off the big pack.

"Your possessions all are here," she whispered. "Your ropes, the claws for your feet, the clothes you must have for the ice and the cold. Denny gave them to me and I have brought them fast. I know shortcuts across the hills."

I reached for her, but she pushed me back with gentle fingers.

"Dress!" she urged. "I will keep watch. Soon come the Executors of the Primate's Will. We must be ahead of them toward the River of Bones. It is forbidden that they follow us farther."

I recognized the necessity. I dressed as directed, but with deep content, and asked no questions. For me the tension was gone. Marya, however, told me more as she watched downslope.

"Yesterday my father went beyond the wall. He was very small, and Elg carried him and all his goods on a shoulder. Already his memory of me grows dim. He will be happy, for I told him I would be with the man I would always love. This contented him."

She took my glasses, adjusted them, swept the country along the back trail. They were good, compact binoculars. Always they had fascinated and mystified her. Suddenly she gave a little cry.

"They come! But first, far ahead, comes Denny! I don't know the meaning of this at all, but we must be first into the fissure!"

I wsted no time in looking. I shrugged into the big pack. She took the rucksack. The magnum was again snug in its holster against my thigh. We moved at good speed down through the boulder field and I marveled at the stamina of my fine strong girl, who already had come twenty miles without rest, carrying the pack now heavy on my shoulders.

We reached the mouth of the fissure. A hundred yards away Denny came into view over a rise, running easily. His baby face had a happy grin; his long yellow hair blew back over his shoulders as he ran. He was stripped to breeches and moccasins. His great chest heaved as he came to a bouncing halt beside us.

"My," the big fellow said, "we do have fun!"

"Denny!" I said urgently. "What's the story? Are you outcast too? The fools! You didn't take the coffin!"

"They're a mile or so back." Denny grinned. "The way those boys can go, that's three or four minutes. The Executors of the Primate's Will. A posse, old son!" He thrust out a hand. "So get you both gone. I'll parley with 'em here until you get down into taboo territory. A wedding present, sort of."

"No!" I said it violently, but Marya pushed me aside. She reached up to kiss the big man swiftly on the cheek, then pulled at my hand.

"Here they come!" Denny's voice went up. "Beat it, you fool! Let me handle this. You'll have your own problems."

He wheeled his big body at the mouth of the fissure, and his laughing voice came over his wide shoulder.

"If the first one's a boy, maybe you could name him Denny! Now scram!"

We were well down the fissure, at the first turn, and we had to look back. The posse loomed up beyond Denny, who stood with powerful legs spread, blocking the trail. There were maybe a dozen young men, all stripped to breeches and moccasins, each carrying the oaken hunting club. Earnest, honest, mighty young men, determined to do the job they had been sent to do by the authority, the oracle of their world. They knew Denny, liked him, respected him. But they didn't intend for him to stop them.

Denny's voice came down to us.

"Are you men or pack dogs? Will you all do together what no one of you can do alone? What kind of shame is that?"

He tossed his yellow hair, laughing at them.

"I have no club. Will you use yours? Come now, who is man enough to use his bare hands and remove me from the trail?"

We simply knew, rather than saw, that each man tossed his club away as he came on. We were out of sight when the first solid smack of flesh on flesh came to us. Then we heard Denny's explosive yell, and we knew that it was loud so we could hear.

"Next!"

We went down at breakneck speed, though a slip or a twisted ankle would have ended everything for us. And we made it. Before I realized the lapse of time the cliffs loomed high, the sky was a slit far above, and we came out onto the slimy, skull-strewn bank of the grisly river.

Nothing had changed. All was as I remembered. It almost

seemed that the last three months could have been a dream, something that hadn't happened at all.

But there was a difference. The spasmodic clutch of a slender hand on my arm reminded me. It wasn't Denny who was with me now, but a tired, wide-eyed girl, staring with sudden horror at a sight no Elkan had looked on for many generations.

I covered the clutching hand with mine, soothingly, but for a few moments I said nothing; just stood and let her look. From my body, through my nerve-ends, I tried to let reassurance flow into her. And, after a bit, I could sense that she was slowly relaxing. Finally I turned to face her.

Her eyes had left the shadowy canyon, the murky river, and the bones. She was studying me intently.

"You do not fear."

It was not a question. It was a statement.

I patted the hand that still clung to me. Then, as casually as I could do it, I shrugged off the straps of the heavy pack frame and eased my aching shoulders.

"I do not fear," I said, "but for that I do not deserve credit. There is nothing to fear. This is only a canyon, ground out and worn by many hundreds of years of action by ice and water. That is only a stream, and its waters come from the melting of ice. The poor creatures whose bones you see lived long ago. They can hurt no one."

She slipped off the straps of the rucksack then and looked back at the river. Her face was still pale, her golden eyes sunken. But I marveled once again at the adaptability, the solid common sense that were so large a part of this woman, and of her race.

"It is true," she mused, as though I were not there. "We have not known this place as it is. Mosses grow on the bones, and the little green water threads make the rocks slippery. The gray stream bird lives here, as it does in other rapids and waterfalls. This is only a canyon, filled with water and shadows and dead bones. Even the Primate does not know that there is no harm here."

She leaned against me with a sigh. Her sturdy body sagged with weariness. I put an arm around her.

"We have had no chance to speak of it, but I know you will try to go back through the ice. But first I must sleep. No man will come for us here."

I unstrapped my sleeping bag from the pack frame, and for the first time saw Denny's bag beneath it.

"Denny gave to me his bag of feathers for sleeping," Marya said. "He said I would require it in the ice lands."

I unrolled the bag in the best spot I could find on the boulder-piled bank. The girl slipped into it. Almost instantly her eyes closed.

"Poor Denny!" I said. "I wonder. . . . What will they do to him, Marya?"

The long eyes opened briefly, and a faint smile crossed my girl's face.

"Perhaps the Executors of the Primate's Will wonder also." Her sleepy smile was almost an amused grin. "He was very great, was he not?" The golden eyes hooded. "But he will go to the Primate, and the Primate will dispose. I will not grieve for Denny, for he did what a man would do, and the Primate is very wise." Her voice trailed off and she slept.

For long hours I sat, my seat the rolled sleeping bag, my back comfortable against a water-worn boulder. I stared unseeingly at the murky rippling water, trying to adjust to things as they were. Events had happened too swiftly for me. I needed the rest, but even more I needed the time.

I scarcely noticed when the shadows of the canyon deepened, the strip of blue sky darkened, and stars came out. Marya slept on, the complete sleep of one who has no doubts.

Finally I roused myself. I unstrapped and inventoried the big pack. And again I blessed Denny. We had kept our survival rations, our little packages of dehydrated nourishment. They were all here. The flashlight, the thermometer, the altimeter, all were neatly fitted in. The fine ropes, not as thick as Marya's little finger, were coiled in their places. There were even more cartridges for the magnum.

I looked again with wonder at the quietly sleeping girl. She had carried a sixty-pound pack, life for two people, across twenty miles of rough country in a few hours. She had descended a mountain goat trail into a gorge that violated all the traditions and taboos of her people. And all she needed now was sleep. Then she would be ready to follow wherever I chose to lead. She had decided. I was her man. And I knew that nothing would change that.

I repacked, made everything handy. Then I slept a little, I guess. Anyway, the next thing I knew there was sun on the canyon walls, and Marya was stirring in her sleeping bag. I think she watched with amusement while I struggled back to consciousness.

"Are we to travel," she inquired gravely, "or will we measure our home plot here? We could build a house of stones."

I pulled her from the bag, set her on her feet, and finished the kiss Apt had interrupted—was it hours or days before? Anyway, it had kept nicely. Her face was rosy when I let her go.

"A first thing you must learn," I told her, "is not to make sport of your man. When you do, that will happen."

"I learn slowly," she retorted. "I can prepare food, though, when there is a fire."

We made our first meal of powdered stuffs and fruits dried hard as bullets, brought back to a kind of edibility by soaking in water from a seep. Marya heated them over the small fire I built, and turned up her fine nose at the results. She ate, though, a full share, as I did. We didn't know what lay ahead. We only knew that it would tax us, perhaps be more than we could overcome.

Privately, I wondered about the tunnel. Was it still there? There were good climbers and ice men at Kluane and there must have been searches for us. They knew where we had gone, but none had come through as we had.

Well, we would soon know. As I remembered, the fissure was four or five miles from where the stream flowed out of the ice. I settled the pack frame on my shoulders, packed now to my tolerance and liking. Marya carried the repacked rucksack. There was a coil of rope across her shoulder, she wore her thin knife at her hip, and, to her great delight, my field glasses swung from her neck. Of all the wonders we had brought, I think these fascinated her most.

She was dressed as I had never seen her dressed. She was fitted for the cold: woven breeches, heavy jacket, a fur-rimmed hood, and knee-high, heavy moccasins. She was a woman who had grown under the sky. She would follow where I led.

The game trail along the rocky river seemed less rough than I remembered, for I was an Elkan hunter now. The bones, and especially the skulls, grew more huge as we strode along. But if they disturbed Marya, she gave no sign. In fact, I'm sure they didn't, for once she stopped beside a skull that towered higher than she. She ran a finger along great teeth, peered into manhole-sized eye sockets.

"How great he must have been when he walked," she said. "One feels a sadness that they all are gone."

"They had their time," I said. "They enjoyed. Our time is now, before we join them."

And she smiled.

By the time the game trail ended the air was wet and chill. Mists rose from the river, which grew ever more milky and turbid as we neared the foot of the glacier. The canyon narrowed. I remembered that it turned sharply just before we had discovered the game trail.

I stepped into the stream, then looked anxiously back at Marya. She followed without hesitation.

"You have spoken of this," she said. "I have prepared. The moccasins pull higher, and inside I have fur. I will not be wet or cold."

So we splashed along through the icy water, around the last twist of the cliff-rimmed canyon—and then we stopped. The great ice wall blocked the way.

I didn't remember it as it appeared then. Up and up it reared, glistening in the sun, frozen waterfall atop frozen waterfall, a thousand vertical feet of ice. Long friezes of icicles festooned it. Clouds of mists ballooned across its faces. Wet, cold air currents flowed from it. We were chilled inside our Arctic clothing.

Once again Marya clutched my arm.

"We go there?"

I didn't blame her. I've seen a hundred glaciers, but even the edge of the Malaspina was not the sight that loomed before us now.

"We came under it, Denny and I," I said. "I believe we can go back. Will you try?"

It was a needless question.

"What has been done can be done." It was as if Arn the Artisan were speaking. "It is frightening, but also it is very beautiful, is it not?"

She stood, the milky icy water swirling around her knees, and her hands strayed to the binoculars. She focused them, sweeping back and forth and tipping her head far back to see the crest of the glistening barrier.

"It is very great," she said at last, "but I know that it is only ice." She replaced the caps on the binocular lenses. "I am ready," she said.

We were maybe a hundred yards from the piled and broken ice, the boulders, the bones, and the rubbish that lay at the base of the ice wall. As we watched, a whole segment cracked free and came crashing and shattering into the jumble below. The echoes bounced from the canyon walls.

I was worried. The water that formed the river spewed and trickled and seeped from dozens of crevices in the shattered ice, but there was no sign of the tunnel mouth. Where it should have been, ice lay piled. A curtain of ice, one of the many frozen waterfalls, lay above and behind the pile. I knew these formed in the long summer days, when melting was fastest. And this was September.

We stayed close to the granite wall of the canyon, where I hoped we'd have most protection from the breaking ice. But it was dangerous. I motioned to Marya to wait while I explored. But when I started on again she was close behind me. I said nothing more. Perhaps, I thought, that was the better way. We would live or be killed together.

We clambered quickly over the ridges of piled ice. A small shelf of granite jutted out above our heads, offering partial protection from further falls. Here I shrugged off my pack frame. I pulled my ice axe from its loops.

"Here you stay," I told Marya. "I know what I search for. And if I have a hurt you could not help if you were injured too."

She caught my face between her mittened hands, kissed me briefly, then gave me a little push.

"I will stay," she said.

It wasn't much of a search. The tunnel, if it still existed, was blocked, choked by the ice jumble. The ice wall where it had been was smooth and glistening and wet, with water trickling and beading its face as high up as I could see. Again and again I swung my axe against the ice face. Nothing. It was as solid as the granite.

I saw then what a forlorn hope the whole idea had been. It was too simple. We had not just come under a glacier, Denny and I. We had done far more than that. The Primate had been right. I was here for all time.

I leaned against the wall, tried to choke back the disappointment, tried to think. And above me, with a ripping, tearing roar, the world rocked. I had only a glimpse of Marya's horrified face. Then the cascading ice chunks were a curtain that shut her out. I rolled into a ball, facing the wall, my head between my knees. The horrible rumble filled my ears and was the only sound in the world.

Chapter 14

How long it lasted I don't know. Two, three minutes? Probably less. I was almost buried in ice splinters, and my body was numb from the impact of heavier pieces. But I could move. My arms and legs worked. Beyond me a new ridge of great chunks lay, and I knew that the fall had overshot me.

Marya! I was climbing the ridge before I knew that I had moved. And she—she was climbing from her side, climbing frantically. She fell sobbing into my arms and we clung together atop the great piled masses of new ice.

Clouds of chilling vapors swirled around us as we stood there. There was another thing, too, and even in my relief, as I held the shuddering girl in my arms, I noticed it. It was the dank charnel smell of the tunnel. What I and my ice axe could not possibly have done, a multi-ton block of ice had done easily. There was a jagged breach in the ice wall, and behind it lay dark space. The tunnel still existed! Somehow we went back to the spot that had sheltered Marya. The fall had not quite reached it. We shouldered our packs, worked our way over the ridge and down through the break into the shadows beyond the ice curtain. And, looking out, everything was familiar again. Back of us the black hole of the tunnel led into the heart of the glacier.

Had I been Marya, I doubt that I could have gone on. The stresses she fought I could only dimly guess. The complete violation of her people's greatest taboo; the chill and gloom of the ice cave where we stood; the after-effects of shock, when she thought I had been crushed in the ice fall. . . . She stood against me, her head on my chest, the fingers of one hand nervously exploring my face. As I had done at the fissure mouth, I held her gently and said nothing. Finally she lifted her head and looked at me.

"You have hurt?" she asked. Her voice was low and steady.

I grinned in a way that I hoped was reassuring.

"Bumped a little," I said, "but I'm okay."

She swept her eyes around the shadowy cavern, then back to where it pinched into the tunnel mouth.

"This is where you came?"

I nodded.

"This is it. I know, now, that I can go back. But it will be very different, Marya. You can still return to Chan-Cho-Pan. As you have said, the Primate would dispose wisely."

The long golden eyes regarded me steadily. I watched the fear and dread leave her face, the sturdy confidence return. Oo-ah, the daughter of Arn the Artisan, peeked from behind the mask of Marya.

There is only one place for me," she said, almost gaily. "With you. I am ready."

With Denny's little squeeze flashlight in my hand, the water rippling around our ankles, I led the way into the tunnel. I could almost hear the doors to a lovely land close behind us.

Looking back, it was not so bad, that hike. The first part was the worst, of course. Darkness, and the dripping, trickling water and the moldy, charnel-like smell. We passed where the great ribs thrust out into the tunnel, and I was reassured. Finally the gloom lightened, the tunnel widened. There was only slushy ice underfoot. We could see each other. I stowed the flashlight in its place in the pack and brought out raisins and chocolate.

Sitting there on our packs we ate them. There are no finer raisins than those of Elkan, but my girl had never had chocolate before. Denny and I had saved it; saved it for this, the return trail.

"It is as you have told," Marya said. "Beyond it will be wide and beautiful and have great animals in the walls?"

I nodded. I was thinking beyond the tunnel, thinking of the climb out of the crevasse, thinking of the vast white reaches of Seward Glacier in September. And I realized how slim our chances were. Already the blizzards were beginning. We had a little cache—a tent, a tiny stove, more food—if we could find them and dig them out. And how could we leave the white lands? Even the most experienced snow and glacier man would not try to cross the Divide now. And the chances of a plane pickup—nil. It was too late for even Jack Wilson or Pete Swan. Probably landing would be impossible, in the unlikely event we were actually discovered. I thought of going back down the tunnel. The Elkans would be kinder than death in the blizzards of the Icefield Ranges—both for Marya and for me.

It was only a thought, though, rejected as soon as formed. I was committed. I would follow through. I remembered the Primate's casual remark about courage, that day we spent telling him of this tunnel, and of the world from which we had come. And now I added, mentally, that courage is sometimes just carrying on when you haven't much choice.

So I swung up my pack, smiled at the eager girl, and again set the trail pace. The corridor widened, vaulted upward. We could travel with Elkan stride, six miles to the hour. We now had good light, blue, cold, almost metallic. The hours passed. We reached the ice jam, climbed it. After the tumbled, splintered new ridges of the ice fall that had nearly done for us, this seemed tame.

The light was dim, almost spectral, when we came finally to the mammoth, and I knew that outside it was night. Probably the winds were ripping across the vast snow stretches, new snow flying. I was tired, not so much from the hazardous day as from stress and worry. Marya, secure in her confidence in me, probably was not so weary.

"Could you sleep here?" I asked. "Would he disturb you?"

She had shrugged off her pack and was studying the great frozen beast with astonishment.

She flashed her wonderful smile at me.

"I am sure he will be very quiet," she said. "It is sad that he must stand here, all those many years. I can sleep here. He will be company."

"We must rest well," I said soberly. "With the next sun we must climb out of the crevasse, out onto the great snow fields. It will not be easy."

We unrolled our sleeping bags. We each disposed of a C-ration, hungrily, and a handful of raisins besides. And, somewhat to my surprise, we slept. The light was rosy when I awoke. The ice walls glowed as I remembered. Out of the sleeping bag it seemed cold. I checked the thermometer. 10°

F. Up on the ice field it would be lower. I had trouble turning a cheerful face to Marya. But I managed. And strange and new and different as this adventure was to her, she missed my concern. Back in the familiar Elkan country I could not have deceived her for a minute.

We packed, ate frugally, and I led on again. At the Elkan pace the trail was not much longer. It was not three hours later that the vaulted ceiling of our corridor thinned and we could see the open crevasse ahead, a bleak ice canyon into which snow was sifting steadily. The stinging cold of the Arctic wind struck our nostrils. In spite of my forebodings, I felt a sense of homecoming. Of all the climbing and exploring I've done, I think the great stretches of the high ice fields have affected me most and deepest. Without Marya to care for I would have welcomed the challenge now.

I could see at a glance that the crevasse was different. Its walls had sloughed, splintered. Ice ridges, snow-covered, lay where before the walls had been glistening, clean-fractured cliffs. In several places ice almost choked the great fissure, and we worked our way over the piled masses with caution. It was easy to see that we would not climb out as Denny and I had come down. Then I realized that this probably was a "good thing," as Val might have said. And when the end of the crevasse came into view, I knew it was.

Hundreds of feet of the walls had collapsed into the ice canyon. Great blocks of ice lay in an awesome jumble. The new snow partially covered them. At first glance it would have seemed suicide to venture among them. But, after studying carefully, I knew it could be done. And with Marya, who knew nothing of rope and piton climbing, it would be easier than up the wall. That quarter mile of unstable, treacherous ice chunks was a veritable Giant's Causeway to the snowfields above—if we had luck!

I can only say—we had it. Roped to me, with Denny's crampons adjusted and bound to her small feet, Marya was magnificent. Only a woman of the open, of the wild, could have done it at all. And actually, although it was tricky, brutal going, we had no trouble. We made it in an hour.

Finally we stood, in powdery new snow halfway up to our knees, stood well away from the splintering edge of the crevasse and looked out across the endless distances of the Icefield Ranges and of Seward Glacier, bordered and broken by the ice-and-snow-sheathed spires of great peaks almost unknown to all but a handful of mountain men—and women. For a moment I forgot our plight and just, as the Elkans say, "appreciated." The girl beside me clutched my arm and stared with awe.

Then the miracle happened. Or, I should say, two miracles. Or perhaps it was three. The snow had been thinning as we climbed. Now, with the suddenness that the high ranges often show, the clouds above swept away in the upper winds and we stood in dazzling, blinding sunlight. And, as if caused by it, the very ice plain on which we stood seemed to rock. Across from us the crevasse wall seemed to break away in slow motion. Acres of ice went plunging into the fissure. A shuddering, muffled roar came up from the depths. And on our side spidery cracks went zigzagging in all directions, small fissures appearing all about us. The great glacier was shifting ever so slightly in its bed, and when the shuddering had stopped I took Marya firmly by the hand and we ran.

Then came the third miracle. As we paused, panting, beyond the last wavering crack, I heard it. The little plane came sweeping down the wind, its motor roar ever louder. The sun glinted on it. I could see that it was red. Pete Swan! Daredevil Pete, taking a chance to cross the Divide and have the last look of the season at the great crevasse.

He must have seen the wall break away. Probably the spiderweb of cracks on our side was much plainer to him than to us. I knew he would circle, take a good look, perhaps take pictures. But would he see us? No one who has not experienced them can picture how tiny, how completely inconspicuous two human beings can be, lost in the stretches of those vast white wastes. And, if he saw us, would he land? Would he chance what lay under that drifting foot of new snow? Our only hope would be that he *was* Daredevil Pete.

He saw us! The Helio circled, as I expected it would, and we ran, waving our arms. Then it swept around again, much lower. I could imagine Pete's astonishment. Two little figures on Seward's ice in September, no tents, no evidence of how they could have gotten there.

The ice field shook again, slightly, but the Helio made its approach, its skis plowed deep into the powdery snow. The cockpit door popped open.

"Get in!" Pete cried. "For God's sake, whoever you are, get in!"

It took a minute. Marya was snug but terrified on the

packs and bags back of the seats. I sat by the pilot. The motor roared, and with agonizing slowness the plane began to slip forward. The wind was behind us, and that was both good and bad. The pilot was completely concentrated.

We gathered momentum. The skis shook off the clinging snow. Ahead I could see a long fissure bisecting our path, but before we reached it our action smoothed and the hiss of skis on snow died. We were airborne!

For a few more minutes Pete nursed his little ship, lifting as fast as he dared, hoarding every foot of altitude. The snow plain dropped away. We swept in a great circle. Below us the crevasse was again a crack, and seaming out from it in all directions was a network of fissures, an incredible sight. And as we watched, the crevasse collapsed in on itself for almost its entire length. The cracking roar rose faintly to us above the steady noise of our motor.

"Good-bye, crevasse!" Pete Swan said it almost with a sigh. "That was short change there, people. We just made it."

The swarthy little man leaned back, grinned at me, and only then did he recognize me.

"Vin!" he cried.

You've done something when you surprise Pete Swan. And even in this extremity, as serious as things had just finished being, I admit I enjoyed it. I tried to look as nonchalant as possible.

"Hello, Pete!" I said.

That ushered in the strangest year that Marya would ever know. For me, too, it was a time of endless problems.

We told our story, simply and honestly, but it was not a story that could be believed. I had friends. They listened, and nodded and smiled, and acted as though I had recently escaped from some institution for benign mental patients. But Marya puzzled them. She was so obviously different. Her speech, her wonder at the simplest mechanical and technical devices, her genuine distress at the dust and pollution of the Alaska Highway, her cringing at the, to her, endless noise—it was evident that those beautiful eyes were looking on a different world.

Beyond a point, it was not a thing that could be explained. So I did what I felt was best for us both. Back in a little valley that I knew, under the eastern edge of the towering St. Elias, I built a cabin, a snug, tight little home in the wilderness. And there, away from the noise, the curiosity, and the doubts of the world, we lived almost alone for a year.

I taught Marya. I explained as best I could all the things that confused her. Little by little I brought her into contact with people, sympathetic people who would be friendly, who would even listen, though none of them believed. How could they?

And after that year Pete took us again, Marya and me, far out across the St. Elias, beyond the white emptiness of Seward, on over the vast and varied ice jumble that is the Malaspina Glacier. This time Marya sat with Pete. This time the trip was a marvel, not a nightmare. We circled and swept low, we studied the terrain with powerful glasses, we took many pictures. This was where it had to be. But it wasn't. It was as if Elkan had never existed, and, I thought, here it never had.

But then, I looked at my wife. Lovely, with her long golden eyes, one of the world's beautiful women, she certainly existed. And she came from there.

And Denny. What about Denny? Where was he now?

We knew, Marya and I. We knew that somewhere Denny still lived and enjoyed, laughing and wrestling and making the guitar of the man Smith to sing.

But it haunted me. The whole strange story haunted me, as though it were something that had happened to somebody else; as though I had dreamed it all. But Marya was no dream.

I wondered about her, though. When we had lived our lives, loved for our time, had our babies, and grown old, when my face wrinkled and my hair whitened, would she diminish to a lovely miniature and spend her last days in a rocking chair I could hold in the palm of my hand?

So I thought, then pushed such thoughts out of my mind. Before they were problems, we had a whole life to lead; to, as the Elkans said, "live and enjoy." And those things I was determined to do. I had brought Marya into a strange new world. No matter what it would take; no matter how it would be achieved, I was determined that she would not regret.

That was my task, my challenge.

Chapter 15

Marya, my wife, was sitting quietly on the wall I had built before our cabin. The westering sun was low. The spruces were shuddering gently in the breeze. It was June, but the breeze came out of the north. And it was north that Marya was facing, her shapely head flung back, the beautiful cameo profile that to me is the final perfection in woman etched clear against the sunset.

I came softly along the wall, on moccasined feet, but she heard me. She turned with a smile. Only I could have seen the faint wistfulness in it.

"How you can come close to the moose or the wolf, so that you can make their pictures or take their skins, I shall never understand. I heard you many paces away."

"Compared to you, moose and wolves are dull people," I said. I sat beside her on the wall and put an arm around her shoulders. "Also, you love me, and love has keen ears."

She leaned against me with a little sigh. Automatically her fingers found mine and clung tightly.

"Yes," she said, "I love you. And I would know your boot sound or your moccasin sound anywhere."

"But there are other things you love, and you were thinking of them, as you often do when the breeze comes from the north."

"I would not wish to forget," Marya said. "I could not if I wished. They are all good memories."

"Marya," I said seriously, "if there were any way, any way at all, I'd take you back. I've searched. We both have. There isn't anything I haven't done. You know that, don't you?"

She turned her smile on me. The long, almost golden eyes looked at me with an open, transparent honesty. When we spoke to each other, we spoke what was in our minds, in our feelings. There was no guile in Marya.

"Vin," she said quietly, "I have spoken this before. I will

doubtless speak it again, when the longing comes. Remember, we chose. I came because I wished to come. If I had to choose again today, knowing what I now know, I would come again under the glacier. I would come gladly."

I tightened my grip around her slender, sturdy body. The fine vitality of this woman flowed through me, a feel unlike anything else I had ever known. And once again I was aware of my good fortune, my luck, if you will. Not many would ever know the complete oneness that we shared, Marya and I.

"Thank you," I said. "I understand that. You know I do. But occasionally it helps to hear you say it."

"You must never regret," she told me earnestly. "What has any woman had that I have not? Without you there would have been no Marya. There would have been only little Oo-ah, the daughter of Arn the Artisan, roaming the land with big Tor, and never knowing that her heart was empty."

"But it was a beautiful land," I reminded, "and no one could miss what she had never known."

She released my hand, pushed me away as she slid lithely from the wall.

"I prefer to know," she told me gaily. "And I hear in the forest the whirlwind for which I will also always be glad."

It was a good comparison. And in a couple of minutes they came into view among the spruces, the boy giggling as he ran, and the malemute rushing around him in circles and occasionally leaping high in the air.

But when they neared us they slowed to a decorous walk. Half a dozen paces away the boy stopped. The dog still frisked about.

"Fang, have respect!"

The malemute promptly sat, flattening his pricked ears. But his red tongue lolled over formidable white teeth, his mouth still wide as he grinned.

The boy clasped his left hand with his right, bowed his small dark head.

"Mother. Father. Live and enjoy!"

We bowed in our turn, clasping hands in the graceful fashion of a beautiful lost land.

"Denny, have happiness!" Marya said.

"And you too, Fang!" I added.

Then Marya bent and held out her arms, and our son flew into them. I put my arms around them both. The blaze-faced dog raced round and round us and finally, with a tremendous leap, went over the tops of our heads.

"It must have been a good playtime," I said. "Fang seems happy."

"Do not feed him," Denny said. "He has already eaten. And because of him, somewhere around there are babies that are hungry."

"I hope you didn't scold him," I said seriously. "What did he kill?"

"A snowshoe. I was searching along the riffles for mussels, and did not see until it was dead. It was a mother. But I could not help it, so I let him eat it."

The boy turned his long eyes, so like his mother's, on the cheerful malemute. "Killer!" he said.

Fang seemed puzzled, but he was not too depressed. He knew that he had done something for which he wasn't being praised, but he couldn't imagine what. He also knew, in spite of the tone, that his friend and playfellow wasn't really angry.

"Now wait," I said. "The time to learn is when there is a problem. What do we feed Fang?"

Denny looked at me gravely.

"We feed him meat," he said.

"And to get meat, something must die. Is that not so?"

"That is so," the boy admitted.

"You have seen me butcher moose and caribou and mountain sheep. For that matter, I have also taken snowshoes and grouse and ptarmigan. So I am a killer too."

Denny considered.

"It is not the same," he decided. "You do it so *we* may have food. And you do not kill mothers."

"I might," I said, "if I knew no better, or if I were hungry enough. It is Fang's nature to kill his own food. You would not expect him to eat bark like a beaver or chew cones like a pine squirrel, would you?"

The idea amused the boy. His long eyes crinkled and he giggled.

"That would be silly," he chuckled.

"Then we must be careful not to confuse him. He will do as you tell him, because we have trained him well. He is your good friend. But unless he is told, if food comes under his nose he will behave like his cousin the wolf. We won't scold him for something unless he disobeys. You did not tell him not to kill the hare."

Our son stood, small, slender, and sturdy, but an imposing man for six cycles of seasons. I was proud of him.

"I was not fair, you think?"

"You made up for it. You allowed him to eat the hare. If you were not too pleased, I don't think he holds it against you. And if ever you were lost in the woods with only Fang for companion he would find food for you both. Remember that."

"I will remember," the boy said. For a minute or so he seemed lost in thought, shutting us all out, a habit he had had since he first began to talk. Then he said, "I think perhaps Mother should teach me something of cooking. I would not care to eat the flesh raw as he does."

I smiled at Marya over his tousled head.

"A good, practical suggestion," I said heartily. "I wonder if she would care to show us what she has cooked recently. I'm sure I am much hungrier than Fang!"

"That is because you have not eaten a whole hare! Come, Fang! We must wash ourselves for supper."

And away they ran, the lithe small boy and the big wolf dog shoulder to shoulder, a small hand gripping the malemute's heavy fur. They disappeared around the corner of the cabin.

"Never do they walk!" Marya said. She smiled pensively. "How they would love the hills and the fields and the forest lands of Chan-Cho-Pan. It seems as if he belongs there, does it not?"

"It's your thinking that puts him there," I said. "To him there is no finer land than the black spruce, the muskeg, and the cold streams of Yukon. I admit that he didn't think much of Vancouver or Portland or San Francisco. Even in Whitehorse he says it is noisy from many people, and the air smells bad."

"Also, Fang could not go to these places. That he missed most of all."

I shook my head. I knew I still had problems. More than one.

"Marya," I said carefully, "we must be wise. It would be fine to see our son one of the great tall men of Elkan, but we know that is not possible. This is his land. And it includes cities and aircraft and technology and pollution and too many people. We cannot hide him away. He must know all these things. This is the only world he has. He must stand tall in it."

My beautiful wife once more faced the north. She raised her head as if to listen, sniffed as if she searched for something alien in the breeze. And this time she did not try to hide the sadness in her smile.

"You have truth, Vin. This is Denny's world. And I have been slow to see that it is my world too. Always, far deep in my thinking, I could see a road back, back to where everything is simple, and everyone lives and enjoys, and when problems arise, the Primate disposes. Somewhere, we know it exists. But for us it is only a dream."

"There's my woman!" I said. My voice must have expressed the relief I felt. "As you said, we chose. I think we knew that it was a choosing for all time. We could not take it back. We know that there is happiness here. There is even yet space where a small boy and a big dog can be free for a while. We can live our lives well."

"Come eat," Marya said. "The meat is hot, the milk is cool from the snow water. Marya of Yukon can prepare food quite as well as ever did Oo-ah of Chan-Cho-Pan."

In that, at least, she was certainly correct.

But later I could not sponge away the sadness, the wistfulness of my wife's smile. She knew, but she could never forget. She did not regret, but the memories would always be there. I brooded and thought. And finally I decided what we would do.

When *your* wife requires cheering up, when you want to make her happy again, you buy her presents, or take her to dinner and the theater, or to a game or a party, whatever she likes best. If time and your money permit, you may even take her to London or to Paris, where life is supposed to reach its peak in our civilized world.

These are simple remedies. My problem was far greater. My wife was sad because she had lost a world, and there was nothing I could buy for her that would take its place. But I did what I thought would please her most.

I announced it in the stately English of Elkan.

"In five sun-spans," I said, "we go north. We will put the big canoe on the Yukon, and it will take us to where the northern geese and the swans go in summer, to nest and rear their young. Denny has never seen white water under the canoe. He has never seen the sun shine at midnight. And Fang has never seen such hunting as he will find on the tundra and in the marshes."

Denny's eyes shone, but he made no outcry such as most small boys might. Somehow the silence of big country has always been in him. The dog felt the excitement in his young master, and beat his tail on the cabin floor.

But Marya said, "But what of the work you must do in the warm time so that we may have what we require when the snow comes again? This is not Elkan, where all men share."

I laughed.

"It is necessary for you to go north too, for you are beginning to think like the women of this land who do not trust their husbands. From the banks that you still do not understand there will be money for our needs. I have placed it there. So for three, four ten-spans of days we will live and enjoy with the caribou and perhaps, if there is time, even the white bear. We will feel the wind off the ice packs, and breathe the best air left in this world. Then we will return, and take up our lives here, and have pleasure from what we cannot change."

Marya understood.

"I will make ready the packs," she said cheerfully. "Denny shall use for the first time the frame you have made for him. And Fang, too, shall have a small pack. Whenever we leave the canoe, each will carry his share."

Somehow it pleased me particularly, that unconscious stating of the basic tenet by which the people of her world lived. It was the core of Elkan thinking. "Each will carry his share."

Chapter 16

Those were good days, wonderful days, as the big canoe drove steadily northward. Living was easy. There was little work with the paddling, for we simply kept our craft where the current was swiftest, and the great northern river bore us smoothly along.

Of course the boy had often been with me, in the small canoe when I fished and hunted waterfowl, and in the large craft when I carried supplies. He had his own small paddle which I had carefully fitted to his strength. His stroke was knowing and skilled. And now he was proud to sit in the stern seat and take his turn at the steering. He knew that he only steered in smooth water, and that a mature eye was always on him. But we could almost see him grow.

We passed Dawson. The Klondike pushed its clear stream like a silver tongue into the murky flood of the Yukon. Denny wrinkled his nose at the stink of the passing ferry, and the malemute growled at the shouting, waving people on her deck.

We didn't pause. We had no need, and I think we all were reaching ahead, looking forward into the untroubled quiet lands that stretched and spread northward for many hundreds of miles. It was not a vacation land for most, I agree, but it fitted the need we had, all of us, as nothing else could have. For the families on the ferry we had just passed it would have been forbidding wilderness. For us it was friendly. In a way, it was home.

"Two or three sun-spans more," I said, "and we will leave the big river. We will follow a small stream, find a pleasant spot, and there we will camp. Even if our campfire smoke goes straight up into the sky, there will be no one close enough to see it. For a little while, this will be our land alone."

"I will climb the hills," Denny said, "and Fang shall hunt what I tell him. No mothers," he added sternly, with a look at the dog.

Fang wagged his tail. Apparently the terms were satisfactory to him. And Marya said, "I will prepare food, different food such as you have not had for long. I will take fish from the stream, mushrooms and roots and leaves from the forest. And when Fang makes a kill, Denny shall learn how to prepare it best."

"I will put away my guns," I said. "Once, long ago, I took a token with the bow. I have it here, that same bow. It is old now, but it is still good. It was made by a master at working with wood. I will take our game with it."

So we planned, while the spruce-clad banks of the Yukon slid past, and the nights grew always shorter.

We knew our stream when we saw it. It came out of wooded, gently rolling hills. Its mouth was wide, and it sent a broad wedge of clean icy water into the ever-increasing volume of the Yukon's flow; one of a thousand streams without a name. I swung the canoe into it, dug my paddle deep, and slowly we pushed our way against the current, on upstream into the peaceful hills.

We found our camp spot, too. For a week we did the things we had planned. Denny and Fang explored, I practiced with the bow, and Marya fed us as only she could.

"If only the bitter cold did not come, I would love a home plot here," she said. "You could build a tight cabin with the spruce logs. There is food everywhere. We would have a wide land for our own. There is nothing lacking."

"It's a pleasant dream, my dear," I said, "but that's all it is. We couldn't live as the wild things do, even though we could keep ourselves fed and sheltered. One thing would always be missing."

Marya looked at me steadily for a moment, her strange, beautiful eyes seeming to insist that the dream was real. Then she sighed.

"I know. Still I like to run away, don't I, Vin? People would be missing. This is beautiful, but we cannot live outside the world."

Denny was listening intently to us, as he usually did, so I tousled his dark hair and brought him into the talk.

"How about it, son? Would you like to live here all your life, hunting and fishing and prowling the hills with Fang, and never seeing a single soul? Does that sound good to you?"

He surprised us.

"That would not be possible," he said. "There are people here."

I glanced at my wife. She seemed stunned. And I'll admit that I was pretty astonished, too.

"Denny," I said seriously, "when have you seen people? And why didn't you tell us?"

"There has not yet been time," the boy said. "Only this morning I have learned of them—and I have not really seen them."

"Tell us."

"Two hills away, there," he waved to the northwest, "eagles have their nest. Fang and I have watched them. And near the nest tree is a tall spruce, with low thick branches that I might climb. I went high, to look down into the nest and see the young."

He looked from me to his mother, then back to me again. Our concern seemed to amuse him, but he hastened to reassure us.

"There was no danger. The branches were thick. I could not fall, and the big birds could not strike me. And from the top of the spruce I could see far across the hills."

He stopped and mused, shutting us out while he thought.

"What did you see?"

"Three young. They are large, almost ready to fly. The old ones feed them fish."

"The people, Denny. What about the people."

"The eagles come from far away with their fish, and when I had climbed high I could see where they got them. There is a lake, four, five, six hills over. It is blue in the sun. It may be very large, for I could not see it all."

He brooded again, his long eyes mirroring something within his mind.

"I think our stream flows from there."

We waited.

"On the lakeshore there was the smoke of a campfire. I watched until Fang grew tired and barked. He does not like it when I climb because he must stay on the ground. I saw no person, but it was a campfire. There is someone there."

Then we were all silent, each thinking his or her own thoughts, and the malemute looking from one to another almost with puzzlement.

"Well," I said finally, "it seems to be harder to find an empty land than even I thought. What shall we do? Go back to the big river and on north toward the Porcupine, or stay for a while and learn to know our neighbors?"

"They are not close," Marya said. "It is not likely we should ever see them. I find this a pleasant land."

"If we can see their campfire, they may perhaps see ours," I pointed out. "They might decide to visit while we are asleep."

"Fang would not allow," Denny said. "He would know."

"True enough. So what would you like to see us do, Old Woodsman?"

The boy grinned slightly. He reacted to my joking very much as his mother did, with loving tolerance, and as though he did not quite understand the reason for it. But he had his answer ready.

"I would like to see the lake. It may reach far among the hills. There would be ducks and loons, and more eagles, and different kinds of fish. Also it would be pleasant to swim there, and to watch game from the canoe. You have said you would teach me new ways of diving. This would be a good place for that."

"Hum-m!" I said. "You *have* thought it out."

I glanced at his mother, then back to him.

"And what about the people? Suppose they do not want us there?"

"It is a large lake," Denny said. "No one owns it. We would have a right to our share."

I liked that. Here, at least, was a man who did not need to hide. He liked the world the way it was, and was confident of his place in it.

"How about it?" I asked my wife. "Shall we go to the lake? The people will only be people—and it is still a big, almost empty land."

Marya studied us gravely, one after the other, even including the alert, interested dog. He always seemed to know when there were new things afoot.

"I would be alone if I did not wish to go. You would like to know who else camps in this land. Denny wishes the lake because it has many birds and fish, and what Denny likes, Fang likes. Very well. What my family wishes, I wish. Perhaps you may teach *me* a new way of diving as well."

Chapter 17

It would have been perhaps a few hours of traveling on foot across the hills. By canoe, up the smoothly flowing stream, it took the whole of a long Arctic summer day. But at the end of it, when the sun lay low behind the spruces, we could see the lake shining in the distance. The current became more than our paddles could match, so I knew we would have to portage that final half mile or so in the morning. We made a fireless camp, ate cold food, and slept as weary people sleep. Only Fang, who had not had to paddle, watched. He was enough.

In the crisp cloudless morning I built a cheery fire. I swung my axe vigorously against a dead spruce, and the sound of it echoed through the woods. My small son looked on with appreciation.

"You are saying to the people at the lake that we are here," he observed. "This way, when they see us come, they will not be surprised."

"Exactly," I said. "I am also making firewood, so that your mother may have all she needs while she prepares our breakfast. I *think* I smell flapjacks."

Denny gathered such a load of wood that he staggered.

"There are also steaks from the yearling caribou, and the blue grouse eggs that Fang found yesterday when we ran along the shore while you paddled. They were very fresh," he added. "The bird could lay more."

"You take the wood," I said. "If I go near, my mouth will water so that I might put out the fire."

Denny went, giggling.

Meanwhile I scouted the route we would have to take as we carried the canoe past the stream's rapid origin to the open lake beyond. It presented no problems. On shorter trips along more rocky watercourses Marya and I had often portaged. Only a woman of the open could have done some of the things we did together, but she rejoiced in them as I did.

So after the bountiful breakfast the packs were quickly made up. We lifted the canoe from the water, settled it on our shoulders, and carried it easily. It was of northern birchbark, amazingly light for its length and capacity, but resilient and strong. An old Indian and I had spent much of a summer making it. It carried more than we could, so Fang was left to guard the extra duffle until I could return for it.

"It is a very fine lake," Denny said. "It is large as Kluane is large. I am glad we have come."

He spoke for us all. I watched Marya, but there was no shadow on her beautiful face. She seemed as pleased as the boy and I. The lake evidently wound far among the hills, seeming narrow only because it was so long. We had come out onto a wide beach of white quartz sand, bright in the morning sun.

"Now, don't explore," I reminded Denny. "Wait until I come back with Fang. Your mother may be glad of your company. She hasn't even seen you much since you learned to walk, you know."

Denny's dark brows came down over the long eyes as he regarded me seriously.

"I see her each day," he began. Then he grinned sheepishly. "You make another joke," he said. "We will watch the fish hawks. Already I have seen one dive."

"Plunge," I corrected. "He goes in feet first."

"Plunge," Denny agreed. "It is a better word."

Within an hour Denny and Fang were racing on the beach, and Marya and I had loaded the canoe to our liking. Then we all embarked again. I sent the craft along leisurely with an occasional dip of the paddle, staying far enough offshore so that the beach swell did not cause us to rock.

"Look for smoke," I directed. "Look for campfire places along the beach. We may as well know whom we're sharing this water with."

Marya swept the shore with her binoculars. Denny used mine, but he continually came back to the ospreys and their fishing. Neighbors that flew were his concern. The kind that built campfires did not have nearly so much interest.

"Sniff, Fang," he told the dog. "When there are people on the shore, tell us."

Fang's bushy tail wagged. Of us all we knew that he got the most complete, the most integrated picture of our surroundings. He sat alertly, his sharp ears pricked, his nose twitching at every breeze. There was game in the forest that we could not see, but Fang knew it was there. His ears pivoted with each sound. He watched the plunge of the fish hawk, but he did not miss the fox that darted across an open space behind the beach. Occasionally he looked at Denny as if to ask a question.

We drifted along slowly. An hour passed, and there was no evidence that our lake had ever known man.

I quizzed Denny again.

"Did your smoke come from the forest or from the shore? Or, from the treetop, was it possible to tell?"

"From the beach." The boy was positive. "By now we

should have seen it. Perhaps the people who made it now try to hide. We should walk along the sand. Fang would find them.

I swung the canoe into the shore again.

"A reasonable suggestion," I said. "We will search, you and Fang and I. Your mother will take the canoe along offshore, and just as a precaution she will have the big rifle handy before her. She shoots it as well as I."

Marya smiled.

"You do not really think it will be needed," she said. "Otherwise you would not take Denny ashore. He is a very fine woodsman, but he is not yet a man."

"There isn't much chance," I admitted. "It's possible, though. Unknown things do not have to be the way we expect. So keep the gun on the seat before you. Put it where it can be seen."

"You wish the fire makers to see it," Denny said keenly. "Then maybe they will not ask us why we are here. There is also the magnum. If they know what it is, they will be polite."

I patted the .357, riding as always against my right thigh.

"Smart man," I said. "To be ready for trouble is the best way not to have any."

I went overside and steadied the canoe. The dog and the small boy leaped ashore. Then I gave the boat a push into deep water again. Marya sat in the stern seat and wielded her paddle like no other woman I have ever known. Skillfully she managed the craft so that it scarcely rocked. The rifle lay conspicuously across the thwarts in front of her.

Well offshore the fish hawk plunged. Spray flew in a sheet as the bird went almost under. The long wings beat strongly as it lifted again, a big lake trout glinting in its talons.

Denny was pleased.

"Ha," he said. "Finally he has breakfast for the young in his nest. Several times before he has plunged and caught nothing." He focused my binoculars. "It is a fine, large fish. We would like one of that size for ourselves."

It was, in fact, almost a full load for the bird. It banked and fought to rise in the face of the gentle breeze from the shore. Slowly it gained altitude. At treetop height it straightened its course, heading across the lake. And the thunderbolt fell.

I heard the high strumming of the wind through the pinions of the diving eagle, and at the same moment he loosed his strident scream. The osprey twisted and banked. For a moment it clung desperately to the fish. It knew, though. It was not facing an unknown problem. At the eagle's second pass the fish hawk released its prey. The bigger bird caught it neatly, almost matter-of-factly, as though it were his due. That fish was destined to feed eaglets, not young ospreys.

"He is a thief!" Denny said indignantly. "If I had the big rifle, I would shoot him! He should catch his own fish!"

"They have managed all their years without your help," I said. "This is the way it is between the old whitehead and the fish hawk. They both get along very well. . . . You know," I had an idea, "I suspect that is your eagle. See, he is going out across the hills."

Denny followed with the binoculars.

"Far away I can see the nest, and by it the tall spruce I climbed. From there I saw the fire."

"Ah," I said. "The old eagle is going to be a help after all. He is drawing a line for you. Now perhaps it will be easier to know where the smoke came from."

The boy studied the terrain. The eagle was now a tiny speck, beating steadily for the distant nest.

"We have come too far. It is back down the beach, but perhaps not a great distance."

We found it, but not easily. It had been located at the forest edge of the sand, a pit fire, probably used for cooking. But it had been carefully and neatly covered, the sand drifted over it naturally. We might have passed it by, but Fang left us as we strolled along, veered over to the hidden spot at the edge of the brush, and stood wagging his tail. On closer inspection I could see what had been done.

"Tell me," I said to Denny. "What is the story of the fire?"

"This is a lesson?"

"Call it so if you want."

"If my nose was like Fang's, I could tell you more. But there was a hole dug for the fire. Perhaps they cooked here. When they heard your axe they covered the fire with sand and brushed away their tracks. They went into the woods, but Fang can follow them."

I took a piece of driftwood and dug. There was a deep bed of ashes under the sand. Denny turned over a large, innocent-looking rock nearby. Underneath it was heavily smoked.

"There will be others like this. Shall I look?"

"No, let them keep their secret. If they want to hide, it is their affair. They have as much right to be here as we do."

I covered the ashes again, smoothed the sand.

"We will make our camp at the other end of the lake. There is certainly room here for us both."

We strolled on along the water's edge for a short distance, then signaled Marya to bring the boat in.

Chapter 18

It was a long lake. We paddled leisurely for several miles. Denny and Fang watched the shore with interest, and probably very little escaped both the eyes of the one and the nose of the other. Life was abundant, along shore and on the lake. And it was undisturbed life. Moose and caribou at the water's edge, loons and ducks on the lake surface, a constant traffic in the air overhead; and none seemed concerned by our passage.

"If there have been men along here, they have been quiet men," I said. "Nothing is frightened by us. They do not seem to know that we are danger. They have not been taught to be afraid."

A little peninsula projecting into the lake, with a high ridge for a backbone, plenty of spruce, and its own beach of white sand, was a location too tempting to leave behind.

"The lake goes on and on," my wife said. "We are far from the camp space of those who hide their fire. I like this spot. The sun shines on both sides of it. We can make a pleasant camp here."

"Ideal," I agreed. "Denny?"

Our son looked from one of us to the other. His gaze was speculative, almost quizzical.

"If I said that I did not like, would you paddle on?" he inquired gravely.

"If you didn't like the place, you'd have a reason. I'd listen. That's why I asked."

"I think it is a very good camp place. Fang likes it. And if the people send up smoke again, we can see it from the ridge-top."

"And you don't think they are going away. Is that it?"

Denny looked concerned.

"Fang did not bark at the fire location. He wagged his tail. This is something I do not understand. He does not like strangers."

This, I realized, was good thinking for a six-year-old. For that matter, it was something neither his mother nor I had noticed. When I thought, I knew he had a point.

"You think perhaps that Fang would not stop these people if they came to our camp in the night?"

When I speak to my family, especially on serious matters, gradually I find myself adopting the graceful phrasing, the almost stately cadence of the English as Elkans speak it. It seems more fitting, somehow. And of course Marya has never spoken any other way.

"I do not know what Fang would do," Denny said now, "but he does not think they are bad."

"Perhaps he is right," Marya said.

"Maybe. But I'd like a chance to judge for myself. We'll camp here, but we'll keep closer watch than usual. And Fang may still tell us if someone is near, whether he's friendly or not."

"He will not allow harm to us," Denny said loyally. "I will tell him to guard. Then no one may come near."

The big malemute sat amidships and watched us with interest during this family conference, glancing from one to another as if he understood it all. And at Denny's vote of confidence he ran out his red tongue and looked almost smug.

"He knows," the boy said. "It is just that he cannot tell us all he knows."

"That's good enough for me. That little cove ahead will make a nice harbor. And there's an osprey nest in that dead spruce on the point out there. You'll have something close to camp to watch."

Denny understood. The implication that he wouldn't be able to prowl far afield probably didn't make him happy, but he didn't protest. Further, he knew that I'd take him to explore. He wasn't being confined. I was just being careful.

We have had many good camps, Marya and I. We have

pitched our small tent in deep woods, in mountain meadows, along lakeshores and stream sides, and in the ice fields high above timberline. And I don't recall a finer location than our spot there on the little tongue of rock and spruce and sand projecting out into the blue waters of this nameless northern lake.

Yet it was not restful. Somehow, we could not relax, could not settle into a comfortable routine. Denny sat long atop a high rock, watching the ospreys plunge and feed their brood. Marya's meals lacked the flair she loved to give them. I fished, and practiced with the bow, but I could muster no enthusiasm. And Fang, after watching us with puzzlement for awhile, simply found himself a comfortable spot in the shade and slept.

So it was relief, the second day, when Denny came quietly down from his observation post and reported: "There is the smoke again. It is closer. It lies just behind a curve in the beach, and I can see no one. But it is there."

That posed a problem. What should we do? The fire makers evidently knew we were there, knew we would see their smoke. In fact, it was pretty likely that they intended for us to see it.

"Let's go," I decided. "Let's get this over. Fang will stay and guard the camp. We'll go visiting."

I estimated that the smoke was a mile or so away. We put the rifle in sight athwart the canoe's bow. It would be only a few minutes journey. We dug our paddles deep and the canoe, without baggage, fairly skimmed the water. Kneeling amidships, Denny plied his small paddle with a careful regard for the rhythm of our strokes. Anticipation gleamed in his long eyes.

"Perhaps they will ask us to dinner," he said. "It was quite a large smoke."

It was an innocent remark of a small boy, but it rang a bell in my head. We were just before the curve in the beach that hid the fire, so I didn't turn back. I knew, though, what we'd find.

"I am not very smart," I said. "I should have known."

We were still offshore, looking at the briskly burning fire through binoculars. It was set in a stone-rimmed pit and damped with wet wood just enough to send a good column of smoke spindling upward. Of course, there was no one there.

"They were probably already near our camp when we left shore. Now all depends on what they want—and on Fang."

"To injure him they would have to use guns," Marya said. "There have been no shots."

I spun the canoe and drove for the beach.

"You two will paddle back," I directed. "Keep the rifle handy before you. I will go through the woods. Perhaps I can no longer run all day, but I can surely run a mile. We will trap them yet. But stay offshore until I call to you."

I went overside, gave the craft a push, and before Marya was fairly settled in the stern seat I had crossed the beach and was moving swiftly and quietly along the edge of the spruce forest. As I said, I could still run a mile. Though there was much down timber in the route I chose, I soon left the canoe far behind.

Our visitor must have seen the returning canoe as soon as it came into sight around the curve of the beach. She knew she had time. She came almost leisurely back down the peninsula, a tall, graceful woman striding with a fluid ease. At her heels, escorting her from our property, was Fang.

I watched. The dog was alert, but there was no doubt that he was friendly. And the woman showed no fear of him. In fact, she was talking to him as I settled down behind a windfall out of sight.

"You are a good dog, and I hope you are pleased," she said. "I touched nothing. I meant no harm. You understand that?"

She stopped and faced the malemute. Fang warily retreated a couple of paces, but, after a moment, wagged his tail. It was clear that she was an acceptable person, so long as she did not disturb what didn't belong to her.

The breeze must have shifted slightly. The dog's nostrils suddenly flared as he picked up my body scent. He circled the woman, bounded over to the windfall, and turned to face her again. Not by a twitch of an ear did he show that he knew I was there. But his responsibility was over. I was back. He was there to take orders.

I took him off the hook by rising casually from my hiding place. The woman's strikingly deep eyes widened slightly, but she kept her poise. She even smiled.

"I am not so clever as I thought," she said.

I studied her for a moment before I spoke. I was genuinely

puzzled. Fang glanced up at me, looked back at the woman, then at me again. He wagged his tail tentatively.

"Everything okay," he was saying. "No harm done. I did my job."

"You went to a lot of unnecessary trouble," I told the woman. "You would have been welcome to visit. If you need help, we will give it if we can."

"You know I am alone?"

"I've just realized it. If there were others, the dog would know. And for some reason he tolerates you. Usually he doesn't."

"He is a very fine dog. He would not allow me to go near your tent, but he made no attempt to harm me. He simply stood in the way."

"It's well you didn't push your luck. He had his orders."

She studied me carefully. I looked back at a tall woman in a fringed buckskin jacket, worn blue jeans, and moccasins. It was a strange face, strongly planed, almost patrician. Black hair waved to her shoulders. The dark eyes glowed. I couldn't have guessed at an age, but she was not old. And I especially remembered my distant view of her; the grace with which she moved.

"I am thinking that this is also true of you. I should not push my luck."

"Well," I said, "an explanation *would* be nice. You've tried to sneak into our camp, first baiting us away, and for what purpose I can't imagine."

"The answer for that is simple," she said gravely. "I wished to know if you were danger to me. What my eyes told me did not seem to be all there was. It was not reasonable that a family, a man, a woman, a child, and a dog, should come camping to this far lake. This is deep wilderness. It is not a land for vacations."

"Then it seems less likely," I countered, "that a lone woman would be here. I suppose there's an answer for that, too."

She nodded slowly.

"There is an answer. But it is not an answer easily told. Now, you would not believe it. Later, if you knew me better, you might."

Fang stood watching us. He glanced from one to the other, and his tail waved slowly.

"Fang vouches for you," I said. "I'll take your word."

The woman laughed. It was a genuine, spontaneous peal of appreciation, a particularly joyous kind of laugh.

"His name is Fang? A wonderful name! So correct!"

"He likes it," I said drily. "I see the canoe in the distance. Come and meet my wife and son, and see if they respond to you as he does."

"Wait!" The woman's voice was suddenly urgent. "Before they come, I should say the other reason why I wished to know what you were like. I have great need for help. It is a different kind of help than you can imagine, and I have never needed it before. And you will believe it even less than the reason I am here."

"But I am willing to listen, and so will they be."

She shook her head.

"I cannot tell you yet. But let me share your company for awhile, and you will know."

I considered. The canoe swung around offshore, waiting for my signal to come in.

"You're asking a lot. Still, I don't see what harm it can do. Tell us how you came to be here, and your need for help will be your own affair. You're checking us out before you ask. I know that."

"Would you not, if you were alone as I am?"

"I suppose I would," I conceded. "I'll call in the canoe. What name shall I tell them? They'll think it strange if you have no name."

"Call me Jeanne," the woman said. "I had a husband who was called Pierre. He is buried back in the north, on the Porcupine."

"I am Vin," I said. If she had no surname, neither would I have. "My wife is Marya, my son Denny. Fang you have met."

"Yes," Jeanne said. Again her interesting face showed amusement at the name. "It has been a pleasure to meet you, Fang."

And again I puzzled at the evident fact that the pleasure was mutual. Fang sat and lolled his red tongue and looked complacent.

I left the fringe of woods and showed myself on the beach. When the canoe crew saw me, I waved them in. The woman followed me. Fang brought up the rear, ears up, tongue dripping, tail waving. He definitely gave the impression that he thought he had done a good day's work.

Marya was shy with the strange woman. Denny regarded her silently from under his dark brows. It was impossible to say what he thought. I talked, groping for a way to ease the tension. In a way, I had committed myself to help the woman, without any idea of why she needed help. But there had been a brief time, when she first spoke of need, that she had shown fear and bewilderment. It was gone quickly, but it had been there.

"Jeanne tells me that there are no other people on the lake. She has lived here for a year. Even Indians do not come in, and she has been undisturbed. That is why she did not show herself when we came. It was hard to believe that we were what we seemed to be."

"For us it is hard also," Marya said, gently but plainly. "A woman alone in the bitter cold of Yukon is difficult to think of. How did you live?"

"I will show you."

I could not escape the awareness of openness, of honesty, when the woman spoke. I was increasingly impressed with her unusual grace and ease of movement, with her finely planed, striking face. She was not beautiful as Marya was beautiful. Handsome was a better word. But competent was an impression that overrode every other. If any woman could spend a solitary winter in the Yukon wilderness, I'd have bet this one could.

"I have a cabin in the spruce near where you entered the lake. I have an axe and traps. I fish in the lake and I hunt with the bow. It is miles, but I will take you to see."

"You hunt with a bow?" I grasped at the obvious oddity.

She smiled. It was an open smile, almost a grin.

"I do not blame you for doubting. I told you that you would not believe. But if you will think, a rifle requires cartridges. I used most of mine long ago, except for a very few. These I would use if my life were in danger. I have a skill with the bow, and arrows can always be made. I do not lack for food."

"Nor do we," Marya said. "This evening's meal you will sit with us. Vin has caught fine trout. I have corn meal, and will make cakes that my men love. And there are the wild blueberries for a pie. I think it has been long since you have been a guest."

My wife's hospitality was Elkan both in its nature and its origin. I knew she would never have invited the woman unless she felt that it was an appropriate thing to do. In effect, she joined Fang and me in pronouncing the guest at least harmless.

Then Denny made it unanimous. He had been studying the woman, his long eyes narrowed, his small face inscrutable.

"I will show you where the loon has her nest," he offered suddenly. "She has hidden it in the edge of the reeds. It is not far from camp. She does not know that I know," he added with a grin.

The woman called Jeanne recognized the acceptance. She did not hide her relief.

"When I have helped your mother with the food, I will be glad to see," she told Denny. "It is not often that anyone finds the loon's nest."

Chapter 19

That was a good meal. It was good not only for the excellence of the food, but for the pleasant easing of the tension that had disturbed us for days. When Jeanne told us that there were no other people in the area we felt that she spoke the truth. She talked freely and with ease. She was familiar with the lake. She told us of many things that we would want to see. It was only later, when I thought over what she had said, that I realized how little she had told us of herself.

She had enjoyed the food. Hers was the hearty appetite that would be expected from one who lived actively in the open. She ate as we ate. Marya's small corn cakes especially won her favor.

"I wouldn't think," she said, "that simple corn cakes could be so different. Can you tell me, or is the making a secret?"

I wondered what she would think if she were told where that recipe had come from. The Elkan corn cakes were the first different food that had impressed me when the young Oo-ah had brought my first breakfast, back in that lost land. I knew my wife was remembering too, but she only said quietly, "From my father I learned how they are made. He prepared food very well. And he liked very much to eat. I will show you how I make the cakes."

"I will have another one, please," Denny said. "My father has said that they will make me tall and great. Also, they are good."

"I didn't have them when I was small," I said. "Therefore I never truly got my growth. You will look down on me."

Denny's dark eyes gleamed.

"When you are old I will be able to help you over the fallen logs and carry your pack for you. You will be glad that mother fed me many cakes."

"Now there is a con job if ever I heard one," I said. "My dear, feed him. Then I will have a comfortable and a pleasant old age."

Jeanne smiled, as she was expected to do, but it seemed to me, for a fleeting moment, that the smile was a travesty, that it was almost a grimace. I knew then that she had spoken the truth to me earlier. She did, as she said, have great need for help. She was a fine strong woman, and what the need could be I couldn't imagine. But I no longer doubted that it existed.

In the days that followed it was good to be able to say to Denny and Fang: "You are free. Explore and watch all you want. But tell your mother or me where you are going, and be in camp when it is time to eat. And do not go near the grizzly or the moose. They may not know what important people you are."

"When we watch, nothing knows we are there. We are careful of the wind, and we make no sounds. And always Fang knows when something comes."

"I depend on that. As I have often said, let Fang teach you. He does not think *anything* is unimportant."

"That is true," the boy said thoughtfully. "I should, I think, tell you of what we saw only yesterday. I have thought perhaps I should not, that it was a secret, that she might not wish you to know. But it made Fang unhappy. He held his head low, and would not wag his tail."

"She? Your mother?" I was alert at once.

Denny shook his head.

"Jeanne. She sat on a rock by the lakeshore, and was not like she is with us. She was very sad. She sat on the rock and cried."

"Hum-m. Did she see you?"

"Nothing sees us if we do not wish to be seen," Denny said proudly. "Even the loon does not know when we watch her nest."

"All very well, great woodsman," I said drily, "but do not become too pleased with yourself. Remember, even the moose is occasionally eaten."

Denny studied me with that strange, adult concentration that I have never seen in another small boy.

"I am growing too large for my moccasins, you think?"

"Not really," I said, "for you are a smart boy. . . . Did Jeanne speak to herself as she sat?"

My son grinned.

"I am smart because I have a smart father," he said. "Jeanne did speak, but I could not tell what she said. It was in a different language, not English, not French. Yet," he added, and his dark brows lowered, "it was not too strange. It seems that I have heard it before."

"An Indian tongue, maybe? Tlingit? Chinook?"

"Not these," the boy said. "It was very different—yet I have heard it."

"If you remember where, tell me. And be very pleasant to Jeanne if you meet her in the woods. I think she badly needs friends, even a boy and a big dog."

"I think she does," Denny agreed gravely. "Also, Fang thinks she is a good person. We like her. And she is very good with the bow."

She was more than good. She was better than any Indian I had ever seen perform, and there were still a few left who had pride in their skill. But even they used the rifle when they hunted their meat.

I, of course, had other memories. I would never forget the Games, and the hundred tall bowmen from all the ten garns, and the fact that I had outshot them all. I did not let Jeanne know what I could do, but I did show her my bow. She had examined it carefully.

"This is very short for a hunting bow," she said. "The style is different and the wood is strange. But such fine workmanship! It is beautiful." She had eyed me with some amusement then. "You did not make this bow. Can you shoot it?"

"I have a fair skill," I said, "but you are right. The bow was made by the finest craftsman in wood that I have ever known. He was a very wonderful man. He was also," I added, "my father-in-law."

"Ah." The woman evidently thought she understood. "May I say, while I have this chance, what I think of his daughter? Your wife is beautiful, but no more beautiful than she is kind. She is most unusual, as this bow is unusual. You are a very lucky man."

"Sometimes I have doubts about many things," I said, "but never about that. There'll never be another woman like Marya. And it always pleases me when others see it. So ask anything you want from me. I'll grant it!"

Jeanne smiled, but I fancied that she was glad of the opportunity my whimsy gave her.

"There is a thing I have thought to ask. It is not so large, but you might not welcome it."

"Try me," I said.

"I spoke of the high cliff at the end of the lake, and Denny thought that the golden eagle might have its nest on it. I know that you plan to take him to see. Might I go with you, in the canoe? It is a long day's paddle. I know the paddle very well. I would find it pleasant to use it again. And it is good to talk with friends. I have been alone for so long."

I didn't have to consider. Our contacts with this lonely woman had all been wary, casual, and, to me at least, never satisfying. Here might be the opportunity I wanted. So I was easy and cordial.

"We will be most pleased to have you come. We will take food and small packs and have an overnight camp. It will be a picnic for us all. We probably need company as much as you do. Marya will thank you for coming."

Jeanne hesitated, as though she were regretting her own request.

"I would not wish to take your space," she said, "but it is a large canoe. Perhaps there is room."

So it was arranged. Later she spoke with Marya about food. By the time the simple planning was done it seemed that we knew each other better than in all the days before.

I realized that the woman was deeply troubled. No matter how solitary and self-sufficient she had been, now she seemed to dread being alone. Her request to go with us, when she found that we were to be away from our camp, was out of desperation. She was afraid. And finally I faced her with it, plainly.

"Jeanne," I said, "on the day you first came to our camp you told me you needed help. You have not mentioned it since. But it was clear then that you spoke the truth, and it's even clearer now. You are terrified of something. I told you then that we would do anything we could. So perhaps you'd better tell me."

She studied me with eyes that seemed more deeply shadowed than ever before. The skin was drawn tightly over the bones of her cheeks. When she smiled, it was a death's-head smile.

"You are helping," she said quietly. "I have been frightened, but that is going. I cannot tell you yet. Soon I will not have to tell you. You will see."

"If it's a mystery, why not clear it up? We are your friends."

She shook her head.

"Not yet. You would think me mad. You would not believe. But when you can see for yourself, then I can explain."

"But why wait until something happens? I have no idea what your problem is, but we can't solve it until we know."

"What will happen you cannot prevent. Nothing can. You can only help me accept it."

"I you have an illness—" I began.

"Do not fear. It is nothing that is danger to you, or to your beautiful wife or your fine son. And Fang will find it mystifying, but it cannot cause him harm."

"If he finds it any more mystifying than I do at this moment, he is going to be a very puzzled dog!"

The woman's laugh rang. It was, I recognized with astonishment, genuine amusement.

"Do not worry, Vin. More and more you are helping. Just to allow me to go with you when you go to the lake's end is the best thing you can do. This is what I need, and I thank you."

That was the way I had to leave it. It was pretty evident that I had no choice. I would get no more from Jeanne. So we made up the small packs, and Denny was eager to be off. We worked at sealing the canoe, he and I, two men together. Fang watched.

"We will start with the sun," I said. "Jeanne will come early. She will show us where the cliff lies. She also knows an upland slope covered with blueberries and the tiny upland cranberries that grow with them. We shall all get as fat as bears."

"Perhaps there will be bears there," Denny said. "They love the berries too."

"If there are," I admonished, "you and Fang will stay close. I don't have so many sons that I can spare one for bear food."

Denny grinned, but the remark seemed to remind him of something. His small face grew thoughtful.

"There is a thing you wished me to think about," he said, "when I said I had heard the speech Jeanne used when she sat on the rock and cried. I could not say where I had heard it. Now I have remembered. But perhaps you will not believe."

"That's not what you mean. You know that when you speak seriously, you are always believed. You mean that you have remembered something unusual."

"That is true." Denny stood, suddenly lost in thought, shutting me out while his mind traveled back over what he had remembered. Then he said, "When I was small, before I could walk well, I would run and fall and bump myself, and knock skin from my knees. Then I would cry. Mother would pick me up and kiss me and say pleasant things. Soon I would forget my hurt."

"Mothers are like this," I said. "Actually, they are pretty nice to have."

The boy smiled. "Mine is," he acknowledged. "But it is from her that I heard the speech. Some of the words she would speak, when there was no one near but me, were soft, singing words. They were not English, and they had no meaning to me. And when I tried to speak them, she didn't say them anymore. But I remember. Jeanne's speech was like those singing words."

I think I was stunned. Anyway, my face must have startled Denny. He dropped the spruce gum paddle and clutched my hand with his small sticky one. His long eyes were wide and anxious.

"You are ill?"

I came back to myself. I composed my face and then I smiled at my son.

"I'm fine. You surprised me, that's all. I think you have remembered a very important thing."

"It will help you, you think?"

I nodded slowly. The implication was fantastic, but I realized even so quickly that it was possible.

"It already has. But I will need time to think about it. So, until I tell you, do not speak of this to Jeanne or to your mother. Do not even mention it to Fang. You might be overheard."

Denny grinned.

"I might," he said. "But Fang would not speak of it. He keeps secrets very well."

I glanced at the watching dog. Seeing that he was noticed, he beat his tail vigorously on the ground.

"I trust you both," I said. "Still, if you don't speak, no one can hear. There'll come a time when we'll all talk of this together. Meanwhile we have a canoe to mend so that we may see a different eagle tomorrow!"

Chapter 20

I dipped my paddle and drew it with the slow, economical stroke that years of practice finally teach. I could paddle as easily as I could walk. And the paddler ahead of me had that same effortless motion. You see it at its best on the lakes and streams of the north.

"By noon we will come to a place where I have often camped. It might be good to have lunch there. The lake water is good enough, but there is here a cold spring that throws water into the air. It would interest Denny to see."

Jeanne glanced back at the boy just behind her and smiled. It was easy to see that these two were friends. It was not the first time she had spoken of something to please Denny. In fact, when I thought of it, this trip was for the boy. It was Denny who wanted to see the golden eagle on his home crags.

Marya leaned back luxuriously in the middle seat, which I had fitted with a back.

"I would be happy to help with the paddling," she said, "but since I am not needed I will watch with the glasses, and tell you what I see."

Jeanne had insisted on the paddle.

"I would like the feel of it again. I came here in my small canoe, and I lost it when wind broke it free and dashed it to pieces against the shore. When I go out again I will walk."

"When will you go again?" Denny asked.

There was a break in the smooth rhythm of her paddle. She seemed to crumple in place for a moment. I would have given much to see her face.

"I do not know," she said in a tone so low I could hardly hear.

Even Denny realized that here was something that should not be spoken of. When we began to talk again it was of other things.

The artesian spring, it seemed, was the wonder it had been advertised. Jeanne had taken Denny and Fang to see, while I helped Marya with the food. I had already resolved that the mystery of Jeanne should be uncovered as soon as possible. And the more I thought of Denny's report, the surer I was that it was no longer a mystery to me. It was a hard thing to believe, but I thought I knew. If I was right, Jeanne's trouble was a very real thing. So, while she was gone, I broached my plan to Marya.

"My dear, there is something I would like you to do. I hear them coming, so I must speak quickly. After we have had our food, when we are reloading the canoe, we will all be talking together. When you speak to Jeanne, I would like you to change, in the middle of your speech, from English to the speech of your land. Speak to her in the Elkan tongue."

My wife looked at me in astonishment. Then slowly her long, faintly golden eyes widened and grew intent. Her voice, when it came, was almost a whisper.

"That is it! Always there has been something I could not quite touch. Vin, I think you have truth!"

"To anyone but us, it wouldn't be reasonable; it wouldn't make sense. Of all the people in this world, we alone know. The man Smith somehow went over the winter mountains and came to a land that didn't exist. Two men went under a glacier and came to that same land. And a man and a woman came back under the glacier to this world again. What has been done can be done."

"She has been long in this world," Marya said. "She speaks of many things up and down the great river. There was a husband called Pierre, who died in a cabin on the Porcupine. Also, they were here and built together the cabin where she lives. When he died, she came back here again. About this her talk is always strange. She does not wish to speak of it at all."

I nodded slowly. Either I was building a fine fiction in my mind or I had resolved something of the mystery of Jeanne. Other things became clearer. The stilted phrasing of her speech, which I had assumed had French origin, was like Marya's speech. There still clung to it vestiges of the English as taught by the man Smith. So I reasoned, and I could see that Marya agreed.

"If we are right, she could be older, much older than she seems."

Suddenly my wife smiled.

"Vin," she said, "we are making a story. We are causing ourselves to believe. It is far more likely that she is just what she says, a lonely French woman who has come again to the place where she was happy with a husband who has died."

"Possibly," I admitted. "Still, I like my story. So you will speak to her, won't you, after we have eaten?"

"I will speak," Marya said.

And when the meal was finished she did.

Denny and Fang were romping on the beach. I was loading the canoe. Jeanne was detailing Denny's wonder at the bubbling jet of the artesian spring. I was close enough to hear Marya's answer to a question, a soft series of unintelligible sounds, the sounds that Denny had called the singing words.

The effect was everthing I could have expected or wanted. The woman simply stopped, in mid-motion. Her classic features were as if carved from stone. Only her deep eyes moved. They were tragic.

Marya's face mirrored her astonishment at the reaction to her own words. Then it was flooded with a gentle pity for the obviously suffering woman. She spoke again. I couldn't understand, but I knew what she was saying. It was soothing speech, reassuring, friendly. It was saying that we understood, that we were her friends.

And finally Jeanne spoke, harshly, in English.

"Who are you?"

I took two strides, and stood beside my wife.

"There was never any doubt as to who we are. We are

Marya and Vin and Denny and Fang. But you are not Jeanne. So the question really is, who are you?"

She looked at us both, studied us for perhaps a minute. The rigidity went out of her tall graceful body. She turned, almost groping, and sat on the nearest stone. Her breath came out in a long, quivering sigh.

"She spoke words I have not heard for twenty years. She spoke them because she knew."

"I did not know," Marya said. "We only suspected."

The woman smiled then. It was a wan smile, and a tired one, but she seemed to be adjusting.

"You would have to know to even suspect," she said. "This is not a speech of this world. There is only one way you could know it. Somehow, you too have come from the land of this speech. Can it be that people now come and go, and I never knew?"

I shook my head.

"For your sake, I almost wish it were true. But it would not be a good thing. Can you see earth movers ripping up the hills of Elkan; aircraft in the skies overhead?"

"I would not wish this," the woman said. "I would only wish to go home."

It was a simple, poignant statement, at once longing and hopeless. For a moment we had no answer. There was nothing to say. But I knew that somewhere deep in Marya's being that little speech was echoed. She too dreamed of going home. We had come here to forget that. And now she was remembering more vividly than for years.

Denny and the dog came charging up, breaking the spell, the melancholy mood.

"It is time that we should go? May I help with the paddling?"

Almost as he spoke he realized that he had interrupted a serious talk among adults. Promptly he bowed his head, clasped his small hands.

"I am sorry." He looked at me. "I have been impolite, you think?"

"Thank you, Denny," I said. "You have not been impolite. You have done us a favor. You have reminded us not to spoil a picnic with grown-up talk. And yes, you may help with the paddling. You may take the bow seat, and the ladies may sit in the middle and be idle and elegant."

The boy smiled. He was relieved, for we had made manners important. But that grin was knowing, too. He understood that I sometimes joked to hide what I was thinking.

"Idle I know, for you have said that of old Jim Joe at the post. He does no work. But elegant—this is a new word. Does it mean that they should just be beautiful?"

I am convinced that a response like that is not a learned thing. It is built-in, a gift, and the man is lucky who has it. Unerringly, Denny had chosen the right word, used it with a grace that couldn't be improved on. But of course he was not dissembling. He simply spoke what he thought.

I nodded, and hoped he could see that I was pleased.

"In this particular case," I said, "that is exactly what it means. Everybody in the boat! If I understand Jeanne, we have a good long paddle before we camp tonight."

Jeanne rose from her seat. Her grave, striking face was calm again, her movements easy and graceful. As she strode across the beach I could see why her walk had disturbed me before. It was an Elkan stride, Elkan grace. Marya has it. Once learned, it is never lost.

"The sun will be low when we reach the cliff. I know a pleasant camp spot. Even if the clouds I see yonder give us rain, we will be under a ledge, comfortable and dry."

"And in the morning there will be the golden eagles, and perhaps ravens. They also like the cliffs, I think." Denny had thought it all out.

"One or the other, but not both," I said. "The eagles will not allow the ravens on their cliff."

"The ravens would try, I think," Denny said. "They do not like to be told what to do."

"You know them well," I agreed. "Now, take slow, easy strokes. That way, the boat and the water will help us and the paddling will not be work."

The boy gave serious attention to his paddling. Fang sat just behind him, watching critically. Occasionally Denny glanced back at me, adjusting his strokes to my rhythm. Few adults could have done better.

The women sat quietly. There was none of the chatter of the morning. Each was, I knew, lost in her own thoughts, trying to adjust to the strange revelation of the noon camp; wondering, no doubt, about the many things that had not been revealed.

I was doing some wondering, myself. We now knew Jeanne for what she was, but we knew nothing more. It seemed evident that she had been in this world for years, but only recently had come the fear, almost the panic, that she had confessed to me. I cudgeled my brain for answers, and got none.

Still, this was not a time for further talk. Later, in the overnight camp under the eagle cliff, we would fill in the spaces. Perhaps Marya and Jeanne would even speak Elkan together.

When the boy's small shoulders began to show a weariness he would never have admitted, Jeanne spoke.

"If Denny would now allow me the bow paddle, I could better direct our course. It has been long since I came here. I will remember better with the paddle in my hand."

Denny looked at me.

"A good idea," I approved. "I have seen signs of big lake trout close by the boat. Maybe if Denny would do some trolling, he could catch our supper. One would be all we could eat. And he's a good fisherman. The fish hawk could learn from him."

Denny grinned. To help was his greatest pride.

"I could not plunge as he does, but I can catch a bigger fish. You will see."

"All have tasks but me," Marya said. "Shall I remain idle and beautiful?"

"Yours is coming," I reminded. "No one prepares food as you do. And Fang will have a camp to guard, so he too may sit now and watch."

We were putting on an act for Denny, for it was his trip. I wondered how much he should be told, what he could understand, of the strange story of Jeanne. I knew it could not be kept from him entirely. He was too alert, too aware of everything. We would have to tell him something. But I was concerned that he should not become bewildered and confused.

"Here the lake grows wider," Jeanne said. "It becomes a great fan, and to the left the hills are highest, and rise from the water's edge. There will be the cliffs. If the clouds were not so low, we would soon see them."

"I've been watching those clouds," I said. "They are dropping fast. I've seen them do that too often to be fooled. I think we're going to get wet after all."

I dug my paddle deep. Jeanne picked up my rhythm, and her long body swung with a smooth ease that is seldom seen.

She was a superb paddler. I'm pretty good myself, so the canoe knifed through the water.

"We may beat it," I said, "but I doubt it. Perhaps we'd better head for the nearest shore. Drying out takes time and isn't much fun. I'll go left. We can follow the shoreline after the storm has passed."

As I said, I knew these northern rainstorms. They swooped with no more warning than the eagle gave the fish hawk. Sometimes there were winds. I saw no point in taking chances with the only family I ever expected to have.

But even as I swung the canoe I could see the rippling lake surface torn by gusts of wind. Waves began to rise, long rollers that soon became broken and choppy. Whitecaps showed. The canoe reeled as the air blast struck it broadside, so I fought to swing the bow into the wind again.

"Now you have a task," I said to Marya. "Lash all packs to the thwarts. Wet bedrolls are better than none. And Denny, stay low. I wouldn't like to have you swept overboard. There are better places to swim."

It was all fun for Denny. He sat on the bottom of the canoe and made Fang lie flat beside him. He held the thongs while his mother tied the duffle tightly to the thwarts.

Jeanne and I kept the nose of the canoe directly into the wind. I didn't dare turn toward shore now. We would have swamped in short order. We were simply waiting it out. Such storms were brief, often only minutes long. But I knew we'd get a soaking, and we did.

The wall of rain rolled over us. We were drenched in an instant. And the clouds, which had been so low that it had seemed we might touch them with a paddle, now dropped to the surface of the water. We plunged into a fog bank, and visibility became little more than the length of the canoe.

The rain squall passed. The wind steadied, but it was still too strong to risk turning the canoe. So we drove blindly forward through the cold, wet mist.

"Everybody okay?" I asked. I hoped my voice was cheery. I was warm with the continuing exercise, and my sodden shirt was beginning to steam.

"I am *wet*," Marya said. "But I will not melt, and when we reach the shore clothes will soon dry."

"Fang has his own raincoat," Denny said. "Under the long outside hairs he is not wet at all. He is warm and dry. It is pleasant to lie against him."

"Let him warm you," I agreed. "He will be glad to share his coat with a friend. Jeanne?"

"I am very cold." I was not expecting the weak, shaken voice. "Perhaps Marya should take the paddle. My strength is leaving me, and it would not be well to lose the paddle."

Marya did not need my glance. Quietly she worked her way forward, took the paddle from the suddenly exhausted woman. Somehow she managed to help Jeanne back to the seat amidships, to cover her with a sodden coat. Then she was in the bow seat again, and my job eased with the addition of her strong paddle.

"It will not be long." Marya spoke soothingly. "The wind is not less, but it blows only from one direction. When the fog lifts, we will soon be on shore. Your illness will pass."

The tall woman shuddered as she huddled under the coat.

"I am not ill." Her voice was low, but it seemed to have gained strength. "It is this that I have feared, these last weeks. Soon I could not have helped myself, alone in this land. And no one who came by could have understood."

"You may trust us," I said, though I didn't understand either.

"I know. It is a marvel. Of all the people in this world, those who would believe did come by."

The wind was certainly not less, as Marya had said. I fancied that it was giving a louder wail, a song I had never heard on an inland lake. But it was a sound that I knew, a sound I had heard before.

The fog drove past. It was so dense that I could scarcely see Marya's sturdy back sway and straighten as she swung her padde. The water beneath us developed long rollers, which grew higher and higher, with deep troughs between them into which the canoe dived steeply, before climbing to the top of the next roll. It was not canoe water. If the rollers began to break and crest, the boat would fill.

I spoke calmly, pushing the panic back deep inside me.

"There is a chance, just a chance, that the boat will swamp. I have never felt a lake behave like this before. We should be ready. We are keeping our bow into the wind, but we are being blown backward just the same. I can hear the water crashing on the shore behind us.

"Cling to the canoe if you can. It won't sink. If you are torn loose, just stay afloat. Don't fight the waves. You will be blown to shore. We are all strong swimmers. Denny, stay near Fang if you can. Do not be frightened. It isn't possible to guess what the shore will be like, but we should not be too far from the cliffs. I will not pretend. Large rocks will be danger, in this wind. Do not cling to each other. Each will be safer alone. And call whenever you can."

The first roller broke. Fortunately, the canoe had almost reached its top, and the crest boiled under us. Sprays of water sheeted high. The already soggy equipment took another dousing, but the boat shipped little water. I could not spare a hand to mop my splashed face. My eyes stung, and I spat water.

Unbelievingly, I licked my lips. I was automatically keeping the boat's bow steady into the wind, but my mind was in turmoil. *For the water was salty!* And I realized that the smell of the air had changed. Now it fitted with the driving landward wind, the fog rolling shoreward in pulsing clouds, the rumbling crash of the breakers on the shrouded beach behind us and toward which we were being blown.

Then quite suddenly the wind shifted. Long streamers of spray blew from the wave crests. The canoe twisted from the sidewise lash of the wind above and the different pull of the waves beneath. We fought, Marya and I, digging our paddles with every ounce of strength we possessed; a brief violent battle that we never had any chance of winning.

The boat skewed into a deep trough; a wall of dark water loomed over us.

"Hold your breaths!" I roared, and later I wondered if anyone had heard me. The next instant the wave crested, rolled forward and buried us.

Chapter 21

At least I followed my own advice. I let myself be thrown free. It was simply like a deep, deep dive, and I didn't struggle. I let the water carry me. I had ridden the surfs from

Malibu to Waikiki, and I knew the feel of the long waves. Automatically, I knew what to do.

When my head broke the surface behind the crest of the roller, I needed to breathe, but not badly. I took a deep draft of the pungent salt air. And I understood, without knowing how I knew, that this was not the lake. There was a feel of bigness, of endless distance, that did not fit with a body of water among the hills. The disembodied cries of gulls from the invisible shore confirmed it. This was ocean. What, how, where, there was no clue. But it was true, and I knew it was true. It was like a dream, but the Arctic water was no dream. Already my limbs were stiffening from the cold.

The whole happening seemed long, though in truth it had only been moments. My sense of the present returned. Where was my wife, my son, the strange woman of Elkan? They would not know how to adjust, as I had, to the different feel of big waves on an ocean shore. I even thought of Fang. Would his instinct, so close to the wolf, make him hold his breath when the water buried him? Could he, would he, swim toward shore?

I realized that the fog was lifting; the shore wind subsiding. I could see the beach. Thankfully, the jumble of jagged rocks that I had feared was not there. It was a great beach, wide and smooth and stretching away in either direction in a long curve. Behind it dunes lay piled. Beyond them a massive cliff reached up and up, much of it still cloaked in the swirling fog. The big waves went rolling far up the sand, thinned and foamed and died, then drained backward into the next incoming wall of water.

I have no memory of any conscious effort to adjust, to stay high behind the cresting roller. What I did I did automatically. But I rode the wave in. It was a big one, high and deep. It deposited me onto the sloping sand almost without a jar.

Drenched, half dazed, I staggered up the wet beach to the wave line. The air seemed gratefully warm after the frigid water. Even the wind was mild.

I knew what to do. My soggy clothes were keeping me cold, so I stripped them off. Anxiously I scanned the beach while I swung my arms, flexed all my warming muscles. It had, after all, been only a short ordeal. In minutes I was fit again; fit and desperate. For there was no sign of the canoe. Nothing lay or moved on the beach. I could only wait.

My eyes picked it up while it was still well out from the beach, a dark body tumbling in the foaming, spreading water. The wave rolled it almost to my feet. It was the dog, and his sagging, sodden body and flopping legs told the story. Nothing in his ancestry, nothing in his training, had prepared him to compete with this. He hadn't been able to hold his breath, to breathe only at opportunity.

I dragged the heavy body by its hind legs up beyond the dry sand line. Water gushed from the open mouth. Sand clung to the limp, dragging tongue. I knelt to arrange the sprawled legs, but my eyes went continually back to the empty beach and the long rollers breaking and foaming.

So I saw Denny when he came in.

I do not remember leaving the dog. I cannot recall crossing the beach, splashing through the surf. Suddenly I was there, the lean small body in my arms, and I was plowing out of the surf again.

But this was an active body. It had come in on a wave crest, as bouyant as a chip, and had landed on hands and knees when the water spread. Denny had remembered. He hadn't panicked. He clung to my naked shoulders as I strode up the beach, but soon he squirmed.

"Do not hold me so tightly," he said. "I have not drowned." He shivered. "But the water was cold!"

I set him on his feet, and stood between him and the body of the dead dog.

"Off with everything!" I ordered. "The air will warm you."

Obediently he began to strip.

"Where is mother? When I was far out I saw her. She was swimming well. But I did not see the canoe."

"Mother will be here." Suddenly I believed it myself, and the relief I felt would be hard to describe. "She is a very fine swimmer. But she does not know how to ride the waves, so she will come in more slowly."

Then I saw her, and I left the boy and ran.

She was alive! She was not even in distress, though the waves threw her onto the sand more roughly than they had either Denny or me. By the time I reached her she was on her feet, water streaming from her clinging, sodden clothing, her long wet hair plastered against her face. I could see a smile starting as I reached out my arms and pulled her fine, strong body against mine. This was Oo-ah of Elkan, and her courage and strength had never failed. For a moment I simply stood and held her, the water swirling around our ankles, and was thankful.

"Father! Mother! Please help! Fang does not breathe!"

"I shouldn't have left him," I whispered. "I forgot he'd see. The dog has drowned."

Denny's small naked body lay on that of his friend, and he was working purposefully. Artificial respiration! I had taught him, and what I taught him he remembered and believed.

"He is filled with water," the boy panted. "It comes out each time I press. He tries, but there is no room for air."

"Denny" I began, but Marya said "Wait!"

Her quick eyes had seen more than mine. She knelt beside the dog. Fang's great jaws sagged wide, but the dragging, limp tongue had been drawn back into the mouth. Denny pushed hard on the big rib cage, and the body shuddered. Water bubbled from the nostrils. The mouth closed and opened again, convulsively.

"Denny, let me," Marya said. "There must be more snap!"

Astride the dog's limp body she once again showed that precision of touch, that instinctive feel for exactly the right move, and she worked with a delicacy few women could have matched. She moved with faith and with sure strength. She *knew* the dog was alive. She would not let him die.

Hers was not the only strength. Anything with less than the vitality and toughness of the big northern dog could not possibly have survived. But in brief moments Fang's legs kicked. I pulled the forelegs forward as Marya pushed and snapped her hands away. Fang struggled weakly. Then he retched and heaved. His jaws clicked as he took a mighty breath.

Marya leaped clear. We all stood away as Fang struggled dizzily to his feet. Then he sat on his haunches, lowered his head, and was very sick on the sand.

"I hope he doesn't hold it against us," I said. "Nothing like a bellyful of salt water to make a man lose faith in everything."

Fang staggered a few steps. Then he sat again and eyed us sadly. But we could see strength return as he breathed deeply, coughed, and breathed again. I caught Denny as he started for the dog.

"Wait a bit. Fang doesn't know what happened. He must have time to remember us. When he is ready he will come to you. But now he is still cold and sick."

"I too am cold." Marya shivered and shrank in her clammy clothing. "So much has happened, I did not notice. I will be comfortable like you."

In a moment her beautiful body was warming in the pleasant air, while she wrung the water from her discarded garments and looked about for a place to hang them.

The fog had lifted. The wind was only a gentle sea breeze, and as we watched the recovering dog, yellow sunrays broke through the overcast and shone warm on the beach. As far as we could see the ocean stretched away. The long waves rose and crested and came boiling and foaming up the beach. It was familiar, but it was not a place I had ever seen before.

"Vin," Marya said quietly, "this is not the lake."

I nodded slowly. I was grappling with the unlikely, and yet somehow it was making sense.

"The salt water would tell us that, even if we could not see what we see. This is ocean; the western ocean, from the position of the sun. It is afternoon, just as it was before the storm, but it is a different afternoon."

"We were going to the cliff of the eagles. There is the cliff behind us."

"It is a cliff, surely, but the one we were looking for would have been tiny compared to that. That is the end of a mountain wall. See how it seems to reach on inland, to lie like a barrier against the northern wind? Yukon has nothing like that."

Marya didn't answer.

After a moment I looked back at her. She was standing, rapt, the sun warm on her sculptured body, her clothes in a pile at her naked feet. The breeze blew her long black hair. Her lips were slightly parted. There was a look of delight and wonder on her beautiful face.

"Marya!"

Slowly she shifted her gaze from the great sunlit wall. She looked at me, and tears rolled down her cheeks.

"Vin," she whispered, "since I am born I have looked far across the hills and have seen that in the distance. Always it flashed white in the sun, and the bands of color were marvels. But I have never seen it close, because no one could come close until it was time. Vin, those are the White Cliffs!"

It is not very sensible to believe the impossible. Most intelligent people shy away from the word "miracle." But Marya was speaking the truth, and I knew it was the truth. Somehow, out of a Yukon storm, we had come back to Elkan.

"Father! Mother! Fang is running away!"

"Denny, wait!"

By the time I had whirled, my son was in full flight behind the running dog. Fang still did not move with his old ease, but his tail was up, and he bounded down the beach with purpose. Denny halted at my call. His small face was tragic.

"He did not wait! He did not wish me to go!"

I went down on one knee to put an arm around his quivering, naked body.

"Fang is still confused," I explained. "He was almost drowned. It will take him a while to be himself again. See, he had a reason for running."

A hundred yards down the beach the dog darted behind a small piled jam of driftwood. It was now well above watermark. I had already noted that the tide was going out. In a moment Fang reappeared. He stood facing us, and for the first time since his recovery he looked alert and strong. His tail waved slowly. Then he gave a quick, sharp bark.

"He has found something," Denny said.

"Right. He is saying, 'Move! Get down here in a hurry!' "

Denny chuckled, with the swift mood change of a small boy.

"Fang speaks very plainly to those who can understand."

I turned to Marya and silently mouthed the word "Jeanne!"

"Please stay with your mother until I call," I told Denny. "This time Fang is speaking to me."

She was there. She lay on a smooth stretch of sand. She seemed completely composed, peaceful as she lay there. She might simply have been asleep. But to my astonishment the deep eyes opened. A smile showed faintly on the strong face. Fang brushed against my naked legs. He whined softly, and looked up at me.

"Good Fang!" Jeanne whispered. "Again he has found me."

I gave Marya an urgent wave, then went down on my knees beside the woman. She was breathing lightly but steadily.

"You'll be okay now," I assured her. "Where are you hurt?"

She lay motionless for several breaths. Then she whispered,

"I do not think I have a hurt. I have simply used all my strength trying not to be drowned. Also, I am very cold."

Marya and Denny came running up, and Fang greeted Denny with a tail wag and a grin. His job was done. The responsibility was ours now.

"Take her feet," I directed Marya. "We'll put her on the dry sand in the sun. We must warm her. Remove her clothes and cover her with the hot sand."

We carried her carefully up higher on the beach, laid her on the sunniest, warmest spot we could find. Then Marya dismissed us.

"I can do this best alone," she said.

I agreed. My eyes had caught a glimpse of something against the driftwood pile, and I started back down the beach.

"Denny, help me," I said.

Fang threw a last glance at Marya as she worked over the exhausted woman, then came with us. His affinity with the strange woman was something I never really explained. But it was there, and it was strong.

What I had seen was the crushed and broken fragments of our canoe. The waves had battered it against the driftwood, and the fine craftsmanship of which I had been so proud was no more. The birchbark was splintered and shredded. But the sturdy framework, though broken, still held together. And best of all, our duffle, our sleeping bags, and packsacks were still bound tightly to the thwarts.

I pulled the crumpled ruin free of the driftwood and dragged it out onto the sand. Then I tried to untie the thongs Marya had made fast while we had been fighting the storm.

"When your mother does a task, she always does it well," I said. "I cannot unknot this wet babiche. My knife is with my clothing. Denny, go gather all our clothing. Everything should be spread to dry. Let Fang help. Hang garments across his back. That way you can carry all in one trip. And bring my knife to me."

They were a team again, my small naked son and his big wolf dog, and they ran together up the beach. I remember Marya's remark of weeks before: "Never do they walk!"

I looked up to where she was tending her patient. She smiled and made an encouraging gesture. And I had a good feeling. Things were going to be all right.

It has taken longer to remember these happenings than it

took them to occur. We had no time to think. To survive, we had to work fast and hard, and the strangeness of our situation meant nothing yet. There had been things to do, one after the other, and we had done them. Then I began to think. But a small procession came back down the beach, and I stopped my work to laugh.

Denny staggered along with a rumpled mass of wet clothing. Fang was draped with garments from his tail to his ears, and in his mouth he carried my gun belt, from which the magnum swung in its holster. Like his mother, when Denny was given a task, he did it well. Between them they had brought everything. Denny dropped his soggy, sand-covered burden and held out my sheath knife.

"Everything is covered with sand," he said. "Perhaps when they are dry, the sand will fall away."

"We'll spread garments on the driftwood. You may unload Fang. I'm surprised that he allowed you to cover him like that."

"Fang does not mind. He wishes to help. Also, he does as I tell him."

"I thank you both. Now I'll see what I can do about drying sleeping bags, and if there is food that hasn't been spoiled."

Chapter 22

It was twilight; the late, still rosy twilight of the summer Arctic. We had had time to do our work. We again wore our clothes, for the sea breeze blowing in was growing cool.

In the lee of the great cliff I had set up a camp of sorts. The white rock faces still reflected the heat of the sun, and with my leaping driftwood fire we were comfortable.

Jeanne sat quietly on a seat I had contrived for her, and watched us as the camp took shape. The secret of Jeanne's fear and her weariness was a secret no longer. While she had lain and been warmed by the sand she had explained to

Marya. It would have made no sense in the Yukon, but to us it was simple, inevitable fact. Marya reported to me.

"She has lived many years. And finally, only a few sun-spans ago, she suddenly felt that her journey would soon begin. She had always known that it would happen, but when it came she had great fear. For in that world there were no White Cliffs, no land beyond the wall where there would be tiny people like herself. She was alone. There were the beasts that would be larger and larger as she grew small, and finally, there would be the cold. She knew she would die. She has always been a strong woman. It was not pleasant to think of being helpless."

"She had more courage than I would have had," I said. I glanced over at the tall woman, sitting completely relaxed, seeming lost in gazing into the flames. "Does she understand where she is now?"

Marya shook her head.

"She does not know. She is very tired and thinks slowly. When the change is taking place, it is usual to remain quiet and to work little and easily. Instead, she was forced to paddle and swim and use much energy against the cold of the water. Her strength is very low. But I think she is not injured and will soon become interested and curious again. From now on she will eat almost nothing. She needs only to rest."

The spread sleeping bags steamed in the fire's heat. For a wonder Marya's plastic food bags had remained tight, their contents unspoiled by salt water. I had made a small cookfire at a distance from the big one, and she set about preparing a simple meal. Fang slept peacefully in the big fire's glow. Denny had suddenly collapsed, as busy children will, and lay with his head pillowed on his shaggy friend.

"One thing we must have, Vin. Fresh water. All would like to drink, I think, and I need it for the cooking and for tea. Perhaps there will be a rain pool near, or a seep from the wall."

"I will get water," I said. I took the large canteen and set out alone for the cliff base.

It turned out not to be a simple errand. I had set up our camp behind the rolling dunes. It was dry near the cliff and well into the sparse grassland beyond. But I kept near the white wall, remembering where we were. Or where we thought we were.

When my big fire was only a spark in the distance, I knew

that I would have to leave the wall and look for a spring or a pond in the open. And that would have to be done with care. For this was the land of the Little People, and, as Elg had said so long ago, if I walked there I *was* danger.

The sun had set, but plenty of light remained. Past the grassy strip that seemed to follow the cliff, brushy vegetation stretched away in variety. In the distance I could see clumps of lush growth, so I knew there was plenty of water out there. I picked out an area where unnamed plants seemed to grow thickly and set out toward it. I watched carefully where I placed my feet, but there seemed no sign of any human use, no evidence of the tiny houses the Little People were supposed to build and occupy. It was simply a pleasant sweep of rolling, brushy land, where one would expect to find small game. It should have, I thought, a watershed effect, with many little streams. The air was clean and untainted.

I came on it quite suddenly.

The twilight had become starshine, and far off to the east a half-moon had already lifted above the horizon. The little road swept in a long curve around the lush patch of vegetation that I had been walking toward. Beyond the road a small pond glistened.

I knew it was a road, though it was no more than four feet wide, and so neatly kept that it was like someone's garden path. It was made of fine white gravel. When I knelt to examine the surface, it seemed that scarcely a stone was out of place. But it was a road for it stretched on and on, paralleling the great escarpment of the White Cliffs toward the east and, from where I stood, curving southward in line with the seacoast a mile away. I had happened to find it where it made its turn.

I could hear water flowing. Only a few yards away the road crossed a little stream. I could easily have stepped across it, but a diminutive bridge spanned it, a bridge so small I would not have dared to put my full weight on it. But we were to see many such structures, and to examine in good light the strongly set stone approaches, the stone buttresses, and the finely carpentered spans.

I had been gone half an hour. Marya would wonder. Further, she needed the water for her cooking. I sipped at the stream water. It was cold and tasty, so I had a good drink, then filled the canteen. With the moonlight growing stronger,

I was able to return to camp at an Elkan run. It took only a few minutes.

"You have seen the Little People," Marya stated gravely.

I shook my head.

"No, but they are there. I found a road, and a bridge that Denny might cross, but not we. I suspect that the Little People don't live close to the Cliffs. It's dry and barren here, protected, but not a good place to get food. And I would guess that they wouldn't want to travel far. After all, they are very old."

"But you found a road?"

I considered.

"So I did. And that means travel, doesn't it? There'll be an explanation. We'll learn many things as we cross the country—and that we'll have to do to reach Elkan. There's no other way."

Marya poured water into a kettle to be heated, then had a drink for herself, drinking directly from the canteen. In the firelight she looked very serious, almost frightened.

"You know, Vin, that this is something no one has ever done. It will not be understood."

"It will be sacrilege," I agreed. "It was taboo to travel the River of Bones, too, but we did it."

"That could be explained; and it was danger to no one but ourselves. There is no way to explain this."

I nodded.

"They will take us to the Primate, and the Primate will dispose. It will be a very hard problem for him. But, as you have often said, the Primate is a wise man."

My wife stood quietly, looking out across the moonlit countryside. I knew her thoughts were traveling far, reaching back, perhaps going round and round. We had changed worlds, changed worlds again. And the two worlds we now knew had very little in common.

"The Primate was always wise. I have never spoken it, but when I was very small I knew him, before he was the Primate. He was my mother's brother."

"His garn was never mentioned," I said. "I had no idea that he came from Chan-Cho-Pan."

"The Primate does not have a society. He is of the whole world, and diposes for all alike. It would make no difference that a tiny girl once sat on his knee."

"All the better for us. He knows that the world we have

come from is a real world, and that we could not choose how and when we came from it. He will understand that it was necessary to cross this land that lies beyond the wall."

For years Marya had dreamed of coming home. Now suddenly it had happened—and everything was strange. It was a land she recognized, but I could tell that she felt less and less joy at being there. For this was where the people of her world came to die. The most important item that the Little People brought with them beyond the wall was the carefully made coffin. What they did then, how they lived and how long, was not truly known. There were beliefs, stories. Elg had told us those, years before, when we had watched Arn the Artisan grow small.

Chapter 23

"Is there food?"

Denny had wakened, as suddenly as he had gone to sleep, and as usual he was good for us. It was not possible to be introspective and solemn with that small, grinning face sniffing hungrily. Fang too was on his feet, his tail waving gently.

"Soon there will be," Marya promised. "It is not a feast, but we will not starve."

"You may go to the beach and wash yourself at the water's edge," I said. "There is fresh water to drink in the big canteen. You may pour a small bowlful for Fang."

As always, Denny turned to obey. Then he stopped. The firelight fell on his suddenly serious face. The dark brows lowered, and he went away from us as he thought.

"Something strange has happened to us, has it not? The lake water was good to drink, but now it is salt. There were never waves, nor a beach like this. Also, Fang thinks that the smells are new."

The dog had moved out of the firelight circle. He stood, a dark, poised statue of a dog, almost motionless now, limned with moonlight. We could hear him sniff. Then suddenly he sat, threw back his head, and howled. It was a lonely, wolf-like wail, and I had never before heard anything like it from Fang.

Denny's long eyes were fixed on me.

"Fang does not understand," he said.

"Denny," I said quietly, "you are right and Fang is right. Something strange *has* happened. But we are safe now; there is no danger, and there won't be any. It will be hard to explain, but when we have slept, and have sunshine again, your mother and I will tell you all we know. It is another adventure. I think you will both enjoy it. Until morning then, we will not speak of it. Do you agree?"

We often made bargains with Denny. He was very proud when his opinion was needed. So this was a familiar move, and he agreed, his small face cheerful again.

"I understand that we will wait, but it would be well to tell Fang to guard. Otherwise, when we are asleep, he will go out to see for himself."

"A wise suggestion," I said, "and I might not have thought of it. Thank you."

From the heat of the sun earlier, and now my good fire, the sleeping bags were usable. My bow and quiver of arrows, in their plastic cases, were unharmed. And after we had had our scanty meal, I sat in the firelight and carefully cleaned and oiled the magnum. I had rarely used it, even in the Yukon, and only once in this world. But it was my final recourse, my last defense, and I would have felt naked without it riding snug against my thigh.

Jeanne had become almost a shadow person, sitting silent and withdrawn before the fire. She did not speak. The vigorous, dynamic woman we had known was gone. She would not eat, but silently drank a cup of tea that Marya brought to her. Fang watched her with concern. Once he glided over to her on noiseless pads and thrust his head against her knee. She smiled faintly and probed behind his ears for a moment with gentle fingers. Then the hand fell into her lap again, and she resumed her unseeing stare into the flames. When Marya spread her bed for her, she went to it without comment or question, as docile as a tired child.

We all slept. Fang was under orders, so he did not leave camp, but once when I woke I could see him prowling restlessly just beyond the fire. I could imagine his puzzlement. The air must have been rich with new, different scents and also with the *feel* of the presence of many people. How the Little People registered to his keen senses I had no way of knowing, but they could have been the strangest of the new things he felt to be there.

When the sun touched high on the white wall behind us, I was already rebuilding my fires. Overhead, gulls soared, familiar and yet somehow different. Beyond the dunes I could hear the surf foaming up the beach. The air made a cool fresh sting in my nostrils. The only smell in it that was not natural was the tang of my own wood smoke.

Fang waited eagerly for the word that would free him for a run in that enticing country out there. After a guard night he always welcomed that release. He would be gone for half an hour or more, and I suspected that he would run for miles. Often he would return proudly with his own breakfast, a hare, a marmot, once even a young beaver.

"Fang wishes to go. Shall I tell him?"

Denny had tumbled out of his sleeping bag, bright and grinning, ready to go himself.

"Denny, I don't dare."

My son showed his astonishment, and I thought that I probably had used the wrong word. The male offspring of a wilderness man would find it hard to believe that there was any reasonable thing that his father did not dare. It was the right time, so I explained.

"You see," I said, "I know what is out there."

Then I told him, as simply and as matter-of-factly as I could, about the Little People, and I was aware as I talked that even to a six-year-old what I was saying was completely fantastic.

"They are only so tall." I held my hand a foot from the ground. "They are very old and live in tiny houses. How many there are no one knows, for no one has ever crossed their land. But their land is that country out there, and it goes on for many miles. Fang's great feet would damage their fields and fences, if they have them. He might not even know they were people, and would think that they were small things that could be eaten."

At that Denny shook his head.

"Fang would know," he said. Then he studied my face carefully, looking for the signs that would mean that I was telling him a tall tale. But he found nothing, and his dark brows lowered.

"You are not speaking a story of fairies?"

When he is really serious, his speech becomes more and more like his mother's.

"I am not," I assured him. "I know how it sounds, but the story is exactly as I have told it. And you will be able to see for yourself, for we must all cross that land. Only that way can we go home."

The boy stared out across the brightening landscape. His face became vacant as he withdrew into his own private world to think. Fang watched us both impatiently. Then Denny returned.

"There is much more than you have said," he stated. "You will tell me when I need to know."

I went down on one knee so that I could put an arm around his sturdy, tough little shoulders.

"You are the most completely satisfactory son I ever had," I stated positively. "You may take Fang for a short run up into the brushland, but make him stay in sight. Half a mile from here, or a bit farther, you might come across a small stream. The water is good, and you and Fang may drink. Later I will get camp water from there."

Denny's eyes were gleaming now.

"Will there be new animals?"

"Nothing big. But if Fang starts a hare or a cottontail, let him take it. We do not have much left that he likes to eat. And," I faced him seriously, "if you go farther than I think and come to a road no larger than a path, *do not cross it.* Come back by the time the sun is there." I pointed. "Breakfast will be prepared by then."

"Fang! With me!"

Denny started, then came to a stop again. He looked back at me, his long eyes crinkling, the hint of a grin on his face.

"You have had no other sons," he said.

The night had done wonders for Jeanne. When she left her sleeping bag she walked to my revived fire almost with a normal stride. Her face was drawn, her dark eyes sunken, but she managed a smile as she passed me and held out her hands to the flames.

"I still feel the cold of the water," she said. "I think I will never forget it."

I was glad to be able to answer her.

"We survived it," I said. "We were lucky. But we won't

have to risk it again. From here we travel by trail. After you've had Marya's flapjacks, you'll feel as gay as Denny and Fang."

Slowly she shook her head.

"I do not think so. There will be no strength in me until my journey is complete. I fear that I cannot travel. You will have to leave me here."

"Ah yes," I said. "Leave you here without weapons or food. Leave you here to grow small alone, with the winter coming." I nodded solemnly. "No doubt about it, that will be the sensible thing to do."

"Vin makes a joke." Marya had come up silently behind me. "Always when things are most serious he makes jokes. But this is not a good joke."

I pulled her into the curve of my arm.

"Jeanne knows, my dear. And she knows that we have no intention of leaving her. She was in the world of Yukon and Alaska far longer than you. She knows that we will all talk together and decide what will be best to do. And then we will do it together."

Marya leaned against me with a sigh.

"Was your Pierre so? Never have I wished any man but this one, but there are times. . . ." She smiled at me and left the speech unfinished.

Jeanne had seated herself again on the rude seat I had made for her. Her deep eyes glinted in the familiar way.

"You are my friends, so I will tell you what no one else knows. There was never a Pierre. He was only a story I have told, for men of the north seem to feel that all women should have men. But if I already had one, this they could understand."

"But if he never showed up, didn't people wonder?"

"I was never very long in one place. I prepared the food in lumber and mining camps, all up and down the great river. I served food in small eating places, when the roadways came. But always, when I had money, I came back to this lake, for it was here that I first found myself when I came to this world."

Jeanne gazed into the fire and again extended her hands toward it. To me it was the beginning of a fine balmy morning, and I realized how different she had become, to be cold in the increasing warmth of a summer day.

"How did it happen?"

The woman shook her head.

"I do not know. It was said that the man Smith became lost in the snow peaks, in the blizzards, and finally came to our land. It was not so with me."

Jeanne paused, gazed vacantly into the distance, withdrew into herself almost as Denny did. She seemed to have forgotten that we were there. Then she began again, speaking softly, remembering.

"I had walked far among the hills, something I loved to do when I had few years. I rested under a big oak tree on a hillcrest, where the view was fine. It was a summer afternoon—and I slept. When I woke, there was no oak tree, and there before me was the lake."

I gave Marya a small squeeze. We realized that Jeanne still thought she was by the lake, though the piled dunes, the air tangy with salt, and the splash and purr of the hidden surf could scarcely have been more different. Since the ordeal of the storm she had been dazed, much of the time barely conscious.

"You thought that somewhere here there might be a door, a way to go home. So you came back again and again."

Jeanne smiled, but it was a wan, resigned smile.

"I did not really think so. The man Smith ended his days in Elkan, and no way back was ever found. But I could not live in his world as he did in mine. It was possible to come here away from the people, and this is why I came. Here the animals and the birds were not so very different, and I could see in my mind women who were strong and beautiful, women who enjoyed, and great tall men who did not smell."

Marya gurgled.

"Vin does not smell. Perhaps if you had looked, you might have found a man you might have loved. Perhaps there could have been a Pierre."

Jeanne's classic features showed more feeling than they had since the storm. Her brows lowered sternly and her deep eyes flashed.

"If a strange happening took you from Vin and you could not come back again, would you take another man?"

Of course, that would be it. I watched the swift pity and sympathy flood my wife's face. She drew away from me, clasped her hands, and bowed her beautiful head. I could see the tears drop onto her fingers.

"I am sorry." It could have been Denny speaking. "I have been most unkind. I did not think."

"You could not know. And of all the women I have known in this world, none have been kind as you have been. Please do not be unhappy."

The stilted speeches of those striking, different women look cold on the printed page, but I could wish nothing better for you than that you could feel their warmth as I did.

Jeanne smiled gently.

"I remember a big quiet man, a man who enjoyed. When he came to me he already had many years. No man in the garn was wiser, and his hands could do marvels. All loved and respected him. He will have gone to the White Cliffs long ago."

Behind her the mighty wall lifted up and up, growing brighter minute by minute as the sun rose higher. I wondered what effect it might have on her if she suddenly knew where she sat. I had queer, unreal feelings myself as I thought of the possibility that that remembered husband still lived, lived as a tiny man no more than a foot tall, lived perhaps only a few miles away in that green country out there.

If he were there, could we find him? Would she know him? Would he remember? Nothing was known of how the Little People lived, when they went beyond the wall. It didn't make sense that they would still be concerned with the lives they had left behind. It was, I knew, generally believed that all ties were forgotten, all experiences sponged away, and that the Little People spent final years unclouded by what had gone before.

"And children? You had children?"

I don't know why my voice had urgency, but suddenly it seemed the most important question I had ever asked. "His hands could do marvels." That was the key.

"No small, busy son such as you have, Vin. And there is only one thing finer. A little daughter. I have had pleasure remembering, for I know she lives and enjoys. She is a woman now. Across the years I still hear her laugh."

I knew. It was coincidence, unbelievable, but no more so than the fact of the existence of Elkan, where everything was different.

"Jeanne," I said gently, "please listen to me. I call you Jeanne because I never heard your name. But your daughter's name was Oo-ah. Your husband was Arn, who was called the Artisan. I knew him very well."

The tall woman came to her feet with the old lithe grace. The small store of energy she had been building and hoarding since the wreck she squandered heedlessly now.

"Speak, man!" she commanded, and gripped my arms with strong hands. "Tell me all you know!"

For the first and only time in my life I felt like Omnipotence.

"I will say only one sentence," I said, "and then you'll have no further need of me. —It was Arn who made my bow."

I left them then. I simply turned my back and walked slowly away toward the dunes. So I don't know how they met. I don't know what they said. Not until I had reached the crest of the highest dune did I turn and look back.

Jeanne again sat in the rustic seat. Marya was beside her on the sand, her arms around her mother's waist, her dark head in her mother's lap. For a few minutes she must have become the little Oo-ah once more, while the dimly remembered shade of her mother suddenly gained substance as this fine, tall wilderness woman. But what they felt, what memories they had, these were things in which I could have no part.

Chapter 24

I would have stayed away longer, given them more time, but from the crest of the dune I could see far up the slope. Denny and Fang were coming in, and as usual they were coming with a rush. I moved to intercept them.

Denny was breathless, but it was not from the run. His dark eyes glowed with excitement.

"Father, we have found the small road! As you have told us, we did not cross it. There was also a bridge. It was very tiny, and made a way across the stream. Fang went over it. He thought it was very fine."

Fang carried a small rabbit in his jaws.

"There are many of these little hares about. They are not snowshoes. I have never seen them before."

"They are cottontails," I said. "There are no hares in this land."

"It will not make a very big breakfast, but he can take more. I made him bring it, for I wished to tell you about the moose. It crossed the road and went on into the Little People's land. Won't it cause harm? Fang would have followed, but I would not let him."

"Now wait," I said. "You are so full of information you are leaving me behind. You saw a *moose*?"

Denny slowed his headlong recital. He sensed that something was not quite right.

"Is this strange? There are always moose."

"In the Yukon, yes. But not here. Denny, in the land of the Little People there are only small animals. Nothing big ever comes here. And in this whole land there has never been a moose."

My son eyed me gravely.

"Would I not know a moose?"

"You certainly would. And that is why I am disturbed. There is something here I do not understand."

"It was a great bull, with a wide rack of antlers still all in velvet. He was frightened of us and ran. I will show you his tracks."

"Hum-m. He ran? That's not too usual either, as you well know. A big bull in his own territory might ask you why you were there. Especially so since you are not very large."

"That is true." Denny thrust out a lower lip, and his brows contracted as he thought. "I do not think he was at home. I think something had happened to him, though he ran well."

I was more concerned than Denny knew. For three memorable months I had hunted the forests, the swamplands, and the open country of Elkan. I had talked to the hunters of the garns. I knew what they hunted. There were elk in abundance, deer in plenty, mountain sheep on the crags. And I also knew that none of these would cross the wall into the land of the Little People. No one understood why. But they didn't.

The hunters of Elkan did not hunt moose. They had never

heard of a moose. There were none in their land. But I didn't for a moment doubt that Denny had seen one. Nor that there was an explanation, though I couldn't imagine what it might be.

Fang had laid his rabbit on the grass and was standing patiently, waiting for permission to eat it. Denny watched me. I must have been lost in thought for minutes before I shook my head, grinned at my son, and came back completely to the present.

"You have brought me more puzzles than I can possibly solve before breakfast," I said. "Eat, Fang! You have already done work today."

"So have I." Denny grasped my hand like the small boy that, after all, he was. "Will there be flapjacks—and more of the honey?"

"There will be," I assured him, "if I have to make them myself!"

"But why should you? Mother does them better." He caught himself and gravely bowed his head. "I did not mean to be impolite," he said.

I held on to the small hand and chuckled.

"A man can live with honesty," I said.

There was a convenient boulder at the edge of the sand. I sat on it, and stood Denny before me.

"I had a reason for saying what I did," I explained. "Today a very wonderful thing has happened for your mother. For us all, for that matter."

Then, as carefully and as simply as I could, I told him as much as I thought he could understand of the story of Jeanne. I made it a good story, a happy story. If it was also an unbelievable story, it was only one of several the boy had heard in the past few hours. And, as I had hoped, he accepted it because I told it. Later, he might wonder. But by then there would be proof.

It is not always easy to know how a boy thinks. I emphasized his mother's happiness at knowing her mother after many years. Denny was more intrigued at the idea of a grandmother.

"Billy Tom, who lives by the river, has a grandmother. She is very old, and her face is wrinkled like tree bark. She moves very slowly, with a stick. Also, she has no teeth. Jeanne is not like this."

"No," I agreed. "She grew tired, though, when the boat

was wrecked, because she is older than she seems. But she will be very proud to have a grandson."

"Will she soon grow old, with white hair, and lose her teeth?"

"No," I said, and was glad I could say it truthfully. "No, this will never happen to Jeanne. She is a very different kind of grandmother from Billy Tom's."

That what would occur instead would be far more incredible was something I wasn't ready to try to explain. There was a little time yet. I'd face it when it began to happen. But at least she would never resemble the wizened, toothless old Indian woman that to Denny meant grandmother.

I am not quite sure how the next hour passed. But somehow Denny and I got our flapjacks and honey, and even Jeanne was persuaded to eat. But for the most part she sat quietly in her seat, alternately looking dazed and unbelieving. And always her deep eyes followed Marya, as if she would never have enough of looking.

As he ate, I could see that Denny was giving the whole matter serious thought. Several times he regarded Jeanne briefly from under his dark brows. When he had finished his food, he stood for a time near the cookfire, brooding. Then suddenly he made up his mind.

"Come, Fang," he said.

With the big dog beside him he walked the few steps to the larger fire and stood before Jeanne. He clasped his hands, gravely bowed his head.

"I am very happy to have you for a grandmother," he said. "You are much nicer than the one of Billy Tom. Also, Fang is very pleased. We thought you should know."

As she sat, Jeanne went through the ritual. But her classic face was soft; her eyes glowed.

"Denny, live and enjoy! And Fang, we have always been friends."

"It is because Fang has always known, I think," Denny said. "But he could only speak in his own way."

Fang waved his tail slowly, looking up at the boy for a clue. But Denny only said, "You must rest now, so you will have strength again. We will go and show my father the moose tracks. He may wish to follow the moose, and Fang could help."

He had read my mind, or so it seemed. I had removed my

bow from its waterproof wrapping. It hadn't been harmed. The caribou-skin quiver, filled with arrows, already hung from my shoulder. And Denny thought of one thing more.

"If I might carry the small binoculars, I would be very careful. Perhaps we might see the Little People from the road."

I glanced at Jeanne, but she seemed not to have heard.

"A good idea," I said. "You may get them."

I had spoken to Marya.

"It will be better if we leave you today. Your mother has much to adjust to—and so do you. Tell her whatever you think wise. And," I took her beautiful face between my two hands for a moment, "I am very happy for you!"

That was all.

I led off up the slope through the brush land, taking a pace Denny could follow. Fang ranged in sweeps around us, but he often stopped and looked at me, watching for a signal. He knew the trip had a purpose. He knew I would tell him what to do. He was saying that he was ready.

The great splayed tracks of a striding moose are like nothing else in the northern woods. These were fresh, and they were huge and spaced far apart. It was exactly as Denny had repoted; a big bull, running hard, perhaps almost in panic.

"Very large," I said. "I have rarely seen so long a stride."

Denny grinned happily. Fang waited alertly for the command to trail. But I disappointed them both.

"We know where he went. I agree that he may cause trouble out there, but if we don't crowd him he may find a marsh and stay there."

I considered.

"I know he doesn't belong in this land, so it is more important for us to learn where he came from. We must backtrack him. If the trail is badly mixed, Fang can tell us. But this is so plain it will be good practice for your eyes."

"It is a lesson?" Denny asked.

"A good one. Lead on. Show me!"

Denny enjoyed the challenge of the wilderness puzzles I gave him every time we went out. This one was easy. He followed the line of tracks at a trot. Fang glided along with him, looking somewhat bored. He knew that the moose was in the other direction.

For a mile the trail meandered through the grassland and patches of scrub. Before Denny and the dog had started it, the moose had not been in flight. The string of tracks often looped back on itself. There were spots where the animal had stood, shifting its feet, probably watching. But this was not the usual pattern of the progress of a feeding moose. Gradually the message came through to me. This was a puzzled, a bewildered animal. That moose was as alien to this land as we were.

"Here he slept," Denny said.

The flattened beach grass showed where the animal had lain. The bed was not far beyond the innermost tier of dunes, and from it the tracks led up over the sands, a wavering, almost erratic line of depressions.

"He came from the beach," Denny said. "He was very tired, I think."

We trailed him on over the dunes. The line of tracks ended at high tide mark.

"This is most strange," my son said. "He came from the ocean."

It did not seen likely. From as far as we could see them the gentle, almost oily waves came curling in, thinning and foaming up onto the beach. The morning sun glinted on the water. There was just enough wind to support the blue-mantled gulls cruising above the advancing tide.

Still, I nodded slowly. It could have happened.

"The moose is a water deer," I said. "He often swam the lake."

"But he could not swim an ocean."

My recurring problem for these past twenty-four hours had been to be sure that Denny did not become confused. The incredible transition that we had made from the lake country of northern Yukon to this land beside the sea was not an understandable thing. He had bridged the whole experience simply by having faith in me. The fact that I evidently knew something of where we were must have reassured him. "When I need to know, you will tell me," he had said. I depended on that now.

"Denny," I said, "I want you to suppose with me."

It was a game we sometimes played. Usually it was another way of learning. The boy enjoyed it. I gave him facts, he put them together and told me what they meant. He looked at me now with his half-grin.

"Suppose," I said, "when the storm struck our canoe, that the moose was also swimming the lake there. We need not have seen him. The storm covered a wide strip. Suppose, when the waves grew great and we were overturned, that the moose was also swept in the same direction. It was very hard swimming for an animal that did not understand. Fang almost drowned. We know what happened to us. Tell me what happened to the moose."

As I had hoped, he simply ignored the impossible nature of the entire picture. He was concerned only with the moose.

"He had to swim very hard," Denny said. "Perhaps he could hold his breath better than Fang, because he often feeds with his head under water. And finally he came to the beach without being filled with water, as Fang was." His long eyes narrowed, as though he were actually watching the great ungainly animal as it floundered out of the surf.

"He did not know what to do, and he was so tired he could not run. So he staggered and wobbled up over the sand, and when he came to the grass he lay down to rest. He stayed there a long time, I think."

He pondered a moment longer, then looked at me.

"Is this how you think?"

"It is exactly how I think. Now we have a reason to trail him, because we know he is confused. This country is new to him. He won't understand the small houses and fields of the Little People. He may cause a great deal of damage. They won't know what to do, because they have never had a large animal in their land."

"What will we do when we find him?"

"Let's find him first," I said. "Because before we do, I think we will also come to those small houses."

Following the wandering of the moose had taken time, but it required only a few minutes to go back to our starting place. Fang came alert when we again cut the trail of the running animal.

"Now," he seemed to say, "now we'll have some action!" But we kept him close to us, and his disgust was evident. Denny trailed, as he had before, and set the pace.

When we came to a meander of the little stream we paused and took a drink. The moose had cleared it at a stride. I took out a corn cake for Denny and one for me. Fang sat with resignation while we enjoyed them. He did not care for such delicacies and would eat them only when food was scarce. He was eager to follow the moose.

But I noticed a change in his behavior as we had our refreshment. Twice he rose to sniff the air. He seemed puzzled. His tail waved slowly and he looked at me as though asking for an explanation.

"Fang is speaking of something he does not understand," Denny said keenly.

"It doesn't make him angry," I said. "It is something familiar, and yet it isn't."

Denny thrust out his lower lip. He brooded for a moment.

"If he could scent people, and yet the scents were very small, this would worry him."

I swallowed the last of my cake.

"Before long," I said, "you will be teaching me! Lead on!"

I had only seen the little road in the moonlight. The moose's big hooves had gouged the gravel as he bounded across, the only blemishes in the neat white surface as far as I could see.

Fang's interest in the moose had wavered. He stood on the road and sniffed, obviously puzzled. I would have given much to have experienced all the rich impressions he was getting through that wonderful organ, his nose. It would certainly have been helpful if he could have told us what he sensed.

He came willingly when I started off down the road. In the distance I could see the superstructure of the little bridge crossing the stream, and I wanted to look at it in the light. The gravel was firm underfoot, well compacted. It had a feel of permanence about it, as though it had been there a long, long time.

"Father!"

Denny's voice was urgent, and as I whirled my right hand slid automatically to the butt of the magnum against my thigh. But for a moment I could see nothing.

Fang stood just off the road, stood rigidly, but his tail waved gently. About three paces beyond him, half hidden by a grass clump, a tiny man stood. He had a miniature bow raised, an arrow nocked, and he was carefully drawing it to his ear.

"Fang, down!"

The dog flattened. He had been carefully trained. When little more than a puppy he had grasped the thing that is essential in a good wilderness dog: instant obedience. This time I am convinced that it saved him an eye.

My shout froze the little man. He didn't release the arrow. Slowly he lowered the bow. But he stood his ground with dignity as I strode up and stood beside the dog. We stared at each other, and I couldn't tell you which was the more astonished.

I knew about the Little People. I had accepted the fact of their existence. For three months I had carried a coffin and an incredible skeleton in my rucksack. But when one finally stood before me, hardly taller than the breadth of my two spread hands, I had to learn to believe all over again.

Finally I got down on my knees, crouched as low as I could get. Fang had not moved. His head lay on his forepaws, his half-closed eyes did not blink. Even his nose had ceased to twitch.

"The dog meant no harm," I told the small bowman. "He does only what I tell him."

The little man hesitated. He opened his mouth, closed it again. I knew that there was a good chance that my speech was meaningless to him. But finally he spoke, hesitantly, and I thought he had to grope to find the words.

"Is there a break in the wall?"

The voice was small, but it was positive, clear, and resonant. And it was comical to detect in the halting English the well-remembered accent of the man Smith.

I shook my head.

"I do not know. We did not come from the wall."

The little man struggled with the idea. Finally he said, "There is no other way."

"There is one," Isaid. "The ocean. The big water."

He stared at me. This must have been an unbelievable thought. Then he spoke fluently, volubly, vehemently, but his speech was Elkan; what Denny had called the singing words. I couldn't understand a syllable. I held up a hand, spoke very slowly.

"You must speak English. I come from the land of the man Smith. I cannot speak your tongue."

This, apparently, was another poser. The little man looked from me to the prone dog, then on behind me to where Denny stood in transfixed delight.

"It is forbidden to be here. Nothing large must come."

I nodded.

"We know that. But it happened, and we are here. There was nothing we could do. And it is very hard to tell you."

I was trying to keep my speech simple, and I knew I

wasn't sounding very convincing, or very informative either, for that matter.

The little man's attention appeared to wander. He looked at the arrow still against his bowstring as if he wondered how it had got there. In a puzzled fashion he returned it to the quiver on his back. Then he seemed to force himself back to the present.

"Your large animal will trample the fields," he said.

"We'll keep him with us," I assured him. "We will walk only on the roads."

"Not the dog." He said it impatiently. "The very large beast. It looks like an elk, but is not an elk. You should not allow it to run."

"But it isn't ours," I explained. "It is a very large wild deer called a moose. It must have come when we did, but we had nothing to do with it. We cannot stop it from running."

The little man studied me steadily, then suddenly became vague again. "Dogs. Elk. I am remembering again. It is not good to remember. They belong in the Other World."

He half turned away, as though we were not there. "It is not good to remember you, either. You should not be here."

"We will go," I assured him. "Just as soon as it is possible we will go."

"Take your moose," the tiny man said. "It could destroy a house with its feet."

"As I said, it is not my moose," I repeated patiently. "I did not bring it here. Where is it now?"

The little man waved toward the east.

"Over there, half a sun-span away. It is in the marsh. Many men watch it. It is too large for us to kill."

"Half a sun-span," I mused. "But it was seen near here not long ago. There are its tracks."

"Half a sun-span for me. You and the dog could go quickly."

"Are you asking me to help you destroy the moose? If I went across your country, I might cause damage as well."

"You brought it here. You should remove it. It is great danger to all."

"Hum-m! When you get an idea, you don't turn it loose. Fang, up!"

The dog rose in place and stood waiting for orders.

"The dog can find the moose for me. But he would have to cross your lands. I could not drive the moose. It would cause damage wherever it went. I will have to kill it. Is this what you want?"

The little man brooded. It seemed to disturb him to try to face a problem that shouldn't exist.

"I am remembering," he muttered. "Elk were eaten. Could not this thing be eaten?"

"It could be. It would feed a thousand such as you. Would there be so many?"

"Thousand." The little archer held out his fingers, closed his tiny hands, then opened and closed them several times. "I have forgotten thousand. But there are people inside the Great Road, sun-span after sun-span. They would come for meat. We do not often eat much of it."

I sensed the beginning of an idea, a completely fantastic idea. I began to see a picture in my mind: thousands of tiny men and women clogging the little roads, all converging on a huge mound of fresh meat, a mound that I would make from the moose.

In that Other World, these had been hunting people. The bow of the little man attested that they were hunters still, when they came beyond the wall. What they hunted I had no idea. Probably cottontails were the largest game in their land.

They could not carry the meat far, at the speeds that their small size would allow. It would soon spoil. If there were enough of them, could they cook it and eat it there in the fields? I let my imagination go. It was all unbelievable anyway, so I envisioned a thousand, ten thousand little cookfires all sending up spindles of smoke, with the odor of roasting meat lying over the whole area, overcoming and blotting out the usual smells of summer. Acres and acres of feasting tiny people; a Lilliputian carnival!

I shook my head and came back to the present. So far there was only one small man. But even he was a wonder. I was not sure I believed his existence even though he stood before me.

For the past few minutes I had completely forgotten Denny. Like Fang, he had not moved. He stood in the road a few paces away, watching and listening, the half grin on his face. I realized that his acceptance of this whole situation was far more complete than mine. His flexible child mind had not yet had time to set itself within rigid, logical boundaries. I had said that there were Little People, so he was not surprised. He was simply interested. I beckoned to him.

"This is my son, Denny," I said.

The little man stared for a moment in silence. Then: "A child! I remember children." He shook his head in a bewildered way. "They are only in the Other World. It was very long ago."

"My name is Vin," I said. "What may we call you?"

The tiny bowman gazed at me thoughtfully.

"No name. We have no names. What would we need them for?"

But the concept bothered him. He muttered to himself. And suddenly he looked at the boy.

"Denny! I remember Denny. It was a strange name. He was big, and he laughed if a leaf fell. And his hair was yellow. No one else had yellow hair."

"Yes," I said. "I knew him. This boy has his name."

The little man digested this. His memory seemed only to come in flashes.

"Two with the same name," he muttered finally. "It is better to have no name." His thoughts jumped. "Will you destroy the moose?"

I rose slowly from my cramped position and stretched to my full height. The little fellow stared up at me.

"It'll be a poor reward for him, since he survived the storm," I said. "But he can't be left here—and it is many miles to the wall. He will be in danger, just as we will be."

I stood for a while and thought.

"Very well. The dog and I will hunt and kill the moose. Then I will skin it, and prepare the flesh. There will be meat for all who can come. It must be eaten soon, or it will spoil. So I will make a great cookfire, and cook much of it. But if people wish the flesh raw, there will be plenty."

"All cannot come soon," the little man said. "We cannot travel as you do. We are small—and we are old."

That was a poser, and certainly true. Again I stood and considered, plagued all the while by the uneasy feeling that none of this was real. I would wake up before long, back in my camp on the Yukon lake. But the landscape stayed stubbornly solid. Even the tiny man at my feet did not waver. In the near distance, bright and colorful in the sun, the White Cliffs reared high.

"Can those who are far away know about this?"

For the first time I caught a hint of a smile on the little man's almost expressionless face.

"We do not have runners, but news will go fast from person to person. They will know."

"I will give them time. After three sun-spans I will hunt and kill the moose. It will stay near the water, for the food it likes best is there."

"There are many bows around the marsh," the little man said. "If the animal comes out, we will drive it back. We cannot kill, but we can sting."

"Sting only if you must," I advised. "A frightened moose would make my task much harder."

The little fellow nodded solemnly.

"That is true. We will try to remember how elk were driven. No one can think of this for long, but someone else will remember when the first one forgets. We will keep the moose in the marsh."

"Good. We will go back to our camp now. Under the Cliffs we will do no harm to people and things we can scarcely see. When I have killed the moose, then we must cross your land to the wall. You have mentioned a Great Road. Perhaps we could travel that. Could we be guided to it?"

Again the faint smile crossed the tiny face.

"You are standing on it. It runs many sun-spans through the land. It is not straight, but when you have traveled far enough, you can see the wall."

He seemed suddenly unbelieving.

"This is not done. No one has ever gone back across the wall!"

"That is true," I agreed, "but we are not small. We could not stay here. We must go back."

The little man turned away.

"I do not understand. But when the moose is killed, and you are gone, things will be as they have always been. That will be good."

"In three sun-spans," I reminded him. "Do not forget. Let the people know."

He drew himself up with a dignity that must have had its origin long before, when he was a large person.

"We do not forget what is here," he said simply. "We only forget the Other World. The people will know."

Chapter 25

Jeanne was growing smaller. It must have begun even before the storm, though in the first stages it would not have been a noticeable thing. Further, we had had many other concerns in those past few days. But now that we knew, it suddenly seemed to go more and more swiftly.

I could not even imagine what was taking place to reduce that fine strong body to a miniature. It was, of course, metamorphosis, a form change. In the world I knew, it was not unique. It was the way of life in some fishes, in amphibians, in thousands of insects and their relatives. And it was the way of life here, too, with the people of this world. Why, how . . . ? I made my mind go blank and refused to think about it.

But it was happening to Jeanne. This was a reality, and could not be ignored. Because of it there were problems that otherwise would have not existed. They were our problems, and we would have to resolve them.

There was the problem of Marya. This, as was soon evident, was not a problem at all. In Marya's thinking her mother's journey was natural, normal, inevitable. It was the way things were. She had never understood the aging that she had seen in her seven years in my world. It had seemed to her a pitiful thing when people grew feeble, helpless, wrinkled, often of impaired mind. She was glad that her mother's aging was of a different kind; that she would live her last years happily, vigorously, with no clouding memories of unhappiness before.

There was the problem of Denny. Denny had too many new things to think about. They were coming too swiftly, too close together. He was only a little boy, and his life had been simple. He had had few contacts with the people of even his own world. His days had been largely occupied by trees and streams and birds and animals. For the most recent half of his life his chief friend and companion had been a big wolf dog. Billy Tom, the small Indian boy, was less a person to him than Fang. What effect this sudden widening of perspective would have on him, including things that would not have been believed by the adults of his world, was hard to predict.

In those three days, three sun-spans, I knew he thought a great deal. Often he withdrew into the quiet recesses of his own mind, shutting us out while he struggled with some strange fact that had never been true before.

I did not try to intrude on his thinking. I never volunteered an explanation. When he asked, I answered. But mainly, I *accepted*. I acted as if each new happening were an expected thing. From my behavior he never suspected that this whole adventure was strange, exotic, unbelievable. And since I had taught him most of what he knew, both of people and of his wilderness world, to learn more was what he expected to do. So finally my only real concern was that the lessons were coming too fast.

There was the problem of Jeanne herself. For her, too, life had changed too swiftly. After twenty years of hoping, when there had been no hope, suddenly all that she had dreamed of had come true. And in the transition she had had to endure more than in the hopeless years before.

There had been the terror of knowing that her journey had begun, in a land where the White Cliffs were not even myth. There had been the trauma of the storm, when the energy that normally was used for change had had to be used to save her life. A tiny daughter dimly remembered had become real as a kind, beautiful woman. And finally, in a fashion as strange as her going away from her world, she had returned to it.

If Fang had problems, he hid them remarkably well. I was sure that the drifting scents of the Little People puzzled him. But he hunted cottontails under Denny's eye and never even approached what the little man had called the Great Road. After all, Fang's world was not just a location. His world was people. And since his people were all here, his world had not really changed.

After three sun-spans he was ready, when I went to keep my promise to the Little People. He could sense that this was a hunt. Together we had killed a dozen moose. I regretted this one, but I knew it had to be done. As long as the moose was alive he was danger to an entire small world.

"You may have to go very fast," Denny told me gravely. "I am not yet big enough to follow you. I would not be help. So I will stay with mother and Jeanne, and come to the road when they come. But when we see your smoke, perhaps I might help with the skinning?"

"You certainly may," I agreed heartily. "You have thought it out very sensibly. Thank you."

He clasped his left hand with his right, bowed his head with dignity. I kissed Marya, put my hand on Jeanne's shrunken shoulder, then set off through the brushy land toward the Great Road.

It felt good. I fell naturally into the stride of the Elkan hunter, six or seven miles to the hour, and half a dozen feet to my left and a body length ahead of me, as he had been taught, the malemute moved with effortless ease. His tongue lolled, and he looked back at me with a grin. He had missed this, missed it as much as I had.

We made short work of the distance to the road. The moose's trail was still plain to my eyes, and though the scent was cold, Fang could follow it. My plan was very tentative. I couldn't possibly know what the country would be like, nor how the tiny bowmen around the marsh would respond to our coming. Would they do what I asked? Their safety was paramount, but it was, after all, their land.

The Little People were there. Almost as soon as we crossed the Great Road we began to see them. Before long their small houses dotted the landscape, sitting in the edges of little fields, among the occasional clumps of low trees, even on hill-tops. Some were of stone, some of small logs, some seemingly made of whatever variety of materials the environment afforded. Few were taller than my waist. All gave evidence of great age, of constant repair. Perhaps some had been in use for millennia.

The countryside was crisscrossed with roads. No house was far from one, but there were not even paths to the dwellings themselves. Small fields were everywhere, without fences or enclosures of any sort, their boundaries set at odd angles to each other, with little patches of woodland and wild growth between them.

I was acutely aware of all this, for the moose's trail led straight across country, with no regard for the tiny artifacts. We had to follow, Fang and I, without causing damage. For short distances we could use the roads. We might have used them more, but they were already in use. They were choked with people! And since they were rarely more than two feet wide, we were completely out of scale. We chose the firmest route we could find, and followed the moose by scent and by eye.

There were times when there were scores of people under my eyes. Yet I felt alone. Though the miniatures moved along briskly, giving every evidence of life, they did not feel alive. They all looked at the dog and me as we passed, but there seemed to be no surprise. I sensed that there shouldn't be. We were why they were here. They had been traveling, some for perhaps a couple of sun-spans, in response to the message about meat.

I didn't try to communicate. My job was to find the moose and kill it. They all knew this. So when the hunt was over and the meat prepared, perhaps then we could talk.

I spoke to Fang instead.

"I couldn't hazard a guess as to what you're thinking," I told him, "but this must be one puzzling situation for you. And why not? It is for me."

The dog seemed at ease. He checked the cold moose tracks with an occasional deep sniff, but he trod lightly and scarcely left any tracks of his own. The Little People he ignored. But he carefully circled any artifact. Once, where the moose trail had crossed one of the small roads, he had a decision to make. There was a continuous line of people, some pushing or pulling tiny two-wheeled carts, strung out where we needed to cross. The dog never broke stride. The Little People cringed as he cleared the parade at a single bound. With such an example I simply murmured "Excuse me!" as I stepped over the line of traffic.

It was a strange hunt. But the half sun-span of the little man was hardly an hour for us. We came over the crest of a ridge and looked down a long open slope to a small marsh in a stream valley at its foot. There were no roads here. I had noticed that the Little People had gathered in groups in the fields behind us. They were the early arrivals, and they were waiting.

I motioned Fang to heel as I went quietly down the slope. From coverts and shady spots all along the edge of the marsh tiny bowmen rose to meet me. They were very much alike, but when one came forward purposefully I recognized our friend of the Great Road. He made no random speech. He came straight to the point.

"The animal is there, in the tree clump in the middle of the marsh. You can see the shadows shift as he moves. It is your hunt. Tell us what to do."

I was as direct as he.

"Call all bowmen away from the marsh. There is no way to know what a frightened or an angry moose will do. I do not wish anyone to be hurt, and I must send the dog in to bring him out. Tell everyone to go to the top of the slope. As you say, it is my hunt now. I will wait."

The word went around. The little bowmen came trudging up the hillside, seeming to spare me scarcely a glance. Actually, each was watching me curiously whenever he thought he wasn't observed. There were more than fifty of them, and some came from the far side of the marsh.

"It was necessary to sting the animal," the little man said. "He wished to come out and eat the corn. There are arrows in his nose."

I examined my own bow with care.

"There must be one in his heart," I said. "The first one, if I haven't lost my touch. He must not run. With all the people on the roads and in the fields, that would be danger. I am ready now. You may follow the others up the slope and tell them I am sending in the dog."

For a moment I thought he might refuse to go. Plainly, he had expected to stay nearby. As he had agreed, it was my hunt, but it was his idea. His hesitation was brief. Almost with a shrug he turned his tiny back and followed his friends.

Though I knew now that the Little People only remembered their previous lives in brief moments and flashes, I hoped that they could appreciate as Fang brought out the moose. They had all been hunters. They had taken the wild elk and the bear with dogs. They had never before seen a moose or a malemute, but the pattern was the same.

Fang watched me alertly, his brush waving gently, his eyes eager. I gave him his signal. He moved into the marsh like a shadow, not approaching the clump of trees directly, but making a gradually tightening circle across the flooded land. He would be a wet dog before his job was finished. He put it off as long as possible, though. He bounded from hummock to hummock, choosing his route, taking his time, neither panicking nor angering the watching moose. When he reached the trees, little more than his pads were wet.

The moose would run before the wolf pack, but he would fight a single animal. Fang moved tantalizingly in front of him. The bull charged, and the dog slipped easily aside. The saplings were too closely spaced for the moose's wide and still tender rack of antlers. Fang dodged in and out. The big animal could not pivot in close quarters; shortly he was confused. He was handicapped, too, in a way that he did not then know. The tiny archers had done more than sting. One arrow had pierced an eye. The moose was half blind.

Fang knew that he must drive the moose toward me. When the frustrated animal was facing in the direction of our shore, the dog nipped his hind legs savagely. From my stand a hundred yards away I could hear his deep growl. It worked, as it always did. The bull ran.

He plunged out of the covert at full speed. Sheets of water flew as his long legs plowed through the shallows. Fang leaped from grass clump to grass clump, and when the moose reached the foot of the slope he was there.

Now the bull had room to move, and he turned again on the tormenting dog. Fang went round and round him, holding him in place, not allowing him to run again. I was ready. Finally the moose stopped, at bay, his great head down, his one eye on the dog a couple of yards away. Fang's red tongue ran out, and he glanced at me, scarcely thirty yards distant. I raised the bow with the swinging draw that was always my trademark.

I had luck. I could scarcely hear the arrow thud. That meant that it had not struck ribs, but had gone cleanly between them and on through the heart beyond.

For a moment the moose did not move. His forelegs spraddled widely, holding him up a few seconds longer. He was literally dead while still standing on his feet. Then the legs crumpled and the heavy body crashed.

I stood for a moment. Fang faced the slope alertly. For from all along the crest, almost like a low soft wind, a sound came rolling down through the grassland. "Ah-h-h!"

Hundreds of tiny people, for a fleeting moment, remembered the Games of that Other World, and appreciated in the old way.

I went swiftly across to the fallen game. I drew the keen edge of my hunting knife across the hairy throat back of the bell, to drain the carcass so that it would cool more quickly, and to insure that it would be good meat. I made a sign to Fang. Like a wolf he moved in for his reward, a drink of fresh hot blood.

Chapter 26

It was twilight. The red coals of my cookfire glowed as a breeze blew fitfully up from the marsh. Above the fire, on an improvised spit, Marya turned a whole big haunch of the moose. And all over the slope small fires flickered as clusters of tiny people roasted meat. Days before I had envisioned this scene. Now, sitting wearily on a boulder near the fire, I was not sure I believed it.

For me, it had been a hard day. I had sent Fang back to the Great Road to meet Marya and Denny and to bring them to the kill. Of course I could not hang a thousand-pound moose, so I skinned and butchered it as it lay. I hung the quarters, cut and piled roasts and filets on all the clean stones about; laid out the great liver. With the axe Marya had brought I cut wood, built fires. Fang and Denny had helped with the skinning. Fang was glad to dispose of scraps. He would have gorged himself, wolf-like, but I made him stop when I thought he'd had enough.

The Little People swarmed. They clustered about while I butchered, watching with interest, looking delighted and confused by turns. I was sure that the familiar procedure triggered memories of their former lives, transient memories that flashed for a brief time, then went away again. They talked continuously among themselves, but always in the Elkan tongue. I could not understand.

"They speak of the great amount of meat," Marya said. "This is something that has never happened before on this side of the wall. Yet they remember large beasts. But nothing stays in their thoughts for long. In their minds there is no real world but this."

"They look very much alike," I said. "Would you recognize one if you had known him before, on the other side of the wall?"

My wife looked at me gravely.

"I would not wish to know. They could not remember for more than minutes, but if they knew me, it would disturb their thoughts. They have had the Other World. They should have this one in peace."

"Of course. Memory would destroy that, wouldn't it? Mother Nature thinks of everything, even in a cycle like this. We must leave as soon as we can."

"The meat is cooked," Marya said. "We can cut what we need and take it back to camp. Also, I would like a fresh piece for drying, so that we may eat until we have crossed the wall. It will be a long trail for my mother. She moves very slowly now."

I nodded.

"Very soon, this will be her world. Does she wish to leave it, knowing that she will have little time on the other side of the wall?"

"She is very sad to leave me," Marya said quietly, "but her journey goes much faster than it might have if she had not had to use her strength in the storm. Three times we have made her clothing smaller."

I stared into the fire. As it did occasionally, the total unreality of the metamorphosis gripped me. It was incredible.

"What will she do for clothing here, when she has become really small?"

Marya smiled.

"Look about you. All wear clothing neatly made, and the cloth is very fine. It has always been believed that they spin and weave, cut and sew. Now we know that it is true. Also, my mother has in her pack the tiny garments she will wear first, when she has reached her size and her strength returns. She made them when she knew her journey would soon begin."

I rose, stretched tired muscles, looked across the darkening slope with its many little twinkling fires.

"Let's wait in our camp," I proposed. "She should not have to make a tiring trek for nothing. We'll stay with her as long as she needs us. Then we can travel the Great Road with speed."

"Her thoughts will turn away from us," Marya said.

"When she can wear the tiny clothes, she will be glad to leave us. But she will be happy about me, too, for she knows I have a life I enjoy."

She turned the spit for a moment and brooded.

"Only one thing disturbs her. She has no coffin. One was never made."

"We'll have one made. After we have been taken to the Primate, and he has listened and disposed, we will bring one to the wall. Could she remember, and know where to come for it? For I know that we can never come beyond the wall again."

"It is a very great need," Marya said quietly. "I believe she will remember."

Overhead, in the deepening, purpling sky, the stars came out one by one. They were the familiar patterns of the north, but just a little different, not quite right, as though we viewed them from a slightly shifted vantage. As I had many times before, I wondered where we really were. Was Elkan of Earth? When we changed worlds, as I had three times, what had we done? I had no answer. But I had no regret, either. Everything I cared for was here, on this pleasant, star-lit slope. And, as the Primate had observed when we first visited him, years before, it was a good land. In spite of the unreal tiny people about me, I felt a strange content.

I watched the shadowy outline of Denny as he made his way carefully among the little fires, followed by the dark silhouette of Fang. Often he stopped, grasped hands, and bowed. Faintly I could hear his voice, speaking in grave, polite tones. The higher, shriller voices of the small people answered. But they must have been starting the conversations. Denny had been told that we were all unbelievable to them.

Finally he came back to the big cookfire. He carried a small filet of roasted meat.

"The Little People wished me to have it, and I could not be impolite," he said. "It is very good. They have cooked it well, although the moose is very tough."

"I know," I said. "We are cooking it too soon. But we had no choice. Did the Little People speak first to you?"

"Each time," the boy said. "First they spoke in the singing words, then English. They spoke as if a child were a wonder. Do they not have children of their own?"

"Long ago they had children. Remember, they do not become Little People until they are very old. Once they were as large as I or your mother."

Denny considered this, gnawing thoughtfully at the meat.

"You have said this," he agreed at last. "It is a hard thing to understand. Perhaps when we have fewer things to do, you would tell me how it happens."

"I'll tell you all I know," I promised, "but not how it happens, because that I don't know. Nobody knows. We only know that it happens here, to these people."

Denny retreated into the familiar isolation of his mind, shutting us out while he rearranged the things that he had heard and seen. When he returned he looked at me with what seemed to be a suppressed excitement, as if he had brought a new idea with him. And, as he quickly proved, he had.

"I have seen that Jeanne's clothes hang very loosely on her. Also, I have remembered that this morning she did not look so tall as mother. She does not eat, and she does not grow rested."

He eyed me intently.

"Does Jeanne grow small? You have said that she would not become white-haired and toothless, like the grandmother of Billy Tom. Will she be one of the Little People instead?"

Until he grows older, a child lives on the pleasant edge of fantasy land. Things are not yet immutable, subject to rules that blunt the imagination. I realized that Denny would accept the fact of the origin of the Little People far more readily than any adult. And the keen observation that was a vital part of his wilderness training would insure that he knew everything that happened. So I had no choice. I nodded, as if it were the most usual thing in the world.

"Yes," I said. "Jeanne will be one of the Little People. She will not be with us much longer, and we must enjoy her company while we can. The changing is difficult, but when it is finished she will be happy. Then we will leave her here, and the Little People will welcome her. She will have more years of pleasant life. We will be glad for her."

Denny finished chewing his meat. He seemed completely satisfied with what I had told him, and accepted it with no comment. He simply had wanted to know. He suddenly appeared more interested in the large roast on the spit.

"The Little People have very small portions," he remarked. "Perhaps we may have a slice of that before we go to camp?"

We did. Each of us had a slice. Then I packed up all the

meat I thought we could use, gathered my axe and weapons. The rising moon would soon make it easy for us to travel, with no danger to the Little People or their tiny artifacts.

I spoke to the nearest group, still busily cutting and cooking meat. Several were small bowmen from the company that had watched the marsh.

"Live and enjoy," I said politely. "We are going back to our camp now. In a little while we will travel the Great Road, and cross the wall into the Other World. The meat is yours. We hope that all may have a share."

One of the small men answered promptly.

"We thank you. The animal would have been danger to our fields and houses. We could not have killed it. But the meat is good. Even those who are still a sun-span away will share in it."

He stopped, hesitated, as if he had forgotten what he was saying. Then he added, as he turned back to the fire:

"The dog is a very fine hunter."

I felt sure that that remark reflected a flash of memory. Long ago, back in the Other World, that tiny man had been a hunter, with pride in the qualities of his dogs. Briefly he appreciated again something that once had been very important to him.

With Fang pacing confidently ahead, the trip back to camp was a silent trek of tired people. I was glad of another slice of the meat and a corn cake and a cup of Marya's tea. Then I went to my sleeping bag. I thought that anything not yet done could well wait for the sun. I had accomplished enough. And I knew that that was an Elkan point of view.

Chapter 27

Jeanne grew small very rapidly. Each day Denny went to her as she sat by the fire or walked slowly about the camp. Gravely he would tell her what he had done the day before, something he had seen, something Fang had done. He seemed to understand the pleasure that this gave her. He never mentioned her diminishing size or referred in any way to the amazing thing that was happening to her.

After this brief visit he would come with me, leaving Marya with her mother during these last days. We swam in the surf, basked in the sun, wandered for miles along the pleasant beach. We surf-fished. Denny caught his first mackerel and his first flounder, and other fishes that I did not think should be there. Fang regarded the waves and surf with deep suspicion, and it was only after coaxing that he would even get his pads wet. Fresh water he enjoyed. But this ocean had not treated him well. He wanted no part of it.

For one long day we traveled along the base of the White Cliffs. We did not go out into the land of the Little People, though occasionally, with the binoculars, we could see small stretches of the Great Road a mile away. Seemingly this was the Little People's boundary. They did not have homes outside the Great Road. I suspected that it encircled the entire occupied land, paralleling the Cliffs to where the snow peaks rose. I knew that it ran inland a scant mile from the ocean. Probably it was routed not far from the wall as well.

After seven years I had my opportunity to examine the marvelous sedimentary wall that was the White Cliffs. Geologically it still made no more sense than it had during those first days, when Elg and Orb had told us it was a thing we could not explore. But it was as beautiful close up as it was from a distance. Denny looked for eagles on it. He did not find them. I wondered if the same strange condition that did not allow large animals to cross the wall also kept eagles from these crags. They seemed ideal. But the Little People would be a good size for Golden Eagle prey. And there were no eagles here.

That was the longest of our days. The moon was high when we finally came to camp again. Fang glided along as though the journey had just begun. I had had all I wanted, though, and a tired small boy slept peacefully on my shoulder.

"Vin, it is time."

From her sleeping bag Marya pointed to the tiny figure busy at the banked fire. It moved briskly, uncovering coals, adding small pieces of wood expertly. Jeanne wore her new clothes, the little garments she had made, in doubt and terror, months before in the Yukon wilds. Somehow, she had known what size they should be. They fitted perfectly.

"She is hungry," Marya said. "She knows that I will prepare food, but we, and this camp, are only partly in her thoughts. She will know us, but her attention will wander. She is ready to go."

For many days Jeanne had had only water, or sometimes a sip of tea. But this morning she had a whole plover's egg, a tiny filet of fish from one of Denny's ocean catches, and a small crumb of corn cake. She ate with gusto. She would speak to us, but it was as though we were not really there.

After the meal she moved restlessly around the camp, examining each item of equipment, often looking off across the land. She stood for minutes before the rustic seat I had made for her, studying it. It was now huge, compared to her tiny body. She would have had to climb even to reach the seat.

Finally she came to me. For a moment she seemed almost herself again, remembering everything.

"They are expecting me now," she said. "I must go. I am glad that Oo-ah has you. She will be happy. And when I remember, I will think of Denny, and be proud. I will even think of Fang, who can almost speak."

She hesitated. Her concentration faltered for a moment, then steadied again. The tiny eyes looked at me appealingly.

"You will not forget the coffin?"

"I will not forget," I promised. "We will go with you to the Great Road."

As a matter of fact she rode, sitting on my forearm, a negligible weight. I could have been carrying a kitten. Marya and Denny walked quietly beside me. Fang followed, his tail drooped.

I placed her down on the Great Road where a smaller road intersected. She stood for a moment, looking around her, as though she recognized where she was. Then, without even acknowledging our presence, she walked across to the small road.

Danny took several steps past us. He stood with hands clasped, his dark head bowed.

"Good-bye Jeanne! Little grandmother. Have happiness."

The tiny figure, already into the small road, turned for a moment. A faint smile flitted across her face, and she raised a diminutive hand. Then she strode purposefully away from us. We had become simply figures in a dim past. She had come home.

Chapter 28

As I had on that earlier stay in this land, I had lost track of time. So many things had happened since first we wet our canoe on the Yukon. The calendar had not been important. And now only the position of the sun in the sky gave a clue to how far the summer had gone. I suspected that July had ended. The peaches would be ripe in the Primate's orchards, and the finest grapes would be on the breakfast tables.

Well, we would soon know. Soberly we dismantled our camp, made up our packs, and removed even the evidence of our campfires. I suspected that none would ever be lighted again at this place. Our being here was as rare and unlikely as the collision of two meteors in space. The best way to accept it was not to think of it at all.

We were still solemn with the going of Jeanne, but as the sun rose high, our spirits lifted with it. We trekked south on the Great Road, which of course to us was not great at all. With the packs it was more comfortable to travel single file. But it was a deep-based, compact gravel path, settled into the landscape by who knew how many thousands of years. It felt good under our moccasins.

"The Great Road is a fine trail for hiking," Denny said. For his share of the time he went ahead and set the pace. Fang glided along beside him. "It is smooth enough for the carts of the Little People. It is very well kept."

"It serves two purposes," I said. "It is the main route of travel from one part of the country to another, and I think it must be the boundary to the land of the Little People. Inside it, they have their homes and fields. Across it, on the outside, is simply wild natural country. Perhaps, sometimes, they hunt there. But usually not even that."

"The Little People are very small." Denny pursued his thought. "How could they mend and repair so long a road?"

"They ate a whole moose," I said. "Size is not as important

when there are many. I suspect that work on the road never stops. If water washes it, or more gravel is needed, whoever is nearest will do the repairs."

"But if they work always on the road, how do they get their food?"

"They'll be fixing the road for everybody. So those who are raising plants or hunting animals will share the food they have. That way, everything gets done and everybody eats."

Denny looked back at me dubiously.

"You are guessing," he said.

"Of course I am," I admitted. "You have seen as much of the Little People as I have. But in the land where we are going, the land beyond the wall, that is the way it works. And before they were small, the Little People lived there."

Denny considered as he trudged along.

"I will have much to speak of, to Billy Tom and the boys who come to the post when their fathers buy. Perhaps I should not mention the Little People. They will not believe it, I think."

Marya and I exchanged glances. Plainly enough, to the boy this was a part of the summer's outing, and now we were on our way home. It was another problem. When we reached the wall, Marya would have come back to the homeland she had dreamed of all those seven years. But Denny would be in a strange and different world.

I had no illusions. The chances of our leaving Elkan were undoubtedly remote. Even I, the only person to make the transition three times, was unlikely ever to do it again. There was no pattern. I did not know what happened. In relation to the world of Earth as I knew it, I had no idea where we were now. There was no way to know.

For the remainder of the day we followed the Great Road steadily southward, into the sun. From our right, but faintly, came the rolling and purring of the surf a mile away. The road paralleled the dunes. We could sometimes see them when the trail sloped upward, and occasionally the glint of the ocean beyond. At Denny's pace, which had to be ours as well, the land of the Little People was not so small after all.

The road was traveled. Often we stepped off the trail to give the right of way to tiny people pushing small carts. Others were simply walking along, sometimes several together. They never spoke, though they looked at us with interest. They knew about us. Whether or not they had shared in the moose we could not know. But the intelligence of our presence had certainly gone from person to person the length and breadth of their land.

Sometimes little streams crossed the road, each spanned by a diminutive bridge. Other roads intersected, but always they ended at the Great Road. With the binoculars we could look along these smaller arteries and see houses off in the distance and small fields evidently cultivated. Occasionally a thread of smoke spindled upward from some chimney probably only inches wide. With everything in scale, the perspective illusion soon became one of a normal countryside. Only when we looked back to the road under our feet did the illusion vanish.

At sunset we made a comfortable camp beside a stream outside the road. I had sent Fang into the brush for the inevitable cottontails, and four times he returned with one neatly held in his mouth. When I skinned them they were not even bruised. Marya discovered with delight a large clump of coarse grass, a clump higher than Denny's head. They both dug under it and brought back a thick bundle of fat, white rhizomes. I remembered them. They were often on the tables of Chan-Cho-Pan.

So we made a meal, and before the moon was up we were asleep. Tomorrow I expected to come to the wall. The land of the Little People would be only a memory, for we could never come back. But I dreamed that we were met by the Primate himself, and that he sternly pointed back along the way we had come, and would not let us cross the wall.

I didn't tell my dream. After all, it was only a dream. Whatever decision the Primate might make, it certainly would not be that. I was silent, though, until we were well on our way again, and several times I surprised Marya watching me with what seemed to be concern. I made an effort, and in soothing her disquiet I cheered myself up as well.

"When we reach the wall, we will still be a number of days' travel from Chan-Cho-Pan," I remarked. "It will be the longest trail Denny has ever taken."

"We will make visits along the way," Marya said. Her long eyes were beginning to glow with anticipation. I think she was only now realizing that she was actually again in her own land. "We will stay in guest houses. Many people will be glad to welcome us."

"Even if they know that we have come from the land of the Little People? From the White Cliffs?"

Marya grew grave. She moved easily along under her well-balanced pack, and after twenty strides she answered, "Even then. We have done no harm, and perhaps we have even helped. We will speak it as it happened. No one doubts the spoken word of a guest."

"But they will see to it that we go promptly to the Primate."

Marya almost grinned.

"We will have guides," she admitted. "They will make sure that we do not lose the way."

That was pretty much how it happened.

It was midafternoon before the Great Road veered from the ocean and began to swing east toward the snow peaks, which lay along the distant horizon like cloud banks, perhaps as much as a hundred miles away. The land became rolling, then hilly. The little highway meandered and twisted to maintain its gentle grade. Often it was forced to climb, and from hilltops and along ridges we looked out on the gracious land of Elkan, just as I remembered it, forest and grassland, glinting streams, small rocky canyons, a used but unspoiled world.

From every elevation I searched with the binoculars and finally I saw it, an unbroken thread dividing the landscape from west to east, going on and on as far as I could see. It was the wall. I pointed it out, and Marya and Denny in turn focused the glasses to look.

"That is where the land of the Little People ends," I explained to Denny. "Beyond it the people are large, and there are different kinds of animals that Fang may hunt. There are towns, and boys of your size. The people are very pleasant."

"It is not a big wall." Denny used the binoculars carefully. "The stones are not stacked high. I do not see how it can keep the deer from the Little People's fields."

"Neither does anybody else," I agreed. "We only know that it does."

When it had approached as close to the wall as I thought it would, we left the Great Road and made our way across open country. We crossed the last of the small streams. We emptied, then refilled our canteens with the fresh cold water, just in case we might need it at the night's camp spot. Then up a last slope, across a small meadow and we came to it, the boundary between the past and the future.

Neither Marya nor I had ever approached it before. To

Denny, of course, it was simply a low, weathered stone wall, amazingly long, but otherwise not so fine as the one before our cabin at home. But I had an idea. I stepped over it, gave a hand to Marya. Denny scrambled over on his own. But Fang, who could have cleared it at a bound, refused to come at all. He seemed deeply disturbed. He trotted back and forth in apparent frustration, as though looking for a break, a way through. Finally he sat, looked at us, and whined as he hadn't done since he was a pup.

"There is something," I said. "Fang knows. I believe that if I try to force him over, he will defy me. He won't want to. But there's something about the wall that he doesn't dare contest."

"But he must come over," Denny said. "We cannot leave him here. If we go away from the wall, he will follow."

"I don't think so," I said.

But we tried. We settled our packs into place and started out across the stretch of grassland that was our logical direction. After a hundred yards we were stopped by a long, anguished wail. Fang sat far enough away from the wall so that he could see us, tipped his muzzle to the sky, and mourned. The wall was no higher than my waist. We were the only beings in the universe that the dog cared for. But he would not, could not, cross the wall.

He was no more baffled than I was.

"This has been a summer of problems," I said "but I'm not too sure this isn't the trickiest of the lot. Fang is held in the land of the Little People. Really stuck there. He can't come out."

"Many times he has jumped twice as high," Denny said. "Why won't he try?"

"For the same reason that the deer, the bear and the wolf will not try. What that is I don't know. It is nothing we can feel. But to them, and to Fang, is is very real."

"I will go back over the wall and speak with him," Denny said. "I will climb over and back. Always he will do what I do. He will come."

We watched him go, running as always. Fang greeted him with wagging tail and an exuberant tongue in his ear. Denny climbed on the wall again, stood there, and commanded. The dog whined and trotted back and forth. He could have been behind a ten-foot fence.

Marya sighed. It was a sound of resignation, but there was something in it that was akin to Fang's bafflement.

"I think there is a way," she said quietly. "Perhaps it will not harm. When stones fall from the wall, whoever passes by replaces them again. It is necessary to do this."

She looked at me, and suddenly I understood.

"Of course! We'll simply tear out a small section of the wall. Then, when the dog has come through, we'll replace it. It'll be just like it was before."

My wife looked very grave.

"It is something no one has *ever* done. Perhaps it is something we should not even tell to the Primate. He would find it hard to be wise. The wall is—as you say—taboo. It protects the Little People."

"And that will be our defense, if we must make one," I said. "We had to remove the dog, for the safety of the land beyond the wall."

I selected a low section of the wall, carefully studied the placement of the stones, then began to remove them. I passed them back to Marya, who stacked them neatly. In a short time there was a three-foot breach in the wall. As Marya said, it was probably something that had never happened before. Fang peered anxiously through the space.

"Go through," I said to Denny, "then come back again. I hope he'll follow you."

Denny obeyed. He gave Fang a pat, then turned and walked back to us.

"Fang, follow!" he said over his shoulder.

At the wall Fang hesitated, then shot through the opening as though propelled by a rocket. He rushed madly around us in a tight circle, occasionally leaping in the air—much higher than the wall. It was almost hysterical relief. He evidently had been much disturbed.

I was as relieved as he was. I turned back to the wall and began rapidly to replace stones. Somehow it seemed imperative to repair that break as soon as possible.

I had reset the foundation stones and was beginning to build, Marya passing the pieces to me in the order in which I had removed them. Denny's voice came from behind us, a low, tense whisper.

"Father! Mother! A man comes!"

The boy did not look in the direction of the newcomer. Neither Marya nor I gave any indication that we knew he was there. But Fang stood, alert and immobile, a statue of a dog, his nostrils verifying what his eyes were telling him.

"Fang, stay!" I said softly. "A friend."

I realized that the fellow had seen what we did. Probably he had watched us cross the wall. Each time I turned I glanced at the approaching man. Fang did not move.

"You may look," I said to Denny. "He knows we see him."

He came across the grassland with the smooth glide of the Elkan hunter. In spite of the fact that I would have much to explain, it gave me a good feeling to watch him come. These were the people we had returned to, and he seemed to be an unusually fine representative. I remembered another meeting, seven years in the past, when Denny and I had come up from the River of Bones and had met Elg in the open land.

This man, I guessed, was bigger than Elg, though far short of height and breadth of the giant Apt. He wore a light sleeveless woven shirt, woven shorts and moccasins. The sheathed, thin hunter's knife was at his belt, a five-foot hunting club in his hand. And he carried a bow hung on his left shoulder, and a quiver of arrows.

He stopped four or five strides from us and stood watching with interested gray eyes. His strong face was tranquil, but it seemed that I could *feel*, rather than see, consternation in his gaze. In a sort of remote way, I admired his calm. What we had done, as Marya had said, no one had *ever* done.

Half the stones had been replaced. The wall was continuous again, without a break. I straightened and faced the hunter. I grasped left hand with right, bowed my head, and said, "A good day to you, friend." Marya and Denny clasped hands and bowed wordlessly.

The man went through the amenities, and his deep voice made a surprising answer.

"The day is almost over, Vin. But I thank you. It has been a good day."

It was the English of the man Smith, as I expected, though just a trifle hesitant, as if he were groping for the words. But he knew me! I looked at him without speaking for a minute.

"I am flattered that you know me," I said finally. "It has been a long time. I am sorry that I cannot call your name."

The man's face softened briefly. It was not quite a smile.

"You would not know it. A hundred bowmen were on the line, all speaking names at once. But all would remember you, for you took the token. Also, you came from another world."

"And I went back again, through the River of Bones, and against the Primate's will. Oo-ah went with me. I should be remembered for that, too."

"The world knows it," the hunter agreed.

He was letting me tell it. He asked no questions, made no accusations. He knew that we understood that he had seen us come from the land of the Little People, tear a breach in the protecting wall. Plainly, the explanations were up to me.

"You saw us," I said. "The dog could not cross the wall. Something prevented him, as it does all animals. It was necessary to remove the stones to let him come through. I have replaced most of them. When I have finished, the wall will not be harmed."

The man simply nodded.

"I saw," he said.

"We have come from the White Cliffs," I went on. "We know that it is forbidden. But this we don't understand any more than you do. *We don't know how we got there.*"

I paused for effect. The hunter's face gave no sign.

"For seven cycles of seasons we have been in my world, also the world of Denny and of the man Smith. We do not know how it was possible to change worlds under the glacier. We do not know how Smith came through among the snow peaks. And we do not know how, in a storm in our land, we came out at the foot of the White Cliffs. But we did."

"It is a strange story," the hunter said.

"Not very believable," I agreed. "Still, there it is. It's the best I can do, for it's the truth."

The man studied me for a moment more, then glanced at Marya, had a longer look at Denny, and, I thought, a decidedly approving look at Fang. His noncommittal features slowly melted into a genuine smile.

"I am called Hod," he said. "My garn is Da-Ma-Ten. It is more than a sun-span from this spot, even longer unless the small man will sometimes ride on my shoulder. There is one in my home who enjoys this."

Denny glanced at me.

"You will be guests," Hod continued. "Then you must go to the Primate. You understand this, I think. He must hear your telling and dispose."

Again I clasped my hands and bowed.

"I am glad to know your name, Hod. This is Marya, my wife, who once was Oo-ah. Our son is Denny. And the one who could not cross the wall is Fang."

Hod clasped his mighty hands and bowed with perfect sobriety.

"Vin, Marya, Denny. Fang. Live and enjoy."

"We thank you," Marya said softly. "Thank you," Denny echoed. And, sensing the pleasant atmosphere, Fang's bushy tail waved very slowly.

Then Hod relaxed completely. He had made his decision about us.

"The guest houses of Da-Ma-Ten will be glad to give you shelter," he said. "All will find your story of great interest. And the stripe-faced dog will attract the eyes of every hunter. Never have I seen one like him."

"He can trail any beast. He guards our camp. And, in addition, he is Denny's friend. Fang is very important to us."

"He has a wise eye." Hod smiled. "I would not care to disturb your camp. I will give him respect."

Then he became businesslike again. He waved an arm.

"There, a few hundred of paces beyond the ridge, you will find a stream, and good spots for camping. You should reach it before the sun is gone. One who can handle a bow as you can, with a hunting dog like Fang, will not need my offer of meat. I will join you again at sunrise. Have comfort!"

He turned and strode away, his fluid pace eating up the distance. In a few moments he was gone.

Marya and I finished repairing the wall. Denny and Fang ran along it while we worked, and Denny seemed to be conducting an experiment of his own. He would climb onto the wall, run along the top, and try to coax the dog to join him. He even dropped over into the land of the Little People again. Fang patiently ran with him, and when he crossed the wall simply sat until he returned. Never before had Fang refused such challenges.

"It is very strange," Denny said, when we finally swung up our packs. "He cannot cross the wall."

"It's something that the people of Elkan have always known, although no one understands why," I said. "But it makes the land of the Little People possible and safe."

"Billy Tom would not believe that either," Denny decided. "There is much that I must remember not to speak of."

I didn't pursue it. Denny would learn many things, as time

passed. It wasn't necessary that he know now that Billy Tom, and all his own past life, were behind him in another world.

We found the stream, made our camp, and ate and rested with a content that I could not explain. Hod came with the morning.

"It is the last of the flapjacks," Marya said. "I have saved them for this time when we have crossed the wall. Also the last of the honey. But there will be some finer in Da-Ma-Ten."

"And grapes!" I remembered. "The best grapes in two worlds. Have they ripened, Hod?"

"There will be plenty," the big hunter said. "This is the best of all seasons for food. I remember that you were known for your eating."

"That is true," I acknowledged gravely. "This is why I have married the cook. She has kept us well fed all these years."

Hod grinned as he accepted flapjacks from Marya.

"You are also remembered for speeches with more than one meaning. I think this is one of them. Is this not so, Denny?"

Denny looked at me, his mouth full of food. He swallowed, then nodded at the hunter.

"That is true. My father always makes jokes. He means that my mother is so wonderful that there is no one like her. No one can prepare food as she does—or shoot, or paddle the canoe, or make the cabin pleasant, or make flowers grow. Also, no one can laugh as she does."

The big man looked almost astonished. And there was no doubt of his approval.

"Well spoken!" he cried. "I will be proud to have you ride my shoulder when we go faster than your pace and your mother and father must carry their packs. Also, when all go to the Primate, I suggest that they let you speak. The Primate is a very wise man. I think he will listen closely to what you have to say."

I had not thought of him for years, but now the craggy face of the Primate, with the long, quizzical eyes, came to me plainly. Hod was right. The Primate would dispose wisely. He would know that the things that had happened were beyond our power to control. And I knew that he would enjoy our son.

"If the Primate is as I remember him, I have no concern,"

I said. "He has great understanding. And, as a man, he enjoys living. I am sure he will speak with us all."

Hod was suddenly silent. He chewed slowly, his face unsmiling. And finally he said, "The Primate you knew went to the White Cliffs three cycles of seasons ago. So there is now a new Primate. But do not have concern. The Primate is always wise. Remember, he is chosen by all the ten garns. Every man feels that he, of all others, can best dispose for this world."

Of course, I had known that it would happen. I remembered that the Primate had been close to the age of Arn the Artisan. He had been the older brother of Jeanne. It had been time for him to go. But it was a blow just the same. As Hod had said, the new Primate would be wise and fair, as he understood things to be, but it would not be the ripe wisdom of experience that had made the old one great. Still, I accepted what I could not change.

"The Primate is the Primate," I said. "He will dispose in the best interests of everyone. And that includes us, I am sure."

"All have been very pleased by his decisions," Hod said. "The garns have never been happier."

"This sounds well for us," Marya said gently. Then she sighed. "Just the same, I will be more at ease when it is over."

We were almost somber as we packed for the trail. Hod watched with interest the rolling of the sleeping bags, the careful arranging of everything on the frames. I knew that to him it was all elaborate beyond any necessity, but I did not explain. Nor did he ask or comment. It would not have been courtesy.

The hunter guided us out across the rolling country, and for a couple of miles he kept almost a compass course, avoiding nothing. But he watched Denny, and adjusted the pace to his tolerance. He was giving due respect to the boy's pride in his traveling ability. Then, when we paused for a moment on a ridge crest, he changed procedure.

"Now we will travel at hunter's pace," he said to Denny. "It is time for you to ride. Later comes a trail, where the walking will be easier for us all."

He swung the boy to his wide shoulder, pack and all, and began to move. I knew what to expect, and of course Marya had been used to the Elkan stride all her days. We could follow, at least for a while. Fang glided along with the hunter, occasionally glancing up at Denny riding in comfort.

It had been seven summers ago that I had first seen that ability to travel. Then it had been Elg drifting along ahead, while Denny and I, with heavy packs, struggled behind him. Denny! Elg! Orb! Suddenly I let myself think of them. I wondered what the Primate had disposed for Denny, who had opposed his will. Did Orb have a wife now, and perhaps sons of his own? How had the Primate disposed for the giant Apt? Did Elg, wise Elg, still serve as the quiet balance wheel for the people of Chan-Cho-Pan? Only Arn the Artisan had had as much respect.

These were not things I would ask. Even if I had, Hod could only tell me what was said. Da-Ma-Ten was the farthest of the garns from Chan-Cho-Pan. He would not know. Only at the Games was there much mingling of the garns. So I would wait.

It seemed to me that the sun moved upward very slowly that morning. At times I almost wondered if it hadn't got itself stuck in place. I was in good trim, and Marya had the marvelous traveling ability of her people, but Hod's effortless, unchanging pace was unbelievable. He was the closest thing to Elg I had ever seen. And, like Elg, he knew just when we had reached our limit, just when to pause and tell us where we were, to point out interesting sights, to place Denny on his feet again so that he might run back and forth and stretch his muscles.

It was noon when we came out of an open woodland onto a broad bench, covered with apple trees. Below us was a stream, with a rustic bridge to cross it, and a trail showing beyond. Hod gathered apples.

"The earliest are ripe," he observed, "though most will come later, when the sun is farther south again. But these are very good. We will have them while we rest by the stream."

He pointed to several stripped and broken trees.

"A bear found this planting," he told Denny. "It was necessary to remove him. Perhaps we may have some of him for our dinner, when we reach Da-Ma-Ten in the starshine."

"Sometimes this must be done," Denny agreed. "May I see his tracks, do you think? Also, Fang would enjoy them."

They left us, with disgusting energy, to go inspect the damaged trees. And I heard Denny say, chattily, "In the land of the Little People my father had to kill a moose. It would have trampled the Little People's fields."

I couldn't repress a grin, for I could imagine Hod's reaction to that. This cheerful small boy was speaking with knowledge of a land which was forbidden, a place no Elkan had ever seen until he had grown tiny. And, added mystery, of course the hunter had never heard of a moose. His face was grave as they moved out of our range of hearing.

Later, by the stream, we ate our apples and drank the cold, tasty water. Marya had brought out corn cakes, like the flapjacks, the last of her supply. Hod approved of them mightily.

"Corn cakes are always good," he said, "but these are finer than most. The boy is right. You prepare food well. I am proud to have the chance to share it."

"Marya does everything well," I said, and Denny nodded solemnly.

It was a long, long afternoon. We stayed on the trail and the footing was not bad. But it seemed to have no end, while the unchanging stride of the big hunter ate up the distance relentlessly. Hod had decided to reach Da-Ma-Ten in one march, though we would arrive, as he had said to Denny, "in the starshine."

"Our coming is known," he said. "A guest house will be prepared, and there will be food waiting. This way is best."

So we had no opportunity to see the garn from a distance. It had long been dark when we finally passed the boundary road and entered the shadowy town. By then both Marya and I were moving mechanically. Denny slept on the hunter's shoulder. Only Fang seemed unperturbed by the long trek.

There was a guest house, and it could have been the one I first remembered in Chan-Cho-Pan. A fire was cheery in the big stone fireplace. There was a tray of hot food, savory meat, streaming cabbages, corn cakes, milk. We ate by flaring torchlight, and didn't inquire how many of those things had got there.

"There are couches and coverings," Hod said simply. "Have comfort!"

And he left us.

Chapter 29

"This is a very pleasant town," Denny said. "Also, Fang likes it. We did not know that a town could be like this."

It was our second day in Da-Ma-Ten. We had slept and eaten and rested. We had met the greeter of guests for this particular ten-sun, and had clasped hands, bowed, and said our names to many people on the roads and in the park.

Of course everyone knew who we were. Like the coming of the man Smith, my coming and going again was legend. And now I had returned once more, it was said from the White Cliffs, with Oo-ah of Chan-Cho-Pan and our son, and a strange big hunting dog with stripes on his face.

We had described the town to Denny. We had explained that the people were much like Hod, and that all used the forms of courtesy that we had taught him. No one would ask questions, we told him, and it would be well to let us tell the grown-ups of our journey. There would be children and dogs in the park. They would be glad to welcome him, and he must be sure that Fang remembered that he was a companion dog, not a wolf.

"Fang will be very polite," Denny said. "He will do as I tell him. He will not strike unless something wishes to harm me. He does not feel danger here. I could tell."

"There is none," I agreed. "Just see to it that he does not try to remind other dogs that he is very great."

"This is not his territory," Denny said. "He knows he is a visitor."

"Then off with you both," I said, laughing. "The roads and the park are free to you. Come back at noon for food."

As always in the garns of Elkan, a guest is a guest of the garn, not of any particular people. No one visited us. No one inquired about our journey or, for that matter, about our well-being. The initiative was entirely ours. We could say much, little, or nothing, as we chose. We knew that everyone was intensely curious, but it could never have been told from their actions.

The current greeter of guests, a big fellow who might, from appearance, have been Hod's brother, made the guest-house arrangements. Nearby families provided the food. If we had other needs, we knew we had only to name them. Somewhere in the garn, someone would see to it that they were met.

If a guest could do the garn a service, he did it. But if there was no necessity, nothing was expected. Since, in the memorable summer when I had lived in this land, I had often been a guest, I knew what to do. And when I saw a big young man busily cutting up a newly fallen tree at a corner, I left Marya to walk on alone.

"Some of these cuts are more easily done by two," I told him. "I have skill with the axe. I would be glad to help."

"I will welcome it, Vin." The young giant mopped sweat with a large square of cloth, leaned on his long-handled axe, and grinned. "I am Don. Many cycles of seasons ago, in the Primate's home, I served you food."

I clasped my hands and bowed.

"Don, I remember. It will be an extra pleasure to help. Let me get my own axe from my pack. It will serve best for the limbing."

So I had spent the morning being a lumberman. We finished with the wood neatly cut and stacked, the road and grass plot cleared and tidy. It was simply a thing a guest would do. Everyone in the garn would know about it.

"In the park," Denny said, "the boys play a game with a ball made of bark. It was easy to learn. I think I will soon be very good at it."

Marya was pleased.

"Children do not change," she said. "When I was a little girl I have played this game—in the park at Chan-Cho-Pan. I, too, was good at it," she added, with a wink at me.

"There are girls who play," Denny said, "but the boys are better." He grinned at his mother. Then he asked, "Will we visit this town, this garn where you were a little girl? Will it be pleasant like this one?"

"If the Primate thinks we should, we will go," I said. "It will be pleasant. Of all the garns, I think I like it best."

Denny reflected.

"There is a boy here called Dan, who also has six cycles of seasons. He is glad that I have come to visit. He showed me how to play the game with the ball."

Marya and I exchanged glances. In them was the relief that we certainly both felt. There was no need to be concerned about Denny, when finally he learned that we were to live in this land. He would adjust. Within a day he had already found a friend.

In fact, I detected a possible problem if we stayed long in Da-Ma-Ten. It was a carefree world for children, a kind of world Denny had never known. This was equally true of all the garns, but he would not know that. I knew that we were waiting for word from the Primate. I hoped it would come soon.

And, very promptly, it did. At our evening meal, Hod quietly brought the message.

"The runner has come from the Primate. It will be his pleasure to have you for guests, while he listens to all you wish to say. It will require five sun-spans of travel. I will guide you." He looked at us quizzically, but he did not smile. "But there will be no fast traveling, nor long, such as we made when we came from the wall. We will stop to look, and have good camps. The Primate has suggested this."

I heaved a sigh.

"I like the man already. You almost walked the ears off us. You know that, don't you?"

"It was a hard march," the hunter admitted, "but at the time it seemed best."

Just why, I wasn't sure. But I was grateful that it was to be a one-time thing.

Hod kept his word. Elg would not have been a more considerate or a more helpful guide. The days were sunny, the south winds blew. For much of the time Denny could maintain our trail pace, but when we all chose to move, he rode quite happily on the hunter's shoulders. Fang ranged far afield and found the small-game hunting rich, the good smells of a game-filled land exactly to his liking. We enjoyed our camps and slept deeply and without worry.

From the high points of the trail Hod pointed out sights. He drew a rough map in the smooth sand of a stream shore and showed the locations of the garns and all the open country of Elkan, from the ocean to the snow peaks. He placed the Primate's dwelling. And he made another small mark in the empty land between Da-Ma-Ten and Char-Che-Po.

"Here dwells Apt," he explained. "As you know, all men live in the garns. Only the Primate's home sits alone, for he is of all the people. But now Apt also lives alone, by the Primate's decision. When he would not follow custom and wished to take a woman against her will, the Primate disposed. It was cycles of seasons gone by. You may have heard."

"I was the woman," Marya said quietly.

Hod glanced keenly from my wife to me. His face was bland, but I think he already knew.

"While all trails go to the Primate's dwelling, none goes to Apt's," he continued. "When a man meets Apt, he bows and passes by. Apt may not visit. The guest houses will not receive him. He is a very strong man, but he may not test at the Games. He hunts as he chooses, but he must be always alone."

"The Man Without A Country," I said, almost to myself. "That's rough!"

"It is just," Hod said. "The Primate is very wise. There must be agreements that all men respect, otherwise it would not be a pleasant world."

"You have me there," I admitted. "You've proved it by making it work."

The shadows were long on the fifth day when we reached our journey's end. I looked down into the wide, level valley, with the sweeping half-curve of the river which flowed past the hill that was crowned with the Primate's home, and the years dropped away. Nothing had changed. The fields were well-kept, the terraces and slopes crowded with neatly pruned fruit trees. The vines still climbed and mellowed the outlines of the great stone house. The gentle south breeze carried the good smells of crops and of ripening fruits.

"The peaches," I said, "and the grapes! It was just like this seven years ago, when Elg brought Denny and me to this spot. It will seem strange that the old Primate will not greet us."

"There is only one Primate," Hod said gravely. "That is the one who lives in that dwelling. Like the peaches and the grapes, the welcome will not change."

"Of course," I said. "That's the key. That's the way it has to be."

We dropped down the trail into the valley. We knew that we were seen, but not a person moved on the balconies or past the windows of the Primate's home. Finally we stood before the entrance, the same great doors of thick wood slabs ornamented by rough, dark metal scrolls. Again nostalgia overwhelmed me, for we simply stood, minute after minute, and no one came. But I knew that this was custom, too, and that the Primate welcomed everyone himself.

I could feel the blood beat in my temples. Marya's beautiful face was eager. Denny looked up with astonishment at the huge heavy doors and the massive stonework of the entrance. Fang's ears were pointed alertly, but he placidly sat while we waited.

Slowly the doors swung open. The Primate strode, with Elkan ease, out across the stone threshold. He seemed even taller, wider than I remembered, but otherwise he had not changed. His face was grave and courteous. The mighty hands that he clasped were the same that had held the ropes and pulled me up many a ledge. His yellow hair fell forward as he bowed.

"Hod. Vin. Marya. Denny. Fang. You are my guests."

We all clasped hands and bowed in return. Hod said, "We are grateful."

Then the Primate straightened, flung back his yellow hair, and grinned, the little-boy grin I remembered so well. One stride, and he had me in a bear hug.

"Vin!" he cried. "Old Vin! Oh, this is great!"

For a moment we pumped hands in good American fashion and neither could say anything at all.

"I've known," the Primate said finally. "Of course I've known. The runners came fast. But I don't think I really believed that you had come back until I could see for myself."

He reached out one great arm and swept Marya against him. He looked down into her smiling face almost with wonder.

"Seven years!" he said. "Seven years, and you've only grown more beautiful! Vin, your going was a good thing. I want to hear it all, step by step." He hesitated, and for a moment his face was grave. "I've worried some, people. There were a lot of things that could have happened. But somehow, I thought you'd get through. I thought you'd make it."

"You gave us the chance," Marya said. "It was what you wished."

"It was what had to be," the Primate said. "I am proud that I had the understanding to know that."

Then his mobile face changed again. He pushed us both aside as he went down on one knee on the stone slab, bringing his pale-blue eyes level with Denny's dark ones. He grinned, and the boy clasped hands and bowed.

"Now here is a man who I hoped existed, and whom I have long wanted to see. Denny, I am the Primate. I am especially glad to welcome you."

"Thank you, sir," the boy said. He studied the big man with no shyness whatever. "You know my father and my mother very well, I think. Also, Fang likes you. I hope I may stay a while in your guest house. I will enjoy it."

"Well spoken!" the Primate said. "I will enjoy it too."

His amused gaze went past the boy to the malemute. Fang stood, poised, his cold eyes glittering, but his heavy brush waved slowly.

"So I have passed muster with Fang. I can see that that is necessary. A malemute! Vin, I never expected to see one again."

"He's a large part of the story," I said. "Fang is no ordinary sled dog/hunting dog. He thinks he's people. He has strong convictions about Denny's importance, and he'll back them up to the last drop of his blood. And you can be sure that his won't be the only blood shed."

"I can believe it," the Primate chuckled. He rose, "Hod, forgive us. As you know, these are my friends." He turned and led the way through the entrance. Briefly, his voice became formal again. "You have all had a long trail. Enter, and be refreshed. When you have rested, there will be food."

"More than one peach?" I inquired innocently, and the Primate's laugh rang.

"There are things a man never forgets," he said. "Come in! Come in, friends. This is a day I have hoped for, but I never thought it would come."

Chapter 30

We spent a week in the big stone house on its perch above the sweeping curve of the river. It was like no week I had ever spent, for we reviewed seven years of living; four lives. We ate well and slept long, but when we were awake there was never an end to the talking. We sat on the wide balconies and talked. We climbed the terraces, strolled along the river, and always there was more to say.

The Primate went with Marya and me through the River of Bones, on under the glacier, and out onto the white desolation of Seward in September. He shared with us the breathtaking timing of the coming of Daredevil Pete and the collapse of the crevasse.

"I knew it would be tricky, out there in the white lands," he said. "That worried me over the years. It was a slim chance."

He listened while we told of the Yukon years, and our searches for a way to come back. Denny was born, and grew, and a squabby, big-footed, big-bellied puppy became Fang. They were good years. We were happy, the way all people were meant to be happy. Because we knew Elkan, we knew the real meaning of "live and enjoy."

And finally we took him down the northern river on our last holiday. He camped with us beside the nameless lake. He listened, stony-faced and thoughtful, to the unbelievable story of Jeanne. He came with us through the storm back to the White Cliffs, a place in Elkan where even the Primate had never been.

The details we could give of the doings of the Little People were the first ever actually known of this second stage in the life cycle of a race. And at this point in our telling I remembered Jeanne's coffin.

"This is as important as any promise I ever made," I said. "I'd like to get it to the wall as fast as I can. There was a pattern of stones to be laid on the top of the wall, and the Little People would watch for them. They would be placed where we crossed the wall. The Little People will know."

"Let me arrange it," the Primate said. "The coffin can go from Da-Ma-Ten. I will ask that Hod take it. He knows the exact spot."

I heaved a sigh of relief.

"Thank you," I said. "It's worth something to be the Primate, after all."

The Primate grinned. For a moment he was just big Denny again, my old friend of a hundred trails and peak climbs. Then, soberly, he was once more the Primate.

"It's worth a great deal to be the Primate, Vin. With the people of this world, it is not so much what the Primate does. It's what the Primate is. The people know what is best to do. They've known, back into antiquity. They know that if each does his share everything will be done. It is clear to them that there can be only so many deer in a range, so many rabbits in a field. Too many, and the food base is destroyed. So the fox plays his part, and the wolf.

"There is only so much space in Elkan, so the garns do not grow. Why should they? Each person has merit in himself. More is not better. One child, or occasionally two, serve every purpose. They live simply, but they are not simple. There is more wisdom here, in each person, than we could imagine in the world we came from.

"So the Primate's function is simply to remind. In this land no one is forced to conform. All think alike, because that way everyone enjoys. If a man is great, he takes a token at the Games. If he is best at a skill or a craft his garn honors him and is proud. What else is there? He lives a life and then he goes to the White Cliffs. And even there he expects to live and enjoy."

The Primate took a deep breath, and smiled apologetically.

"Sorry, people. You need no lectures or instruction. You know."

"Yes," I said. "We know."

Marya leaned forward.

"Just the same," she said, "you must speak more. We have told you of seven years. But in that time you also lived seven years. I think the Primate should tell of those years. If you wondered and thought of us, we also thought of you. We always will."

"You think perhaps that those years will explain how I became the Primate?"

"We know how you became the Primate," Marya said. "You were chosen by all the garns, because of all men they trusted you most. No, we want to know how Denny lived, after Vin and Marya went down into the River of Bones. We know it must have been a very different life. All these cycles of seasons we have wondered—and hoped that it was well with you."

The Primate nodded slowly. He reached out a big hand to a great bowl of grapes on the table at his elbow. He plucked a single grape, regarded it abstractedly for a moment, then ate it with appreciation.

"Yes," he said finally, "it was a very different life."

He had another grape, chewed it reflectively.

"Very well. It was a long, a restless sort of time, but the telling can be short. From the beginning, then: When I was sure you were well into the canyon, I let the posse take me."

"Posse?" Marya's fine eyebrows raised.

The Primate chuckled.

"A good American word. I'm glad you never had any occasion to know it. The Executors of the Primate's Will. I no longer opposed them, and gave them my word. Then we went to the Primate.

"Vin, he was the wisest man I have ever known. We had long talks, and I tried to show him why it was best that you try to go back, and that, because you were going, it was the only place for Marya. He understood. He realized, too, what the story of the coffin had to be. He knew we had never been beyond the wall. We simply did not know what we had found. There was no desecration.

"So he disposed, and I was free to go back to Chan-Cho-Pan, and to live as I had before. But of course that wasn't possible. Arn had gone to the White Cliffs. Vin and Marya had gone back under the glacier, and perhaps had met their fates in the snow country. Several times I was tempted to follow you—but I knew that that would solve nothing. Even if I could get through, it would be better for me here.

"So I became a wanderer. I visited in every garn. I worked in their fields, helped with the lumbering, showed them what I know of keeping food and preserving meat. I prowled the length and breadth of Elkan, from the ocean to the snow peaks, from the wall to the canyon of the River of Bones.

"I climbed farther into the snow peaks than anyone ever has, and believe me, Vin, they are not the St. Elias. The farther I went the less I understood. It is simply another land.

"I hunted everything, from the white bears of the north to the big crag sheep of the snow peaks. I wrestled whenever a man wanted a friendly contest, and I took three more tokens at the Games. But more and more often I would come back here and work in the Primate's fields and orchards.

"This was home, it seemed. The Primate welcomed me. When his duties allowed, we discussed every topic under that bright sun out there. I enjoyed the wisdom of a really original mind—and he learned the good things and the bad of another world. I widened his horizons with astronomy—and he certainly widened mine in many ways."

The Primate paused, stared out from the balcony where we sat, his blue eyes hooded. Far below us, on the riverbank, Denny and Fang were racing. The Primate smiled.

"It's good to have another Denny," he said. "I thank you."

"I am glad that he can have an honored name," I replied. "When he is older and can understand, he will be proud."

"That fellow will need no support from a name," the Primate said. "He is already his own man. If the name has respect, he will add to it. But that will never be his concern."

"We feel well about him," Marya said. "But—Denny is now, and Denny is future. We wish to hear the rest of the past of that other Denny."

The Primate nodded.

"There isn't much more. When the Primate knew that his journey had begun, he had me do many of the things that are the Primate's responsibility. He made his own furnishings and his own coffin. I watched him grow small, just as we three, years ago, watched Arn's last days in this world.

"And when the day came, he insisted that I take him to the wall. He and all his belongings made a very small package. I carried him in one long trek, a day and a night, and set him across the wall probably not far from where you came over. By then he had almost forgotten me. He had become a part of another world.

"Then I came back here, because I didn't know what else to do. The workers from the garns worked on in the fields, and, since I knew, they came to me for direction. We were all waiting for the next Primate.

"In five days they came, ten big men, all men I had

known, one from each garn. Elg was the man from Chan-Cho-Pan. There was no ceremony. The garns had decided. I was the Primate. The whole world knew it before I did."

The Primate resorted once more to the bowl of grapes. He plucked one, rolled it in his big fingers, finally popped it into his mouth.

"When I thought it all over, I could see that it was not a bad thing. I did have perspective—and the old Primate had taught me and thought well of me. What better thing could I do?"

He rose suddenly and smiled down at us, the carefree, open grin of the old Denny.

"So now I must dispose for you, who have done things no one else has *ever* done. You went through the canyon of the River of Bones, which is forbidden. You came through the land beyond the wall, from the very base of the White Cliffs. Further, you brought an animal, which must never be there, and you tore a breach in the wall itself to let it through."

"Don't forget the moose," I said drily. "The Little People insisted that we brought that as well. But when I killed it they ate it with good appetite."

The Primate chuckled.

"Incredible, isn't it, Vin? I think I will have to consult a wiser man. You two sit and enjoy the view, and what I have left of the grapes. I will go down and speak with my namesake. Perhaps he can give me a clue."

In a few minutes we saw the big man emerge onto a terrace below the lower walls of the house. He moved down through the vineyards with the effortless ease that seven years in Elkan had given him. He vaulted a wall, wove his way through an orchard, and shortly came out on the riverbank. Denny and Fang ran to meet him.

We watched them as they strolled companionably along the edge of the orchard. It was too far to hear, but we could see that Denny was chattering happily, as he did only when with trusted friends. And the Primate was nodding solemnly.

They paused, and the boy pointed up into one of the peach trees. The Primate picked him up, held him high, and Denny plucked the particular sun-ripened fruit that had attracted his attention. The Primate broke it in two and they shared it, a half to each. They walked on down to the riverbank, their backs toward us. Our son was a very small boy still, for he reached up, with complete confidence, and held onto the big man's hand. Behind them Fang trailed contentedly.

"Somehow, I think that the Primate has disposed," I said.

"It was never a problem at all," Marya said. "We have given him happiness. This is only the way he tells us."

Chapter 31

It was almost sunset. For two days we had been on the trail, a trail we had not seen for seven years. We were traveling easily now, for the distance was not much more. Ahead of us our guide moved with the matchless gliding trail pace that had no equal in Elkan. It was the first I had ever seen in this land. I had never seen a better.

That, too, was the Primate's arranging. He had sent the runner to Chan-Cho-Pan, and Elg had come. It had been like greeting a brother again. We had had much talk, the four of us, and now we were going back to Chan-Cho-Pan. Once again, for me, the Primate had disposed.

We came over the last low ridge. It lay below us on the plain, a neat rectangle of a city, with its patterned roads and rows of home plots, every angle softened by trees, and the lake glinting in the central, wooded park. Far in the distance, a boundary for the horizon, the White Cliffs gleamed in the last rays of the sun.

Elg came to a halt, smiling.

"Many people will welcome you," he said. "The House of the Maples has been made ready. It was felt that Oo-ah would like this best."

Then suddenly he was grave. He clasped his big left hand with his mighty right, and bowed his head.

"Oo-ah. Vin. Denny. Fang. Live and enjoy! You are home!"